SECRETS

OF

MOTHER

SECRETS OF MOTHER

A CRISTIANE BRADFORD NOVEL

Sirrah Medeiros

Tundra Swan Press
Virginia

Secrets of Mother

Copyright ©2022 by Sirrah Medeiros

ISBN: 979-8-9852025-3-3

Library of Congress Control Number (LCCN): 2022914914

Published in October 2022 by TUNDRA SWAN PRESS, Virginia, USA.
Cover Design by Sirrah Medeiros
Edited by Eugenie Rayner, Magic Lamp Editing Services
Cover photo "A Witch Holding a Glass of Wine" by Joanna Malinowska via freestocks.org is licensed under CC0 1.0

All rights reserved.

This is a work of fiction. This story or any portion thereof may not be reproduced or used in any manner whatsoever without the express written permission of the publisher except for the use of brief quotations in a book review.

The events depicted in this story are entirely fictitious. Any references to historical events or real places are used fictitiously. Other names, characters, places, and events are products of the author's imagination.

To request permission and all other inquiries, contact Tundra Swan Press at info@tundraswanpress.com.

CONTENT WARNING

This book contains material some readers may find disturbing—language, the death of secondary characters, and gore. This book is part of a series.

"Life is a spell so exquisite that everything conspires to break it."

—EMILY DICKINSON

ONE

Cristiane strummed the steering wheel, contemplative as she drove the unfamiliar winding road. There was a vague awareness of when the snow flurries began falling from the heavens. The car headlights caught specks of luminosity as the murky tree line raced by. Cristiane found herself preoccupied with the snowfall, as if fairies were sprinkling their dust along her trail in honor of the occasion. A smile spread across her lips.

Tonight she would meet other witches more advanced in the craft. Her anticipation for the initiation ceremony had heightened her anxiety over the past few weeks. As a result, she'd chewed her nails down to the quick. A nasty habit Cristiane had hoped to say goodbye to when she left for college three years ago. Instead, the habit had become worse. Her schedule was daunting. Between overloading on classes each semester and driving an hour for witchcraft training with Isadora once a week, she had no time to relax or have a social life. But she hoped tonight would change all that. She yearned to make new friends, new witch friends. And more than anything, she longed to find her tribe—people who would accept her.

A fleeting shadow traversed in front of Cristiane's car as a hard thump whacked against the corner, jolting its occupants.

"Ah!" she shrieked while slamming on the brakes. The car slid in the snow as Cristiane fought to keep them out of the dark roadside alcove. "What the hell?"

"What?" Isadora woke with a start and bolted upright.

"I hit something. It was fast and huge." Cristiane's hands shook as she gripped the wheel and took a couple of slow, deep breaths to calm her nerves. She jammed the gearshift into park, then grabbed the door handle. "I'll go look."

Heavy snowflakes fell in the beams of light to the front as Cristiane pushed open the car door. Yet to the sides and rear, the road was desolate and shrouded in obscurity. As she stepped out, the crunch of compacting snow under her feet grated on her nerves. She loved snow, but she didn't want tonight to be ruined by a car accident. Tonight was supposed to be special.

Cristiane trudged to the front while Isadora stepped out and scanned the roadside along the snow-covered ditch.

Two shallow dents defaced the corner of Cristiane's car on the hood and bumper. As she crouched over the car's front end, she brushed a hand along each spot, looking for scratches or other damage. Finding none, she saw no reason to call for an insurance review or police report. The dents would pop out with suction.

"No actual damage." The relief was unmistakable in her voice as she stood, shaking off her concern. "I can't afford—"

"Shh, something is in the tree line." Isadora's voice was low as she scouted the brush and trees in the darkness. She noticed strong, wide prints evident in the snow trailing through the ditch. The footprints were uneven, heavier on one side. It was carrying something and moving fast when hit. Finally her eyes settled on a pair of bright violet eyes peering back at her. The color reminded her of Hungarian lilacs found in late spring until the eye centers flared with crimson. Not raising an alarm, she crept backward to rest against the car as she felt for the door handle. She didn't move her eyes off those in the bushes. By the low, raspy growl, it was fifty yards from her—too close. She knew the creature's nature, but Cristiane was easy prey and knew nothing about what waited in the brush. They had to get inside the vehicle and leave.

"Get back in the car, Cris." Isadora eased her door open as she instructed Cristiane through tight lips. "Do it, now."

Cristiane obeyed. The tone of Isadora's voice was unusual. Commanding, but there was a subtle hint of dread—fear.

After they'd driven away, Isadora broke the silence and spoke of creatures Cristiane had only read about in fables: fantastical beings of all sorts, such as changelings, werewolves, and demons. According to Isadora, Cristiane had bumped into the latter.

Cristiane's mouth hung open as she drove her teacher to their destination. She listened as Isadora talked with her hands motioning this way and that, distracting Cristiane. Her hands cemented at the ten and two positions on the wheel, Cristiane drove with caution as growing concern for her mentor played in her mind.

The lesson was abridged as Isadora soon motioned for Cristiane to pull into a long drive leading to their destination. Isadora spoke quickly, glancing back every so often, checking if what Cristiane hit with the car had followed them. "We should have discussed these creatures a long time ago, but with you in Springfield and our time short when we are together to study, I am sorry to say I have been remiss in teaching you about society's dark outliers. As a witch, you will become more aware, and will need to protect yourself or fight. It is a grave error on my part. I'm surprised my ward has lasted as long as it has in hiding your powers."

Cristiane had little chance to talk. Astonished, she wasn't sure if Isadora was growing senile, insane, or if the marvelous beings she mentioned were real. "So what you're saying is vampires are real, too." Cristiane thought she was being sarcastic as she pulled into the circular drive and slid the gear into park.

"Of course." Isadora opened the door, then stepped out, leaving her pupil speechless.

The creature crouched in the trees, assessing its wounds. Its arm hung limp at its side because of a dislocated shoulder. Two mishaps in one night. Luck was not in its favor. To rush the women would have served its ego, but nothing else. The crone witch's power was formidable and to charge after the women in its damaged form could have proven disastrous.

Xirnan longed for another host—a strong, youthful body. This decrepit, old form would not last much longer—stretched far beyond the normal human lifespan through cunning and sorcery. If only the horrid woman would speak on its behalf to persuade their leader to grant its request for Malin's physicality. Although it found the man's personality abhorrent, the physical body was ideal for its wizardry and was more amiable to society. It could walk among mankind without gawking stares and pointed fingers. As the useless arm hung by its side, it hoped his master would grant a new vessel soon.

To exist in the physical realm for such a time and yet be bound to a disparaging form bristled Xirnan's sensibilities. Once a proud battalion leader of soldier demons for their monarch, it bowed its head, ashamed of the depths fallen after centuries of faithful service. Nothing more than a soldier demon to serve a daft woman's foolishness, restricted to hiding in the shadows because of its position and looks. It growled in frustration and kicked the man it had flung on the ground.

Prey lay in the dirt, bound and gagged at its feet, bewitched into sleep and injected with enough sedative to drop a horse. If the women hadn't hit it, it could carry the man the rest of the distance. But in damaged condition, it would need help to bring in their prize before the sedative wore off. Disgusted, it pulled a phone from the cloak and pinged the location to its least favorite human.

The coven gathered at an expansive estate. American elm trees trailed along each side of the entrance road leading to the front of the property. The lawn was generous with evening lights lining the circular drive toward a large parking area. The front entrance had a casual sophistication with plantings of boxwood, hydrangea, and low-lying groundcover grasses still to sprout their spring blossoms. Yet cameras mounted in several locations ensured the home's boundaries were well monitored. If anyone attempted to break in or approach from the front, the estate's security guards would meet them. Four people, dressed in military style, stood guard for the ceremony. Cristiane mused over the need for such measures but hurried to catch up with Isadora. It was not time to ask such questions.

As Isadora and Cristiane strolled past the house, the backyard opened to trees lining the perimeter view. Large red pines abruptly angled outward after the terraced patio, providing a clear view of anyone or anything approaching across the vast grasslands from the rear. The evening sky showed through snow-filled clouds. Stars sparkled against the blackness, interrupted by puffs of gray dispersing glistening frosted bits down from the heavens. The view of the expansive patio took Cristiane's breath while she considered the small decorative heaters and bushes draped in twinkling lights. A sizeable outdoor fireplace showcased in the center was aflame with a warm, inviting fire. With the spring snow falling as a backdrop to the ceremony, it was a perfect location for the festivities.

The home was once a bed-and-breakfast, explained Isadora. Now Sarah's home and the coven's headquarters, it supplied everything members needed, and offered restful seclusion at the discretion of the owner. Confused, Cristiane pondered whether to ask what she meant, but Isadora interrupted her thoughts. "Join the other two trainees. The high priestess will meet with the sponsors before we call you three over to us. If you're anxious, meditate or sit quietly until the ceremony begins." Isadora pointed toward two others about Cristiane's age.

Cristiane nodded and wandered over to the two clustered near the fireplace and made quick introductions. The coven members gathered at the far end of the patio. The trainees watched as several members opened the circle upon Isadora's approach, then closed around her. A few moments later, the old woman's head popped up slightly over the crowd alongside the high priestess and gave the leader a curt nod, signaling she was ready.

"Then you may begin for us, Isadora."

"I am honored to present my candidate for initiation, Cristiane." Isadora gestured to Cristiane as she beamed with pride. Her young student had trained with vigor over many months and grasped each new skill with ease. Cristiane was ready to learn more from the other members. "I have trained her on my own, but she is ready to learn from each of you, to develop and hone her skills in the craft. She is ready to expand her presence within our community and become a skilled asset to the coven."

Trying to concentrate, Cristiane could hear the parents introduce their children, the other two candidates sitting with Cristiane for initiation. Along with the others, she watched in silence behind the coven circle as the high priestess and her members discussed the ritual preparations and asked questions of each inductee's sponsor.

"Why is her mother not by her side?" High Priestess Sarah directed the pointed question once the other sponsors completed their introductions. "You are the longest serving coven member, Isadora. Why haven't we heard of this young lady?"

"She came to my attention a few years ago through another pupil. Since that time, Cristiane has trained under my apprenticeship while simultaneously completing her college studies. Although there is a powerful family legacy, her mother does not practice witchcraft."

"Ah, I see. Well, don't make me drag everything out of you. What is her family name?" High Priestess Sarah raised her hands, the billowing sleeves of her robe catching the wind as she waited for Isadora's answer.

"Her family surname is Bradford, but we found her witch lineage on her mother's side. We can follow her ancestry back hundreds of years." Isadora paused, looking at her High Priestess. "She is a ninth generation descendent of Carolyn Madison."

The vast quiet emphasized the coven members collectively sucking in their breath. Participants looked to their leader for her reaction. The high priestess did not hide her dismay. Shock froze on her face as she dropped her arms to her sides, dispirited by the revelation.

The high priestess quickly recovered and stood relaxed as she interlaced her fingers. Her eyes looked far off in the distance as she measured her response. Twice she opened her mouth to speak, then closed it again. Finally she said, "Isadora, you should have consulted me prior to the ceremony with such a candidate."

Her coven leader's words stunned Isadora. As if hit in the torso, she stumbled back, caught herself from falling on the stairs, and then remained motionless for several seconds. As she glanced at each colleague, they peered back at her without sorrow. "Why? You have never questioned the intentions of a coven sponsorship. What makes you question Cristiane's intent?"

Cristiane stood up when she heard her name and listened more closely to the exchange between the two women.

"Cristiane is the daughter of Beatrice, isn't she?" High Priestess Sarah asked as she folded her arms across her chest. Her jaw clenched as anger rose from deep in her upper body. She did not expect to have an issue with the initiation ceremony. The potential demon Isadora mentioned on arrival was enough cause for concern. Sarah was becoming increasingly irritated with the course of the evening. With the new inductees watching, she held her temper in check.

"Well, yes. Her mother's name is Beatrice, but she is not a practicing witch. I have guided Cristiane's training in the craft. Beatrice is not involved in this." Isadora's voice rose with a catch as she attempted to control her anger. She took a cleansing breath, then said, "How do you, High Priestess, know Beatrice Bradford? Why would Cristiane's mother give you pause?"

"I'm sorry, Isadora. I cannot welcome your inductee this evening. Her mother is an active witch. If her daughter is unaware, then I suggest you both take great caution and look at why Beatrice has not disclosed or shared her practice with her daughter."

Cristiane stood in stunned silence, her eyes shining in the moonlight as she held back tears. She covered her mouth with her hands, reminding herself not to scream a retort or interrupt to ask her own questions. Her mind raced as she tried to recall when she might have questioned her mother's actions, especially in the past few years. Nothing. *Has Mom lied to me all my life?*

"Be careful, Isadora. As you are aware, we are a modern coven promoting individual enlightenment and holistic practices. Beatrice chose an alternate path—a sinister path.

Until I am confident her practice does not influence her daughter, Cristiane is not welcome."

Isadora, embarrassed and devastated, stormed past the group, wrapped an arm around Cristiane, and steered her away from the gathering.

"Isadora, what's going on? Why is that woman—"

"You mean the high priestess," Isadora corrected, as they turned the corner and rushed to the front of the house. Isadora's short, quick steps belied her age as Cristiane struggled to keep up. "We will discuss this soon. First, I must take you away so the others may continue with their initiation. We should not be here as they enjoy the experience."

Cristiane, exasperated at having to wait for answers, offered to help Isadora into the car, but she was waved off as they caught sight of the high priestess standing at the corner of her home in the dark.

"Get in and wait. I'll be right back."

Sarah and Isadora spoke in the shadows several yards from Cristiane's sedan. Cristiane, with her head down, watched from the corner of her eye, and wondered if they were discussing her and her mother. She didn't start the engine, hoping instead to overhear a morsel of the conversation. As the minutes ticked by, Cristiane chewed at her nails; the anger also brewing until she shook with rage. Feelings of betrayal welled up in her. She and her mother in no way got along, especially as Cristiane started high school and even now living a few hours away at college. She thought the physical distance would help them improve their relationship, but her mother remained distant. Could this secret be why her mom was so hard to reach? *Mother! Nothing makes sense, but the first chance I get, I'm going home to see if what I learned tonight is true.*

Once Isadora finished her discussion with the high priestess, she marched back to the car, buckled into her seat, and offered nothing more to Cristiane. They drove away as an uncomfortable silence filled the car. Cristiane's anxiety, usually flaring with lots of external noise, rose to a fever pitch as she drove along the darkened road back to Isadora's. She realized her hands hurt from the death grip she had on the steering wheel. Her palms left sweat marks as she loosened her hold and tried to relax. The old woman didn't speak until her home was visible.

Isadora cleared her throat and turned toward Cristiane. "We will discuss joining the coven later. The high priestess wants answers about your mother and to get to know you. I should have done my homework and investigated your family, your living family members, before now. I'm sorry tonight did not turn out as we planned." Isadora patted her young pupil on the shoulder. "In the meantime, we will train on nonhuman and humanoid creatures as we investigate your mother. Your first chance meeting with a creature was quite uneventful. We must be grateful for the rare exception. However, you must prepare for any encounter. As you use your magic, these other species have a way of targeting witches and make our lives more difficult or interesting, depending on the creature and the circumstances."

"I don't know what to say. I'm speechless." After putting her head down, she turned to Isadora. Sadness and tears played from the corner of her eyes. "I'd prefer to be alone tonight rather than stay over after everything that's happened. You understand?"

"Of course. This evening has been a disappointment. Try not to be too discouraged."

"I will do my best." Cristiane helped Isadora into her home, then quickly jumped back into the warm car. She drove the dark side streets back to Springfield as the evening's events flooded her mind. She needed space to think. With her roommate gone for spring break, the dorm would be her sanctuary for the night.

Isadora placed the water kettle on to boil, then pulled a few supplies together while she waited for the whistle. Irritated, more with herself than anyone else, she pulled candles, tea leaves, thyme, a dish, and a few other items from the nearby sideboard and slapped them on the small table. *I'm nothing more than a weary old woman. How could I be so careless as to not investigate Cristiane's parents more fully, especially knowing Cristiane's distant ancestry? It is an unforgivable omission to not teach her about creatures. The demon likely would have killed her tonight.*

The kettle whistle began its slow crescendo, which pulled Isadora from her thoughts. She knew not to poke around the ether in her current state of mind. Chamomile tea and a calming spell were to start. Isadora lit the lavender candle and sipped her tea as she reflected on the conversation with Sarah while slowly exhaling the emotions of the night. She chanted the calming spell in between sips of her tea. She was in no rush, needing to ensure her mind was free of hostility and angst.

When centered, Isadora blew out the candle, put it aside, and pulled over a candle made of essential oils and infused with herbs such as dragon's blood, patchouli, clove, juniper, Saint John's Wort, frankincense, rosemary, and sage. When combined, the ingredients provide powerful protection. It was wise to be overly cautious. Rather than simply recite a protection ward, she used several layers of protection before probing through the cosmos. The spells were not only for herself but to protect Cristiane and any thought she had of Cristiane from reaching Beatrice. Isadora wanted to remain hidden while she searched for the truth. If Sarah was right, Isadora had to remain watchful of other forces at play when poking around the Bradford home.

Once adequate protections were in place, Isadora sighed and stretched. It was the middle of the night and she no longer had the stamina for late evenings. Exhaustion wore on her like a drenched wool cloak, but she knew Cristiane was going to her parents tomorrow. Isadora needed to see if Cristiane was in danger.

Isadora cleared the table of items used throughout the evening, except for what she needed for the reveal spell. If not conducted correctly, the spell could allow in unwanted energy, exposing matters to Beatrice or any witch near her. She needed answers without revealing herself, Cristiane, or the coven. At such a late hour, Beatrice would be asleep and her defenses down. Isadora hoped as much as she said the chant and sprinkled thyme into the dish. She then set the red candle in the middle of the dish over the thyme and lit it. Isadora sat back, waiting for the wax to melt and pool over the candle edges into the herb, while her mind cleared of her surroundings. Her eyes closed, she breathed in, slow and calm, willing her mind's energy to press out and find Beatrice.

It didn't take long for Isadora to locate Beatrice—she was asleep but restless.

Isadora did not provoke, but lingered and allowed her force to hover at a safe distance. She waited to experience the powers and aura near the sleeping witch. Beatrice tossed, mumbling in her sleep, clearly suffering turmoil, but as Isadora concentrated, trying to decipher a phrase or two, she perceived a menacing darkness around Beatrice. The blackness served as a barrier and prevented Isadora from grasping Beatrice's words. It blocked Isadora from finding the sleeping witch's hidden truth. The murky aura was suffocating, constricting, and as Isadora continued to chant, pressing to break through the barricade, she felt a sickness fill her abdomen.

Her stomach churned. Slowly at first, virtually unnoticed, but Isadora instinctively placed her palm over her mid-section. Her concentration on Beatrice, she didn't acknowledge the spread of evil filling her insides. Isadora choked on bile, jumped from the table, ran to the kitchen sink, and vomited between gulps of air. The sensation overpowered her with dread. She poured a glass of water and downed it.

Something cloaked Beatrice—preventing Isadora from identifying the truth. Yet that wasn't all. There was evil surrounding Beatrice, holding her down. Or Beatrice invited the evil on her own volition. Isadora was unsure. She could not discern whether Beatrice was practicing witchcraft tonight. One thing was clear: evil lived in the house. Cristiane must be careful during her visit.

Cristiane could not sleep. Although the tequila shots should have helped her fall asleep, she tossed and turned, thinking about the coven's rejection. It stung; Cristiane couldn't deny that the high priestess' words hurt her. And her teacher, Isadora, too, was crestfallen by her leader's rejection. *How did Isadora not foresee the coven leader's concerns?*

For hours, Cristiane paced back and forth with her thoughts racing while pulling at hangers and shoving clothes into a duffle. At least she made use of the time and packed a bag for the few days at her parents' house. When she noticed it was one in the morning, Cristiane climbed back into bed and longed for sleep to take her.

She thought of Isadora as a grandmother, an integral part of her life. Isadora was the salve to a wound Cris didn't know she had until the older woman became a part of her life. Isadora quickly became a cherished source of acceptance and love since her own mother rarely showed affection toward her. There was no point in introducing Isadora to her parents. Although Cristiane knew her father loved her dearly, Beatrice ruled their home. It seemed every time her dad tried to have quality time with her, especially as a teenager, her mom butted in and ruined it. Her mother would not have accepted Isadora. Cristiane realized how isolated and alone she was during her teenage years, and it made her angry. Tears welled up at the corners of her eyes.

Eventually, she slumbered, only for tormented dreams of vampires, werewolves, and demons to haunt her rest. Creatures were chasing her into a clearing surrounded by dark woods. A beacon of hope, distant flickering torches, came into view. Faint voices murmured from the same direction. Help was near. Cristiane ran as fast as her legs would carry her into the open meadow. Yet as soon as she reached the area, men yelled, ordering commands to each other as they swarmed her from all around. Heavy nets landed on her and the creatures at her heels. They tied her and the wolves onto stakes over piles of logs—into the pits to burn. Werewolves howled in protest as the fires were lit. As the hunters set Cristiane's pit aflame, she looked for mercy, but found none. The werewolves contorted, paws turning into hands, fur caught in fire turned to scorched flesh as wolf howls gurgled into the hollers of men. Then, as flames licked at her heels, the men fell silent.

She woke sitting upright and swatting wildly at her arms, trying to abate imaginary flames. Perspiration beaded along her hairline.

Irritated with having another tormenting dream. Cristiane hurried to craft a pleasant dream spell with cinnamon, lavender, and bay leaves and then placed the dish beside her bed. She crawled under the blanket and recited to herself as her eyes closed—*Give me quiet. Give me repose. Comfort my dreams. Anguish close.*

TWO

Cristiane crept along the road toward her parents' house. She caught sight of her mother in the distance and stopped at the corner to watch Beatrice stretch and roll her shoulders as if achy.

Her hair was disheveled in what was originally an updo held with a large clip. The clip freed half of her mother's hair and dangled behind an ear. Her mom put a hand on the opposite shoulder and rubbed at it as if dislodging a muscle cramp while she spun and twisted her neck. Her mom appeared old from the distance. Cristiane sighed and furrowed her lip, remembering the purpose of her visit.

So much for hoping to explore the house before either of them got home.

Cristiane caught sight of movement as Beatrice picked up the broom again and turned the corner toward her childhood home.

Beatrice was at the base of the front porch steps brushing fresh snow off the light post when Cristiane pulled into the driveway.

Cristiane got out of the car and walked toward her. "Hi, Mom." Cristiane gave a quick wave, then took a few more steps to embrace Beatrice. "It's good to see you."

"Hi?" Beatrice questioned as she returned the hug. "You're not pregnant, are you?"

"Jeez, Mom! No." Cristiane snapped back as she pulled away, keeping her hands on Beatrice's shoulders. "Can't I give my mom a hug without going through an inquisition?" She studied her mother's face. Fine lines lurked at the eye corners; frizzy gray hair glistened along her hairline with the mid-day sun. To Cristiane's surprise, Beatrice looked worn and tired.

"Sorry, you're right. I thought you were buttering me up for something."

"Not at all, happy to be home. I thought you'd be at the shop until closing today."

"Chelsea is running the store more often, so I can focus on making products to stock and do vendor purchases. Anyway, with the snow, we won't have many customers."

"Care to help me with a bag?" Cristiane started toward her car. "The snow sure made the drive from school fun. I didn't know we were getting so much of it."

"Sure. We're going to get a lot more of it tonight. It is pretty with the holiday lights, but you know it's unbearable after the New Year and horrible when spring should show by now." Beatrice took the suitcase Cristiane offered her.

"Imagine if we could snap a finger and have it disappear." Cristiane watched her mom's face for a change in expression but received none.

"That would be nice." Beatrice turned toward the house while Cristiane studied her voice, movements, anything that was unusual. She saw nothing. Disappointed, she pulled out her other bag, closed the trunk, and followed her mom's path in the snow toward the door.

Cristiane finished putting her clothes and belongings away and then sat on the edge of her bed, wondering how she was going to discover answers. Lost in thought, she barely noticed an orb hovering in the left corner near the closet door. She was used to the ghostly apparitions popping up from time to time since she experienced her first sighting during high school senior year. Her best friend's boyfriend, Robby, helped Cristiane make sense of her ability when it first happened. He'd been seeing apparitions from a very young age and then introduced Cristiane to Isadora, a wise witch with decades of experience.

Cristiane's ability presented itself after her old boyfriend, David, gave her an emerald necklace he'd found in an old crypt during their last Halloween frolic through the local cemetery. The emerald necklace wound up being a hand-crafted talisman from Cristiane's witch ancestors. Once Cristiane wore the necklace, bizarre injuries happened to those around her, and she started seeing spirits.

Since then, several ghosts found their way to Cristiane. Most looked for help in solving an unresolved issue before leaving her alone. She didn't witness a light or sign of the ghosts crossing to another dimensional plane, but that's how Isadora and Robby described it when the ghosts moved on. Isadora clarified the apparitions can see their exit when they're ready and vanish from our sight.

With a tilt of her head, Cristiane studied the orb, or ghost light, as she liked to call them. There was a hint of gray shadow behind it. Like when she encountered a spirit in her car, maybe this orb was attached to another spirit, or to its surroundings at the time of death. She could not tell. Her friend Robby insisted the spirits make contact when either they were frantic for help, or when a clairvoyant was ready to see them and help in their quest. So far, Cristiane hadn't run into any desperate ghosts and she wanted to keep it that way. Desperation makes souls do stupid things. She could only imagine that frantic ghosts could be dangerous and stupid, a combination that equals trouble. Cristiane stood to move closer and attempt to talk with the spirit when Jeffrey, her dad, popped his head into her room.

His eyes sparkled as he smiled at his daughter. "Pretty soon you'll finish college, and we can convert your room to a warm study. It's cold by the garage in the winter. You know, I've wanted to make this a cozy spot to work on puzzles and models."

"Dad!" Cristiane turned to give him a giant hug. "You've had an empty nest for three years. You could have changed the room any time."

Jeffrey kissed the top of his daughter's head as he squeezed her tight, returning her embrace. "Where would you go if we'd converted your room sooner? You need a place to call home during college. Whether coming home during a school break or to run to when you feel overwhelmed. This is your home whenever you need it."

"Thanks, Dad. I appreciate it, but I'll be done with school by Christmas and who knows where a job will lead?" Cristiane stepped back from Jeffrey, watching to see how her words landed on her father.

"Don't remind me, sweet pea. You're growing up too fast." His eyes glistening, Jeffrey cleared his throat and walked across the room to the frost-covered window. "If this weather keeps up, your mother and I may have to sell and move farther south. Climate change makes the seasons too unpredictable here in the northeast."

"Settle by a warm beach and you may never get rid of me. You know I love the heat." Cristiane walked to the left corner, waving a hand around where the ghost light was a moment earlier. She mentally noted the frigid air before swinging back toward her father. He looked at her with a quizzical, scrunched-up face. "Spider web. You and mom must not clean in here often."

"We don't."

Jeffrey's stomach gurgled. "Ah, that reminds me. Lunch is ready if you're hungry. I whipped up some of your favorites: turkey club, sliced pineapple, and kettle chips with dip."

"I'm famished. Dad, you're the best." Cristiane couldn't help but think about how different her parents were to her. Beatrice could barely hug her without feeling obligated and uncomfortable. "Any chance you have a cold beer in the fridge?"

"Yep. It's that fancy lager you brought home on your last visit, too."

"Nice! With this pampering, why would I want to get my own place?" Cristiane followed her dad out the door. When they passed her parents' bedroom, Cristiane paused as she saw a ghost light hover behind her mother. *Now that's odd. If Mom's a witch, shouldn't she see spirits like I do?*

Dinner with her parents was going well until Cristiane asked her mother about their ancestry. They hadn't talked about their ancestors buried in the local cemetery, even though Cristiane and her friends went there every Halloween since they were in middle school. During the last Halloween outing with her friends three years earlier, Cristiane found her forebears in a small mausoleum in the graveyard. An inscription explained the townspeople had buried her witch ancestors there after prosecution during the historic witch trials around Salem and their hometown. Constance Worthington, a prominent ancestor, had the tomb built for her mother Rachel, and Rachel's mother and aunt, to honor them and serve as a historical reminder to the community.

Her mother rarely talked about her family history, but this time Cristiane pushed for details.

Beatrice retaliated with her own questions about Cristiane's plans if she graduated early. Beatrice continued to press about getting an internship or part-time job now, so it would be easier to get a permanent position. Cristiane wasn't ready to discuss her future. Besides, she was blazing through classes, far ahead of schedule. She was too anxious to apply for internships or think about a proper job. But Cristiane realized it was her mother's tactic to divert the conversation. She didn't want to push her mother too soon.

Thusly, Cristiane jumped at the chance to meet up with her high school friends when Tina called to get together.

"Let me see that rock!" Cristiane pulled Tina's hand into the light over the bar table. "I can't believe Robby splurged for that—it's huge."

Robby beamed with pride as he leaned over his bride-to-be's shoulder. "I can't take all the credit. The center emerald cut stone was my grandmother's. We took the diamond to the jeweler, and they made the diamond-and-sapphire-studded infinity band based on my specifications. Over the past two years, it helped to be very attentive, listening and learning what Tina liked."

Tina leaned away so she could look into Robby's eyes. "Two years? You never mentioned that you had this planned that long ago." She kissed him quickly, then turned to Cristiane, eyebrows raised and mouthed, "Wow!"

"What can I say? I knew you were the one." Robby slid into the booth beside Tina and gave her thigh a light squeeze.

"Okay, okay. Enough with the gushy stuff. I'm thrilled for you both." Cristiane smiled at her friends. She raised her margarita. "Cheers!"

Glasses clanked, and then the air fell silent as they each took a sip from their drinks. As Tina set her glass down, she leaned into Cristiane. "Look toward the door. David is coming in with that group. Are you sure you're okay?"

"Of course, I'm fine. I broke up with him, remember?" Cristiane looked toward the door, curious but calm.

"Well, I know. But he's bringing Joyce."

"Joyce?" David and a bubbly woman came around the table as the question slid from her lips.

"Hey, Cris. Has Tina been telling you about Joyce?" David pulled up a chair and guided the young woman with tight, curly hair to take the seat. "Cristiane, meet Joyce. Joyce, meet Cristiane. You know, the high school girlfriend I mentioned." David and the other men pulled more chairs to the table, then headed to the bar for drinks.

After giving a quick glance to Tina and Robby, she extended her hand to the woman sitting across from her. "Hi Joyce, nice to meet you. No, Tina hasn't told me anything, just your name. I'd love—"

"Oh my gosh, it's so great to finally meet you. David has told me all about growing up with you and your high school antics: school dances, trips to the cemetery. You name it. I'm happy to have a face with the name now." Joyce grabbed Cristiane's hand between her own and shook it vigorously as she cracked a bright smile.

Joyce was effervescent, all smiles, as enthusiasm radiated off her. Joyce didn't appear self-conscious at all. Even the sizeable gap between bright white teeth fit with her personality. Cristiane took a quick chug of her margarita. "How did you two meet?"

"Skydiving." Joyce noticed Cristiane's eyes pop. "David won a beginner skydiving package from the local radio station last summer, and I was the instructor for the course. We've been hanging out ever since." Joyce took the beer David offered and took a few quick sips. "I'm an Adventure Sports Instructor. I specialize in skydiving, bungy jumping, paragliding, air balloons—oh, and mountain climbing. Some people like to climb up, then jump off the mountain. David wants to try that next as he's been training to climb in Yellowstone Park and then paraglide from the mountaintop."

Joyce saw Cristiane look at David with a quizzical stare. "I'm sorry, I talk a lot. Sometimes I don't know when to shut it." Joyce sat back and put her hand to her mouth, crinkling her eyes, as she laughed.

"Oh, no. I'm sorry, you're fine. I'm a little surprised that David is so adventurous. He liked to tell jokes but was otherwise quiet in high school." Cristiane liked Joyce and her sparkling personality. She couldn't help but smile at David's new girlfriend.

"That's what he said, too." Joyce smacked his leg and then took his hand as he pulled his chair beside hers. "I had a tough time believing he was a quiet jokester. But he was shy in his first adventure course. I didn't think about it because many people are timid at first. He loves to tell jokes and, boy, can he make me laugh." Joyce beamed as she looked at David, clearly smitten.

David gave Joyce a quick kiss. "I was coming to grips with the limits I had placed on myself as a kid after my father died. I realized, with help from my mom, that I withdrew and stopped being the adventurous person I used to be as a child. Other than the weird things the four of us would get into as nerdy kids, I wasn't comfortable in my own skin." David glanced at Tina, Robby, and Cristiane. "My parents used to take us on so many adventures. I'd forgotten how happy those outings made me feel. It took time and forcing myself out of my comfort zone, but I started hiking and then joined a rowing team. But when I tried the skydiving class, this lady truly pulled me out of my shell."

Cristiane stood, raised her glass, and waited for the others around the table to follow suit. "Well, I'm glad Joyce helped you crawl out of your shell. Here's to new loves and old friendships." She clinked glasses with everyone and then sat back, smiling with relief that there was no tension between them.

"And to new friends. Let's finish introductions." Robby waved to get everyone's attention and have them quiet down. "Cristiane, these two gorgeous ladies are Claire and Robyn, and these three fine gentlemen are Jarvis, Zack, and Liam. Zack has dibs on Liam, so no flirting with those two." Each tipped their fingers to their foreheads in salute as Robby rattled off their names.

Zack hopped over and gave Cristiane a peck on the cheek with a quick hug. "You can flirt with us all you want."

"I agree." Liam raised his glass. "Flirting for everyone."

The table roared with laughter.

Cristiane laughed and smiled so much it hurt. "To new friends. It's nice to meet all of you."

A brief time later, Cristiane leaned back in her seat and watched the group say their goodbyes to David and Joyce. Cristiane enjoyed the banter between them throughout the evening. Joyce stole the crowd with her spirited talk of learning how to teach the various sports and then gaining certification. David was a different person, lively and engaged when Joyce spoke. He was always funny in high school, but Cristiane could see that he was bolder now, more confident rather than using humor to hide insecurities, like he did when they were younger. She waved to the others as they left the bar after David and Joyce.

Tina walked to the restroom as Robby came back to the table. "So, what'd you think of everyone?" Robby plopped down in his seat, then poured the rest of the beer pitcher into their glasses.

"Clearly, David and Joyce will follow down the aisle right after you and Tina. Those two are joined at the hip."

Cristiane jested before taking a big gulp. "I like her, and David is so different. He beams when he looks at her. You know they're meant to be."

"You might be right. They've been inseparable since the summer. It'll be a year come May." Robby looked at Cristiane from the corner of his eye. "And who is dangling from your arm these days? I haven't heard Tina mention that you're dating anyone."

"Nope. I'm flying solo." Cristiane rubbed the back of her neck and shrugged. "I haven't had time to date, honestly."

Robby and Cristiane fell silent, both looking at the far corner of the bar. A haggard ghost sat at the corner table. He was frail, with patchy clothes two to three sizes too big hanging from his shoulders.

Robby nudged her. "You see that?"

"Yep. Poor guy, by the looks of it, he drank himself to death."

"You're probably right." Robby shook his head. "I tried to engage him a few months ago when the bar was empty. Charlie, the bartender, was in the back getting bottles to restock. I don't want people to think I'm talking to myself, you know."

Cristiane gave an understanding nod.

"I tried, but he didn't want to talk with me. He muttered something I couldn't understand and plunked his head down on the table. I guess he died drunk, so it's hard to figure out what he needs to cross over."

"That's strange. Did Isadora give any guidance on how to handle it?"

"Not really. She said she'd come by sometime and see if she could help. She'll take care of the poor soul when the weather clears and she can drive on her own."

"Speaking of ghosts, shouldn't my mom be able to see them if I can?" With the coven rejection raw on her nerves, she wasn't ready to share everything about why she wanted to know. "I noticed the orb a few times yesterday in my parents' house. It's not shown up at their house before. But it was next to my mom at noon, and she didn't seem to notice."

"Not necessarily. You couldn't see spirits until the necklace David gave you was stuck around your neck. Maybe your mom doesn't know the family legacy and hasn't tapped into her witchiness." Robby shrugged as he struck a finger against the beer stein. "Have you talked to her about any of this since releasing the ghosts of Rachel and Prudence?"

"How do you think my mom would react if I'd told her David gave me an enchanted necklace from one of our dead ancestors? And, by the way," she reminded Robby with a friendly nudge, "the curse assaulted any man who came near me until my friends and a wise witch met in the cemetery with me to release the curse and help the ancestral witch spirits cross into the next dimension."

"Now that you say it out loud, it sounds like you lost your mind." Robby took a swig of his drink.

"You know how my mom is with me. She can barely get through dinner without a bitter remark. I haven't asked if she practices the craft or mentioned anything to her, especially about studying witchcraft or seeing ghosts." Cristiane shook her head and worried her lip. "I brought up our ancestry, but she shut me down. Mom used to be fun when I was little, but since high school, we keep butting heads. I can't talk with her about anything in my life."

"Have you tried your dad? It'd be hard to keep it from your spouse over 20 years."

"Maybe. He is the opposite of Mom. He's so trusting of her. I can attempt, but I imagine he would have said something, or would have insisted Mom tell me. He must be in the dark, or she doesn't practice witchcraft at all." Cristiane saw Tina walking back to the table. "Okay, you two lovebirds. I'm going to call it a night. I hope I can see you again before the week is over."

They gave quick hugs goodbye, and then Cristiane walked slowly to the door. The somber spirit in the corner looked up briefly. His deep, smoke-filled eye sockets pierced her gaze. Cristiane gave a half-smile and quickened her pace through the door, out to the frigid night air.

THREE

"**D**ad wasn't at all helpful this morning. He didn't know about Mom's ancestry related to the local cemetery and said he knew little about her lineage since my grandmother died right before they met." Cristiane cradled her cell phone as she stood looking out her bedroom window, watching her dad leave to play basketball at the VFW. "I need to look around myself."

Isadora blew out an exasperated breath. "Don't play your hand too quickly, Cris. Be careful. I find it hard to believe your mother doesn't know her ancestry when it's buried in the town cemetery."

"That's what I thought. I see nothing unusual around the house, and she hasn't nipped at my hints."

"Don't needle. There are too many scenarios that go to an awful end if she practices dark magic. Be careful. When I investigated, the surrounding presence was formidable. I don't think it was witch magic, but something more sinister." Isadora's concern was palpable. Her voice wobbled with worry. "You'll know the opportunity when it presents."

Not twenty minutes later, the opportunity arose.

"Cris, why don't you go with me to the grocery store? We can get lunch while we're out."

"Thanks, Mom. I'm still whipped from last night. You know I don't drink very often. I think I'll take a nap while the house is quiet." Cristiane was surprised by her mom's invite but knew she wouldn't press. They rarely did well on outings on their own.

"Okay. Text if you want me to pick up anything special for you."

Cristiane heard the front door open. Mom wasn't waiting, which was a good sign. "Thanks. I'm sure I'll be fine. Just need a little more sleep." She heard the door close and lock. Cristiane peeked through a curtain edge and watched Beatrice pull out of the driveway and then take off down the road. *Now the hunt begins.*

Cristiane looked through her supply case and retrieved amethyst and lapis lazuli stones. She stopped in the bathroom and ran the crystals under chilly water, cleansing away any negativity or her own residual energy. Moving quickly from room to room, Cristiane started with the basement and worked her way up to the top floor. She used the crystals to hone her vibrational energy to locate the presence or use of magic. The kitchen held her up for a few minutes until Cristiane realized her mom must use alchemy to prepare meals. Beatrice must have made a recent meal in haste and hadn't cleaned the area of residual magical energy. *She is a superb cook.*

When she reached the top floor and stood at the entry of her parents' bedroom, Cristiane's senses tingled as the stones warmed in her hands. The spell was not revealing anything specific, but rather an intuitive pull held her in the room. Guessing her mother had a dampening spell to mask its contents, she had to find whatever was causing the sensation before either of her parents returned home.

Cristiane opened the closet that faced the front of the house. Her senses deadened. Nothing was in the space other than her dad's clothes, half on the hangers with many haphazardly tossed on the shelves, and a pile of shoes in the corner. She loved him, but he was a slob. There were shoe racks lining the closet floor, but he still kicked off every pair into the same corner and had to dig into the pile whenever he needed something hidden below.

She turned and moved toward her mom's closet at the opposite end of the room. As she approached, goosebumps popped up along her forearms. Something was there. Cristiane noticed the lock her mom had on the door since she was little was now gone. The door frame was smooth to the touch, with bright white trim where the lock used to be. No need to keep a lock when everyone has grown.

Cristiane couldn't recall if the lock had always been there. Her mom said they put the latch on when Cristiane was two years old, after she'd wandered inside and couldn't get out. They searched everywhere that day and had neighbors canvasing the nearby streets. Beatrice had a call in to the police when Dad finally found Cris huddled in the closet, crying because she couldn't turn the door handle. Distraught, they'd put the lock on immediately. *I always thought it strange that I couldn't remember being lost in the closet.* They designed all the bedroom closets the same, but Mom's closet had a lock.

Cristiane opened the door and stood for a moment, taking a mental note of item placement. Beatrice was meticulously neat. Her mother would notice if something wasn't right. As Cristiane looked from top to bottom, the walls popped out as something strange occurred to her. *Who wallpapers their closet with flowers from floor to ceiling?*

Cris knew she'd found a clue, drawing the clothes apart to reveal the back wall. She stepped in and lightly tapped across the wall, listening for a change. A hollowness in the center. There must be a door. As she searched quickly, she stood with her hands out wide, feeling with the tips of her fingers. She felt a slight change in the pattern to her right and followed it around. She found hinges on the left, but no access handle. There was nothing to grab, no handle, indentation, or knob. Frustrated, she put her hand to the wall while cursing under her breath. A faint click startled her. As she pulled her hand back to look around, the wall pulled away slightly—a pressure release. Clever.

As she stepped into the dark space, straightened, and gathered her bearings, the surroundings gave her pause. When her eyes adjusted to the lack of light, she noticed a switch to her left and flicked it on. The room sat above the garage, hidden near the upstairs AC unit where she now stood. The room was larger than she expected, like the size of a bathroom.

At the opposite end of the entrance, a small altar was messy and littered with items—candles, crystals, incense, and herbs. Nothing unusual, but she took a few photos with her cell phone. To the right was an end table with a few drawers. Curious, Cristiane opened the bottom drawer to find a pad of yellowed paper on which there was a list of names and addresses written in scrawling cursive. Not her mother's writing. Cristiane closed the drawer and moved to the next one. This was full of photos—some incredibly old and worn. Drawn to the edge of one, she pulled it out of the pile and held it to the light. She felt weary touching the strange portrait. Two men stood near an odd pentagram backdrop, but the pentagram was different, upside down, with a goat's head etched within it. She didn't like the photograph's aura and hurried to take a picture and put it back in the drawer. Her foot hit a large wooden trunk. She kneeled to investigate. But Beatrice had it locked with a strong padlock. She'd need to find a key.

A car door slammed. Cristiane glanced at her phone. It'd been over an hour since Beatrice had left. Cristiane hurried and took another photo, then turned off the light and slipped out of the area, shutting the entrance without causing a tear to the wallpaper. She moved the clothes hangers back in place and studied her placement before closing the door. *Was it closed all the way? Damn, I can't remember.*

Rushing to her room, the front door opened and Cristiane could hear the rustle of bags being dropped inside as Beatrice muttered, "Damn snow."

Cristiane quickly darted across the upstairs to her own room and jumped onto the bed, pulling the cover over herself as if sleeping. A few moments later, Beatrice pushed the bedroom door open and looked in longer than Cristiane thought was normal. Another moment passed, then the door soon clicked shut as Cristiane let go of an anxious sigh.

FOUR

Anxious, Cristiane sent the last text to Isadora with the photos taken in Beatrice's altar room and waited. She kept checking her phone for Isadora's reply while remaining huddled under the covers. She didn't want Beatrice to come back into the room. Cristiane nodded off when she heard her dad pull into the driveway twenty minutes later. As soon as she heard a noise loud enough to use as an excuse, she went downstairs.

"Hey, Pumpkin. Mom said you needed a rest. Too much partying for you last night, I hear." Jeffrey tousled Cristiane's hair as he sat next to her on the kitchen barstool and then popped a beer open, tilting it toward his daughter. "Little hair of the dog?"

Chuckling, Cristiane grabbed the beer from her dad. "Sure, I can handle it." She then chugged half the beer, watching his shocked expression from the corner of her eye. "Oh, did you mean to keep this one for yourself?"

"I'll grab another."

"You two. Here you go." Beatrice handed her husband a fresh beer, the top already off the bottle.

Cristiane looked at the spread on the kitchen counter. Lasagna, chopped vegetables, and bread dough rising in a covered bowl lay strewn across the counter's length. "How long was I asleep? You went shopping and made all of this?" Cristiane studied her mother's face, waiting for a reply.

"Oh, shopping didn't take me long. I had a lot of time to prepare dinner." Beatrice turned and grabbed a wine glass and wine bottle from the shelf over her head. "It takes less time to cook than you think."

Cristiane watched her mother pour a glass of wine. She knew dinner preparations took longer than the 30 minutes her mother had been home.

The rest of the afternoon and throughout dinner were calmer than Cristiane remembered in some time. Her mother was relaxed and hadn't nit-picked at anything Cristiane said through dinner. Both her parents commented on how proud they were of her achievements in school and that she would graduate a semester earlier than most. Everyone cleared the table together as Cristiane started washing the dishes that wouldn't fit in the dishwasher.

A few minutes later, Beatrice came back into the room, ready to go to her book club meeting. She stood watching Cristiane for a moment. "Did you go into my closet today?" Her voice was short and accusatory.

Beatrice's tone sent Cristiane's mind back to a time in middle school. Beatrice had jumped on her for borrowing makeup to experiment with her friend, Tina, after school. Cristiane had asked permission before school, but that afternoon, as she and Tina had painted on brightly colored eyelids and ruby lips, Beatrice walked through the bedroom doorway and scolded Cristiane for taking the makeup without consent.

Embarrassed, Tina had cowered away from the conflict to wash her face.

Cristiane reminded her mother of asking her that morning and gaining consent. Beatrice then berated Cristiane again and refused to admit that she'd forgotten. Crestfallen,

Cristiane never asked to borrow anything from her mother again.

Thinking quickly on her feet, Cristiane wiped her hands dry and turned to face her mom with as normal a voice as she could muster. "Yeah, I wanted a quick throw. You know, something not so heavy for my nap, but I didn't find anything, so I just climbed into the heavy comforter on my bed. Sorry, did I knock something off a shelf?" Cristiane's eyebrows raised as she waited for Beatrice to respond.

"No, nothing's wrong. The hangers weren't in their proper place." Beatrice studied her daughter, eyes slightly askance as she decided whether to believe the explanation.

"I probably looked on the floor, too. I can't remember." Cristiane gave a quick smile and changed the subject. "Why don't I go with you to your book club tonight? I'd like to meet some of your friends."

Beatrice straightened, clearly agitated by Cristiane's interest in her book club. "No, not tonight. Maybe another time when I can announce you joining us beforehand. Some of the older ladies are sticklers for routine. They wouldn't be happy with someone new popping into our gathering without prior notice." Beatrice shifted in place, her fingers pulling at the raised wood chips in the door trim.

"Notice? You make it sound like a top-secret operation. It's just a book club group." Cristiane leaned against the counter and crossed her arms, glaring at her mother. "What's the real reason I can't go with you?"

"What do you mean, real reason? You just can't go with me tonight."

"But why the secrecy? Dad doesn't know any of them. Are you drinking, smoking pot, and dancing around stone pillars under the moonlight?"

"Now you're being silly. As I said, another time." Beatrice's voice was an octave higher as she stood tall and smoothed her hands over her hips, not making eye contact with Cristiane. She was ready to leave. "I'll find out the next title we're reading and let you know later. We're done here."

"Fine. I'll be waiting," Cristiane stabbed back curtly. "Be sure to give the ladies our best."

"Now you're just being snotty." Without looking, she walked to the door.

"Like mother, like daughter, I suppose," Cristiane spewed to her mother's back as the door slammed shut. She smacked the counter. "Shit, she drives me crazy."

"Now—that's your mother you're talking about, young lady."

"Oh, sorry, Dad. She knows how to push all the wrong buttons."

"It's a shame. You two used to do so much together when you were younger. There was nothing your mom could do that would bother you." Jeffrey gestured to a stool for Cristiane to sit. He popped the caps off a couple of beers and sat beside her. "You used to follow her around like a shadow, mimicking everything she would do. Whether that was folding laundry, planting herbs in the garden, or cleaning around the house."

"I remember bits and pieces. When did we plant herbs?" Cristiane looked at her dad, flabbergasted. "Now we seem to tolerate each other. It's been like this since high school. We bicker over everything."

"Your mom has always been a private person, but maybe it had more to do with you growing up, becoming independent, and less about your mom's attitude. I'm not saying it's all you, because I cringe sometimes when I hear what she says to you, but relationships are a two-way street. You both have to work at it. She's the parent, but now that you're also an adult, maybe you can find a path back to each other."

"Daddy, I don't know. It's hard with Mom, but I'm willing to try. I feel she's hiding something from both of us. You know her ancestors are in that cemetery at the corner of town. How could she not know that history, or share it with me—us? And what's with the room behind her closet?"

"Don't go jumping to conclusions. You've barely been home the past few years. Have you tried asking her about your grandmother's family?"

"Other than the other night at dinner? Well, no. Not yet anyway. It seems like we fight before I get a chance."

"All right then, ask her. That's where you start." Jeffrey patted his daughter's hand. "As far as that yoga room, your mom has had it for years to meditate and relax. Whatever she does, it is her space, and she can light that terrible incense without hearing from me. I have my study; she has her corner in the wall—literally."

"Mom's meditating and doing yoga in there?" Cristiane knew it was more than that, but she couldn't get into it with her dad until she had facts. "I guess that explains the lock on the door all those years ago, after I got stuck in there."

"When were you stuck in your mom's closet?"

"Mom said I was two years old. You don't remember?" Cristiane was confused. Beatrice had recited the day's events when Cristiane had gone missing as a little girl. Her mother was worried that she had been taken, or that she had gone astray in the nearby woods. Cristiane wasn't found until hours later, in her mother's closet.

"You've never gotten away from us. If you were stuck in a closet, she found you before I came home, and it wasn't a big enough concern that the incident stuck with me." Jeffrey looked at his daughter. "I would have remembered if you were ever missing."

"I must have misunderstood Mom." But Cristiane was certain there was another reason for the door lock. "Listen, I'm gonna change and meet some of the old gang at the little pub, Willie's. You want to go with me? Robby and Tina are engaged and David has a great new girlfriend. You'd like her."

"No, sweetie. You go ahead. I've had more than my share of beer today." He took a long swig from the bottle, finishing his drink. "I think I'll watch one of those action movies your mom hates and call it a night."

"Okay, Dad. I love you. If you change your mind, you know where to find me." Cristiane kissed his temple and then tossed her bottle into the recycle bin.

Cristiane drove by the old mill pub. Robby and Tina didn't want to meet, but maybe David and Joyce were there. Cristiane wished she'd gotten Joyce's phone number the other night. David's new girlfriend was a lot of fun. In fact, all the people she met were great. She was the only one who had relocated for college. The others socialized often. A twinge of jealousy tugged at her as she pulled in to cruise the parking lot. She had to go back to Springfield in a week, where it'd been so hard to meet anyone outside of class, much less make friends.

Not recognizing any cars, Cristiane turned right, toward downtown. She hadn't been there in a while. At least it was a change of scenery, and the roads would be clear of the latest snow. As she approached Main Street, a tall figure with hunched broad shoulders turned out of the alley, capturing her attention. She could have sworn he had glowing eyes. Distracted, she ran the light. A passing car laid on the horn, pulling her back to reality.

The horn also caught the figure's attention. It turned toward Cristiane, his glowing violet eyes passing her, targeted at the driver honking and yelling obscenities as it sped by. The man remained standing long after the car was gone.

Cristiane slowed and pulled into a parking space opposite Javier's nightclub. "What the hell is that?" She slid down in the seat to hide. Her eyes were barely over the edge of the window frame as she turned to catch the man's face. Caught in the streetlight, his features shocked Cristiane. His skin was tough, like leather, but a strange translucent quality that made her skin crawl. The bones were visible here and there across his profile. His eyes glowed beyond where eyes would normally fit and he had no eyebrows or other hair that she could tell. He didn't look human. Yet his arm was in a sling and he limped grotesquely. Watching him, or it, walk back into the alley made her shiver.

The SUV at the corner of the alley also made her shiver. Bolting upright, Cristiane pulled the gear in reverse and eased the vehicle back a little so she could read the license plate. There was no denying it—BeaBee2. *Why is Mom at a nightclub?*

As Cristiane contemplated this new revelation, two women stepped out of a side door in the alley. One was clearly Beatrice, based on her clothes and how she walked. The unknown woman was the same height, but broad-shouldered, wearing a sheath dress and heels. Cristiane turned off her car and slipped down into the seat again. A man came out to join the two women, offered them both a cigarette and lit them before lighting his own. *Mom doesn't smoke. What the hell is going on?*

Moments ticked by as she watched the three in the alley smoke, drink, and talk. Cristiane inched her nose to the window as condensation formed from her breath against the glass. She rubbed at it with her coat sleeve, only to smear the view. Irritated, she inched the window down trying to clear the interior fog as the man took out a key and opened the alley door, ushering the women in first before he followed behind them, his hand caressing Beatrice's back as she walked ahead into the building.

Cristiane's mind was reeling. *That is not a book club.*

Her cell phone rang, breaking the silence and causing Cristiane to jump. "Hello? What?"

"Are you okay? What's wrong?"

"Oh, sorry, Isadora. I'm fine. It's—I just saw my mom smoking and drinking outside of Javier's night club. She is supposed to be at a book club with a bunch of ladies." Cristiane settled down at the sound of Isadora's voice. "Did you find anything in the pictures?"

"Your mom is a practicing witch. There are some disturbing things in the photos, but I don't want to get into it on the phone." Isadora trailed off.

"Isadora? What?"

"Be careful and cast a protection spell to shield you from danger. Do it before you go home." Isadora spoke with more urgency. "I'm not sure how much longer my wards will hold. The demon you hit the other night may be near, too. You have to be watchful. I don't know exactly what we're dealing with besides your mom. I need to consult with Sarah before we talk more about it."

"Is that it? That's all you're going to give me? My mom is a completely different person than who I knew. She could be having an affair. The guy had his hands on her. What do I say to my dad?"

"Nothing! Say nothing to your dad. It could put him in harm's way. Hold tight a little longer. I'll be in touch soon." Isadora hung up.

Cristiane stared at the phone. Not wanting to go home, she pulled out onto the street and drove around town. With the side streets covered in snow, she stayed on the main roads until she noticed she'd driven in a wide circle, back where she started. Cristiane pulled into the parking lot at Willie's pub. No cars that she recognized, but she parked and waited a few minutes before going home. She took a deep breath. She turned up the heat and rubbed her hands in the warm air flowing from the vent while gazing around the area. Someone with a familiar face walked along the sidewalk towards the entrance. *Was that Liam or Jarvis? Only one way to find out.*

FIVE

The doorbell rang while Beatrice had her hands in the sink rinsing dinner dishes. "Jeffrey, you're not expecting anyone tonight, are you? Cris, it's probably one of your friends. Can you get the door?"

With a sigh, Cristiane jumped up to see who had come to visit. Once close to the door, an overwhelming sense of dread invaded her mind. She grew agitated the closer she got to the door. Her gut told her to not open it. She shook off the feeling, then turned the handle as Beatrice darted from the kitchen.

"No, Cris, I'll get—"

But the door swung open before Beatrice could stop her daughter. In front of Cristiane stood an older woman of average height. She looked as surprised as Cristiane, but, with a wry smile, she extended her hand.

Cristiane felt gut-punched and stepped back a few paces. She reeled as the realization hit her. Last night, this woman stood in the alley with her mother. She stared at the woman's outstretched hand, unwilling to touch it.

"Well, who do we have here?"

The woman's aura was menacing, as if it pulled the life from anyone in her presence. Shocked, Cristiane waved her hand and slammed the door shut on the woman.

"Don't! No!" Beatrice screamed as she ran to the door. "Go to your room." Beatrice slammed the door behind her as she rushed out.

Cristiane turned to her father. "Dad, what's that about? Do you know that woman?"

Her dad brought an ice cream bowl with him from the kitchen, not concerned with what had occurred. "I don't, sugar bear. Just do as your mom asked. We'll figure this out when she comes back inside." Jeffrey sat in the family room and clicked on the remote.

"I'm not a child. I'm going upstairs so I can watch them from my window, not because Mom told me to like I'm a scolded toddler." Annoyed, Cristiane shook her head at her father. His ability to brush off conflict drove her crazy.

Cristiane ran to her bedroom window. She positioned herself to watch, hiding behind the curtain. Beatrice had her arms crossed, wrapped around herself, guarded or cold, or both. The visitor had a finger pointed at her face, flapping it by her mom's nose. Whomever she was, Beatrice had pissed her off. Cristiane noticed her mother make a tight fist with one hand under her crossed arms the more the woman talked. Mom was holding back.

Cristiane bent down and worked the window up, hoping she could overhear the conversation. She blew out a breath she didn't realize she was holding. With a wave of her fingers, the window eased up a few inches without a sound. She hid once more at the corner of the window and listened.

"Xirnan sensed someone snooping around the club last night. A young woman he spotted lurking around the alley entrance while we had our meeting." The woman's eyes were dark daggers, glowing with a hint of magic. Her words to Beatrice spat out with venom. "Who is the girl inside? Is she your daughter?"

The woman was a few inches shorter than her mother, with a blunt haircut to black hair, making her look formidable with broad shoulders and a wide stance. It was a posture that reminded Cristiane of someone in the military. This woman knew how to handle herself. If they got into a physical fight, Beatrice would lose. If magic was involved, Cristiane didn't know who would win.

"I'm sure I've mentioned her before. Don't be ridiculous, Nissa. She was out with friends and thinks I was at a book club gathering." Beatrice didn't want a front yard confrontation for the neighbors to see. "All of us have kept our personal lives separate from the group. I'm sure I have told you about her, but like you, we don't talk about our families."

"You are not just anyone. You made a promise many years ago. We have not forgotten." Nissa grabbed Beatrice hard. Cristiane watched the fingernails dig into the back of her mother's arm as Nissa moved closer and whispered in her mother's ear. The grip tightened as Nissa pulled back a little. "Once I discover everything you have been hiding, I will be in touch soon."

Cristiane twisted, ready to dart down the stairs to help her mom, when she saw Nissa shove Beatrice away. Nissa strode toward a black SUV at the end of the drive, waiting. Cristiane hadn't noticed the vehicle while the women argued, but now curiosity made her lean closer to the glass, her breath fogging the window. Someone else was behind the wheel as Nissa slid in on the passenger side. As they backed out onto the road, Cristiane's eyes remained glued to the driver's window, trying to catch a view of whomever drove to their home.

The SUV started forward, then stopped for a moment—long enough to glimpse the glowing lavender eyes and translucent skin of the creature she had seen outside Javier's. It stared at her, and as it did, the eyes turned a fiery red, flames dancing in their sockets. Cristiane took a step back, her eyes attached to those in the vehicle, shining like torches in the dark. A smirk spread across his bony face before he turned and vanished into the murky interior. Pushing herself away from the window, Cristiane plopped on her bed, flabbergasted and worried.

A minute later, a shivering Beatrice walked back into the house, closed the door, and leaned against it with her head down. She was visibly shaken. Whatever happened, she looked broken, weak.

"Beatrice, our daughter is upstairs. You need to talk to her." Jeffrey turned from his chair, waiting for his wife to respond.

Beatrice nodded. "I understand. I believed something was wrong, and I was right, but that doesn't excuse me from yelling at her." She trudged up the stairs and walked down the short hallway to her daughter's room. Cristiane was sitting on the edge of the bed.

"Can I come in?" Beatrice waited until Cristiane waved her in and then sat down next to her daughter. Beatrice patted Cris on the knee. "Someone from the book club died and Nissa Marth came by to tell me the news."

Cris knew her mother was lying, but also realized another confrontation wouldn't help her find out the truth. Cristiane kept her head down for a moment until she noted Beatrice was shaking. Cristiane sensed it was out of fear and not sadness or the cold. She looked at her mom, noting the agonizing dread stamped across her face. "Mom, it looked like you were arguing. Who was her driver? He's creepy as hell. What are you not telling me?"

Beatrice looked at Cris for a long moment and then spoke with her normal harsh tone. "It seems you—" She shook her head while putting up a hand. Beatrice stopped, took a breath, and then bowed her head. With a much gentler voice, she wrapped an arm around Cristiane. "Nothing, Cris. I'm processing the news, is all. I don't know who drove her here, but don't you worry about a thing." After getting up from the bed, she turned to Cristiane. She bent down and gave Cris a kiss on the forehead. "I love you. Let's go downstairs and have some ice cream."

Cris was again speechless. Her mother never showed such tenderness. She examined her mom's walk to the door, shoulders drooped, not her mother's normal poise and elegance.

"Mom?" The question hung in the air between them, full of questions and concern.

Beatrice turned, "Let it go, Cris. It'll be okay. We'll be okay."

Cris saw chilling fear. Worry danced at the corner of her mother's eyes before the façade of a smile replaced it. A flicker of something leaped across Beatrice's features—determination or anger mixed with concern. Cris couldn't interpret the expression as her mother turned toward the hall.

"Your father is going to eat all the ice cream. Let's pull out the fixings and make him start the movie over for us."

Despair surrounded Cristiane as it crept into her room with her mother. Melancholy journeyed through the door as a veiled mist, now refusing to budge. The weight of it settled like a heavy anchor, full of horror and foreboding. Something evil lurked around the corners. She couldn't solve the mystery on her own, but it was clear Beatrice was not allowing her in. Cristiane had to let the issue go for the moment.

With a quick grin, Cristiane popped up from the bed. "Sure, Mom. You have stuff to make a sundae?"

"Yes!" Beatrice's voice rang with an excited hitch. "Brownies, hot fudge, and plenty of whipped cream."

"Sprinkles?" Cris came up behind her mom with a squeeze to her shoulders.

"Of course. I'm not barbaric." Beatrice smiled as she raised her hands in an exaggerated wave of mocked offense.

Cristiane laughed as she rushed past her mother. "I saw you holding back outside. Are you sure?" She gave Beatrice a fake jab and then turned to run down the stairs.

"Ha. Ha. Ha. I see you have your sense of humor back."

SIX

The next morning, Cristiane left the house before her parents woke, drove to the diner, and sat in a back corner booth. She tapped her cell phone against the table, agitated that it was a workday for Tina and Robby. After missing Isadora's call last night, she desperately wanted to talk to someone. Isadora's message was cryptic.

"Doing research and will call tomorrow. Don't push your mother; you could be in danger. Spend the day away from the house if possible. Will let you know when I have more. Stay safe."

With Tina and Robby busy, Cristiane hesitated in calling David. She didn't want to bring up history but wanted to keep her mind busy until she heard from Isadora. Hoping he and Joyce were free, she sent him a text message and waited, sipping hot coffee, and looking out the window. The morning sunlight was vivid, shimmering through the trees. It would melt the snow of the past few days before nightfall. A shiver ran through her. She hated the cold and looked forward to a few days of warmer weather.

Her phone vibrated, pulling her from her thoughts. A text from David. He and Joyce were coming to the diner. She took a deep breath; thankful she didn't have to spend the day digging deeper into her imagination and stirring up her anxiety. She was jumpy enough without having to keep the past few days to herself.

A few minutes later, a disheveled duo, David and Joyce, plopped down in the booth opposite Cristiane. After pleasantries and drink orders, David waited for the server to leave before he jumped into why Cristiane sent the text. "So what's the big mystery? Did your mom pull one of her usual stunts?"

Cristiane noticed Joyce didn't look surprised by the question. David must have told her everything about Cristiane's family and growing up together. It would normally irritate her, but she was thankful she didn't have to explain history right now. "No, not really. It's a lot more sinister than that. I'm not sure you're going to believe it, but I must talk to someone. I'm grateful for you two coming out to meet me this morning."

The server came back with a tray. When she finished filling mugs and leaving waters, she took their food orders and left.

"After senior year and finding out you're a witch, I think I'm open minded for almost anything." David looked at Joyce, who nodded her agreement. "You can tell us anything."

"I know I can." Cristiane looked at Joyce and put her hand on their joined hands. "I really appreciate it, both of you."

"I hope it doesn't make you uncomfortable that I came." Joyce's smile reached her eyes as she searched Cristiane's face for a sign of irritation. "We hit it off so well the other night. I want to help, if I can."

"Of course. I am thrilled that you came. Honestly, I wanted to chat with you both, but I didn't have your number." Joyce was genuine. Cristiane loved that about her, and that David was so at ease with them both. After their awkward break up at graduation, Cristiane was relieved that he found someone so exceptional. Cristiane slid her cell phone to Joyce. "Can we swap?"

"Great! Yes." The women exchanged phone numbers as the server approached with their breakfasts.

David eyed the women as they continued to talk while the attendant tried to juggle several plates.

"Are you two done?" David grabbed two dishes from the server and set them down in front of himself. "Serving ladies first doesn't happen when you make the food wait and get cold."

The server stepped back, giving David a terse glance. Joyce and Cristiane stared at him, too.

As he rolled his eyes with a shrug, he reached up and helped distribute the other plates around the table. "Thank you."

"Yes. Jeez, you are grumpy when you're hungry." Joyce glanced at Cristiane, looking for backup. "Am I right?"

Cristiane nodded her agreement, digging into a veggie omelet. She was hungry, too.

After finishing their meals, Cristiane spent an hour telling David and Joyce about the coven leader's accusations about her mom, the findings in the hidden altar room, discovering her mother at Javier's club, the strange, creepy man with the glowing eyes, and finally the visit from Nissa at the house last night. She explained she believed Nissa was the same woman from the club, but there was also a man who put his hand on Beatrice as they went back in the club. She talked fast, but neither one of her captivated listeners interrupted as she spoke. She ended with her own deluge of questions about her mother, including that she suspected her mom might be having an affair.

David's mouth remained agape through much of Cristiane's dissertation. Although he was intimately aware of the rift between the two, Beatrice had always been kind to him, especially after his father died. Mrs. Bradford had an air of sophistication, but not pretentious or secretive. She was president of the PTA while he and Cristiane were in elementary school, and organized parties and outings for the students. She was a lot of fun when they were young, volunteering at the school often. He wasn't sure exactly when things changed. But during middle school, he and the other kids noticed that Mrs. Bradford stopped volunteering at school. And when they'd visited the Bradford house, she was out of sight. Initially, he thought it was because of Cristiane growing up and the typical mother-daughter battles he remembered between his own older sisters and mother. But as his siblings ironed out issues at home, and the bond between mother and daughter grew strong again, Cristiane and her mother grew farther and farther apart.

"Wow. That's a lot to unpack on your own." David eyed Joyce, who looked as shocked as he. "I don't think we can help with all of it, but maybe we can check out the club tonight. It's a public place, plus we had talked about going there soon, didn't we?" David put his arm around Joyce as she nodded and slid closer to him, putting her hand on his knee. "Joyce wanted to see if they have live entertainment nights. She sings and thinks it'd be fun to perform for small groups, like the club."

"You sing, too? What can't you do?" Cristiane was in awe of Joyce and her many talents and ambition. She noticed Joyce blush at her exclamation. Cristiane sat back and thought it over. "I don't know what to say. It could be dangerous."

Joyce waved off her concern. "Don't worry about us. As David said, we were going to go before long, anyway. This gives us a reason to commit to dress clothes for a proper date. We wear climbing gear all the time and a girl's gotta put on heels once in a while." Joyce looked at David, who frowned at the mention of dressing up. "See that look? He hates to put on anything other than a t-shirt. It's a public place. We're more than safe. If we can do some recon for you, then it will make the night that much more fun. We'd be happy to go."

Relieved, Cristiane nodded to her new friend. If someone had noticed her outside the club, then this was the perfect plan. If her mother was having an affair, Cristiane didn't want to make an emotional scene. "Okay, then that's settled. Hopefully, while you're at the club, I will hear from Isadora about some of the other issues. The man in the alley had a key, or key card, to open the side door, so he must work at the club. I'll text you a description. He was tall, wore a tailored suit that fit well, blond hair, athletic. I'd say about six feet tall. Huh, maybe Mom is having an affair." Cristiane contemplated her last statement. Then she dismissed the thought, grabbed her phone, and started tapping away at buttons.

David raised his hand. "Just one thing. You mentioned someone with glowing purple eyes at the club and your house. Do you think he works there, too?"

"Oh, I almost forgot about him." Cristiane smacked her forehead and slumped back in the booth. "He must work there, but not around the public. I know it sounds crazy, but he doesn't look right, or even human. You'll know as soon as you see him." Cristiane sat upright and looked them both in the eyes. "Be careful if you cross his path. That one makes my skin crawl. Oh, and he favored an arm, cradling it, as if it were painful to let drop to his side. He wore a sling or brace, so he'll be easy to spot."

"If he's hurt, then he can't be too much of a threat. That's good news if we run into him." David waved to the server for the check and sat up straighter. "Is there anything else we need to know? I think I'd better get going. I might need to do a quick shopping trip if I must look spiffy for my date." He raised an eyebrow and nudged his head toward Joyce. She slapped him in mock retaliation, to which he winked and kissed her on the cheek.

"You two are so cute. I think that's all. You have his description in the text I sent you both. If I hear from Isadora or learn anything before tonight, I will be in touch." Cris smiled as she got up from the booth and hugged Joyce as she slid out of the opposite side. "I can't thank you enough."

"It's our pleasure. You're doing me a favor. I mentioned that club months ago to David." Joyce shot David a light slap on the arm as he rose from the table. "I'll call after we get home, and we'll fill you in."

"Thanks. I'll be awake no matter the time." Cristiane gave David a quick hug and gestured to the door. "Go ahead. I got the check. It's the least I can do if you need to buy an outfit."

David laughed as he took Joyce's hand and led her toward the door. "Thanks."

It was early, so Javier's wasn't hopping when they pulled into the adjacent parking space. David got out and buttoned his navy-blue suit jacket. Peering at himself in the window's reflection, he smoothed a stray hair back in place and then rubbed at his clean-shaven chin. He looked better than good, even though he didn't like the fitted feeling of the jacket across his shoulders. At least he could move easily because of the stretch of the fabric. He and Joyce may be on reconnaissance, but he wanted to dance and have some fun, too. He walked around the back of the car to open the passenger door for his date.

Joyce wore a deep v-neck dress in a bright teal that hugged her full curves and made her skin look amazing in the evening light. Her tawny eyes sparkled with the metallic teal eyeshadow that matched her dress. She was rounded but quick and lithe during her classes and outdoor activities.

David loved that she was strong, energetic, and didn't worry about every morsel she put in her mouth. He took her hand and helped her step out of the car, holding her at arm's length. She bowed her head, smiling, as he stepped back and let his eyes roam straight down to the heels with long, twisted black, vine-like spikes holding her up.

She pressed into him after completing a pirouette, kissing him hard on the mouth. "See what you've been missing under t-shirts every day?"

David cleared his throat as he encircled Joyce in an embrace. His lips brushed against her own before he pulled on her bottom lip, and then lingered for a deep, passionate kiss. He pulled away a fraction as he whispered across her mouth. "I do. I'm curious, though—those shoes look deadly."

Joyce kicked up a foot and laughed. "These are Dior. I've been itching to wear them. And that heel can come in handy if we find ourselves in a pickle."

"Keep those around later. I can think of other times you can wear those shoes that don't include stakeouts or dancing."

"David!" Joyce smacked his arm and then gave it a squeeze. She turned with him as they began their way across the street to the club.

Inside it was dark, with candles lit on the tables positioned along the walls. They saw a couple of cozy booths in two of the corners, with a dance area in the middle of the club. It was bigger than David had imagined, with plenty of room at the opposite end for a band or piano. David wondered if there was a stage behind the heavy burgundy curtains. A couple of stairs to the left led toward another level with more tables. He noted two couples on that level, with several tables on the main floor taken, and a few people at the bar. There were about thirty people, but the club was not as busy as it would be in another hour.

David pointed and asked for a specific table. The host nodded, and they followed the young man to the middle of the main floor. David offered a chair to Joyce and guided it in before he took the seat opposite her that faced the entrance. He could see the entire business, except for one table above and behind his head. He liked the vantage point to look at everyone who would come and go from the nightclub.

The evening went by faster than they expected. While on the dance floor, David noticed a man walking up the lengthy hallway from the alley entrance. He nudged his chin up for Joyce to look and then spun around and pulled her in close while he monitored the man picking through a set of keys. "If he opens that side door, I'm going to follow him in. You should buy me some time, go to the restroom, and then I'll meet you at the table." They continue to dance for a moment as they watch, and when they see the guy open the door, David gave her a kiss on the cheek and hurried down the hall to catch the side door before he lost a chance to follow.

David walked casually to the wall edge, then darted down the hall to catch the door from locking shut. He waited a few seconds before sliding in through the door and closing it behind him. Stairs led down into the darkness. He caught his breath, listening for footsteps before he ventured into the unknown. Every few steps he stopped and listened to the foreboding silence, then as he reached a landing, a faint light shone in the distance. It was below him, but not by much. David gauged he had another half a flight of stairs to tread and tiptoed down the remaining steps.

The underside area was a hallway, sufficient for eight people to stand side by side. Maybe it was a wine cellar. David felt along one wall as he moved toward the light. No doors on the left side. He made a mental note to check the other side on his way out. As he reached the end, he found a huge pocket-door covering most of the wall. It was ajar enough so he could scurry through sideways. Once inside, he crouched behind a stack of crates, letting his eyes adjust to his surroundings. Opposite his position, a three-tiered shelf held an array of artifacts and goblets. He pulled his phone from the jacket breast pocket, shifted closer, and took a few pictures without a flash. Later, he could manipulate the exposure and lighting to see what he'd found.

No sounds threatened his senses, so he moved farther into the space. A large hanging on the left wall was visible through the narrow stream of light. He stepped back and took another picture. As he stepped, he stumbled over a table. Hastily, he reached out to grab whatever shook loose from his blunder. David righted the object but came away with a tacky mess. Unable to see, he wiped his hands along the backside of his pants before taking a photo of the item. As he put the phone back in his jacket, footsteps echoed, but he couldn't decide from which direction.

David looked for cover. The crates were farther away than he felt safe to travel. Instead, he moved forward and pressed again into the far-right corner, the darkest space in the room. If a light came on, he was screwed. Sure enough, a man swung open a door up from David. The light spread out through most of the room, except where David remained crouched, pressed deep into the corner. Muffled scratches and chirps came from the open doorway. The man looked out over the room long enough for David to see his hair was more of a gray color with blond highlights. David thought the guy looked vain, and he walked with a strut, but otherwise, there wasn't a distinctive trait that David found in the dim light. He could be the club manager or a bouncer, dressed in a dark suit with broad shoulders. The club was lavish and expensive, so their security would dress well to blend in.

As David studied him, he realized the man fit Cristiane's description of whomever was with her mother. Curious, David edged his phone out and snuck a photo before the door closed, extinguishing the light source and the unusual sounds coming from the corner room.

He remained crouched until he heard the pocket-door slide shut, then David stood and stretched his legs. In total darkness, he stood motionless, listening for other noises. Confident no one was around, he clicked on the phone's light and made his way through the room. He bumped against a tall table and felt for the edge behind a curtain as he swung the phone around for a better view.

As David pulled aside the curtain, a metallic, stale stench filled his nostrils while carnage reached his gaze in the beam of light. The putrid air was so potent, he could taste the iron in the back of his throat. David cleared his throat and swallowed hard, keeping down the bile threatening to erupt. Dried blood, remnants of flesh pulled from the bone, lay strewn across an ancient altar. The shock of destruction in front of him paralyzed his thoughts. His eyes darted about, confused over what stood before him, while patrons above enjoyed a fun-filled evening as they ate, drank, and danced in the club. He shuddered, dismissing the rambling thoughts, and concentrated on the sight before him.

The table was slightly taller than normal, with strange carvings at either end. David found the camera app on his phone and began clicking at every angle. To his left, the end carvings were of bird feet with monstrous talons hooked to the table corners. Along the table length were carvings of feathers and skulls, which sprang from what David surmised was the table head. He bent down and took pictures of the sides as he crept along the slab, following the carvings from talons to torso, then to the strange head. Opposite the bird-like feet, a jackal's head with paws at the corners were at the far end of the table. It was a grotesque creature, sporting a long snout and jagged teeth. At the throat of the beast, human breasts protruded from a mass of feathers. David stepped back for a couple of panoramic photos and took several more of the bloody remains along the tabletop.

He caught sight of the time on the phone. David was gone far longer than he'd planned. Not only would Joyce be worried about him, but the staff would notice his absence. He peered around the curtain and made a beeline for the pocket-door at the far end of the room. Once there, he stopped to listen before sliding it open. Silence. He slid through the door and hurried along his left, feeling his way in the blackness.

A door midway down the hall gave him pause. He tried the handle, locked. No time to investigate. He continued to the stairs while listening for footfalls or voices. He rushed to the top and caught his breath before easing the door ajar. The blond man stood at the entrance to the dance floor, his back to David. Another person stood just outside of David's sight, their back also to David. Not knowing when they could turn, David made a quick exit into the hallway and eased the door shut behind him.

He rushed a few steps up and then made haste into the restroom. He splashed water over his hands and grabbed a paper towel to wipe a blood smear off his face. As a stall door opened, he tossed the towel and rushed into the hallway as the restroom door banged close. The two men turned at the sound of the door smacking shut. David pulled on his jacket and buttoned it tight. He nodded to both as he passed, while plunging his wet hands in his pockets.

"Where have you been? You look terrible." Joyce rose as David approached within feet of their table.

"Please tell me you paid the bill. We must go, now."

"Yes, of course. You were gone so long. I was worried. I told the waiter you might have felt a little sick."

"Thank you." David gestured toward the door. The palm of his hand was still dark, bloody, and dirty. Joyce eyed him as he shook his head and quickly slid the hand back into his pocket. "Not here. Let's go."

SEVEN

With a shudder, Cristiane opened her eyes. The room swayed out of focus as Cristiane felt a smooth wooden surface beneath her. She rose from the floor. It was damp and dark, with the faint whisper of waves lapping against something below her feet. A distant seal's bark hit her ears as briny air filled her nostrils. She gained her footing on the slick surface and peered at the shapes forming as her eyes adjusted to the dimness. Walking decks surrounded two vessels nestled in slips, gently rocking against the buoys tied along the deck. A boathouse. But how did she get here?

Cristiane eased along the building's side until her eyes adjusted to the surroundings. She was near a waterway. It was frigid, but no snow reflected the moon's light. Early winter, she presumed, while she walked to a door in the far-right corner. Lights shone in the distance at a higher elevation, then all went dark. People were nearby, although she had no clue where she was.

She stepped out of the boathouse into the crisp air. Late fall leaves of assorted colors sporadically littered the coastline as she made her way from the dock to dry land. Cristiane peered about as she found a lit stairway leading up toward an archway of branches. The lighting dispersed a soft glow as Cristiane made her way up the hill. Once she reached the summit, she turned and gasped at the distant view across an expansive waterway, toward a city.

Behind Cristiane rose a beautiful Tudor-style estate home. A mounted cannon sat on a lush, well-maintained lawn toward her left, edged with dwarf Japanese holly cascading over the hillside into the trees whence she came. Behind that was a lavish veranda with open archways along the entire backside perimeter, offering a viewing deck above, along the second story. Summer mornings must be lovely, with the water's cool breeze tumbling through while sipping hot coffee and eating breakfast. Cristiane imagined extravagant parties, brimming with people sipping champagne and strolling the area, while looking for fireworks or boats traveling the waters. A grand lifestyle she could only dream of living.

Cristiane shivered, rushing to a door. She raised her eyebrows when it opened at her touch. Too easy. She slipped into the dim light of a colossal modern kitchen. A stark contrast to the historical brick exterior. When she edged toward the murky hallway, a child's laughter caught her ear, causing her to duck into the adjacent pantry. A young boy around five years old ran past the door, dressed in dog-print pajamas. A few seconds passed then an older woman dressed in a housekeeper's uniform shuffled through, allowing the young lad to charge ahead without concern of capture. Once the housekeeper was beyond the pantry, Cristiane stepped out and followed the pair through the shadowy hall.

Not hearing doors open or close, Cristiane passed several rooms as she ventured deeper into the darkness. A towering portico opened to a room at the far end of the hall. Cristiane slowed her pace as she approached the entrance. Laughter and giggles rang out louder as the boy begged between breaths and giggles for the woman to stop tickling him. A smile crept across Cristiane's lips as she peeked into the room. She observed the play session for a few minutes, remembering how she and her own mother used to play similar games when she was the same age. Without a thought, she strolled in and leaned against the back of a carved wingback chair. Caught up in observing the playful shenanigans, Cristiane was late in noticing the boy run straight toward her. She stood frozen, expecting him to stop and confront her when he passed by. Before Cristiane could formulate the idea or process their movements, both apparitions passed through Cristiane.

Cristiane then stood outside without a house in sight. A short distance away was a car covered by a fallen tree. Confused, she spun herself around, struggling to understand. How was this possible if she were in a historical home a moment ago?

A thick boundary of trees lined the long dirt road. Cristiane lingered as the scent of fresh pine and cedar wafted past her face. Crickets chirped while tree branches shimmied in the moonlight, casting eerie shadows through the clearing on the road. An involuntary shiver ran through Cristiane as a screech momentarily halted the crickets' songs. Her ears picked up faint crunching as something scurried along the forest floor. She hoped it was a squirrel or deer and not a bear or wolf. Uneasy, she crept toward the vehicle.

She stepped close to the car and covered her eyes from the moonlight. Cristiane wiped the frosty film from the window and jumped back, falling to the ground. Gasping, she shook the fright from her body and stood again. Hesitant but determined, Cristiane strode back to the car. A man sat slumped behind the driver's wheel; the side of his face blotched with glass and streaked with dried blood. She cleared the frost away again and found a thick branch pierced through the man's chest, blood and twigs littered his front.

Cristiane reached into her back pocket for her phone and found nothing. Perplexed, she walked to the car's other side and continued to investigate. A rear door stood ajar.

Cristiane pushed it closed, clearing her route to the front passenger side. No need to gaze through a window. She noticed the figure of a young child exposed through the shattered windshield. The body lay atop the blackened, ash-covered hood.

Her breath caught as she found the upper body burned to a crisp. Distraught, Cristiane dropped her head to her chest, unsure what to do next. She explored the surroundings for a victim's phone, hoping to call for help. As she circled out from the car, extending the search perimeter with each pass, Cristiane picked up branches and kicked away at leaves with her feet to clean up her path. The pine intense in the chilly air, she plodded through her quest, becoming more discouraged with each round. On the third pass, her foot hit something under the leaves.

A skull rolled across the forest floor as fog built up suddenly through the trees. The radiant crimson sockets of the skull haunted Cristiane. The fires rising from the darkest depths toward her face were familiar, but from where she couldn't grasp. But she couldn't glance away. She heard a low, guttural chuckle rise higher and higher as the flaming sockets inched closer. Drawn to peer deeper, she leaned toward the frightening visage as the flaming pupils pulled inward. The scene took over her mind, changing from flames to a bottomless sea of bloody, writhing bodies the size of small children, warping, twisting, and changing into various shapes throughout a never-ending hellish landscape. The sinister laughter bellowed, knocking Cristiane on her back.

Sobbing, Cristiane woke from the nightmare. She took a few deep breaths, then flipped the bed covers away, letting the chilly air wash over her. She sighed and closed her eyes as the realistic smells and images faded from her mind. Vivid dreams, since the session with her ancestors' spirits and the family curse on the emerald necklace, were many times enjoyable escapades with her witch ancestors, Rachel and Prudence, or entertaining times with her friends. But sometimes, like this evening, the dreams were hellish nightmares that stayed with her for days.

At least she didn't waken with a scream that caused her parents to rush into her room like she was a child. With that thought, she pulled herself from the bed, checked her phone for messages, and then ventured to the kitchen for a glass of water.

Slippers clapped against the wooden stairs as Cristiane made her way to the first floor. As her foot hit the carpet, an orb hovered in her path. She'd seen the orb so many times during this visit home she waved it off with a flick of her wrist, continuing her journey to the kitchen. Cristiane got a glass and shuffled to the refrigerator, pushing the water dispenser. She eyed the ghost light as her glass filled with water.

There was a misty backdrop. Sometimes Cristiane thought it was another spirit, but many times the orb appeared alone, leaving her to question if there was something in the accompanying mist. "Just spill it, will you? My patience has run thin." Cristiane took a drink while monitoring the sphere as it floated above the counter.

Perplexed, she put her glass on the counter and glared at the ball. She took a few steps and leaned her hip against the edge. Cristiane crossed her arms and tightened her fists. She felt as if she were having a standoff with her imagination. "Damn it, tell me what you want! Do you need help to cross over? What is it? Liven up and appear better than this ghost light." She raised and flicked her hands in despair toward the object.

Cristiane, annoyed from the dream and brazen, circled around the kitchen island to stand inches from the hovering object. "What—do you—want from me?" Cristiane spoke with deliberation. The apparition had lingered for days at the house. She was sick of seeing it pop up at odd times. The orb moved within inches of her face, then rushed through her shoulder, causing a biting pain through the scar at her collarbone. She rubbed at the spot until the ache eased while she turned, searching for the glowing sphere. It had disappeared. "What in the world?" She waited for something to happen, movement or a sign, but it didn't return.

Ready to give up, Cristiane grabbed her phone and turned to go back upstairs. A male figure materialized from the mist. "Well, that's something." She was beyond being spooked but stopped as a thought tugged at her mind. "Do I know you?" She edged closer and realized the figure was the man from her nightmare. He was the person behind the steering wheel covered in glass, with a branch plunged into his chest.

The figure raised his chin, allowing Cristiane to study his face. She closed the distance between them, squinting as though that would bring him to life. As she opened her mouth to ask him more questions, her phone chimed, alerting her to a text. She glanced at the screen to see the message was from David. When she looked up a second later, the apparition was gone.

Cristiane read the mysterious note. She couldn't wait to hear what he and Joyce found at Javier's. The diner would open soon for breakfast. She rushed upstairs to shower and change.

EIGHT

David spent the morning with Cristiane and Joyce, discussing what he found in the club's basement. Many of the photos needed editing to enhance lighting or adjust for sharpness and clarity because he didn't use a flash. The pictures were disturbing, but David hoped to improve the quality so Cristiane could get the truth from her mother. David agreed to clean them up and then forward the stack of photos to Cristiane.

He was concerned about more than photos. David had touched a few items in the room and transferred a significant amount of blood onto his hands and clothes. He didn't think it was much initially until they were in Joyce's apartment. David was annoyed but also worried because blood covered his hands, fingertips to palms. He had sauntered by the two men in the hall on his way out the basement doorway. If he was lucky, he had closed his jacket and hid his hands in time before they took notice.

Not able to give reassurances, Cristiane offered to elicit guidance from Isadora. "She left a message to meet her this afternoon. You should keep the clothes you wore last night for evidence. I think we will need it as we learn what's been happening in that chamber. I'll text you when I can meet up later. Back at Willie's tonight?" Her friends agreed.

Cristiane arrived at Isadora's in the late afternoon. She'd spent time with her parents and helped her mother. Beatrice had fallen down a flight of stairs at the outdoor mall earlier in the day and the fall left her bruised and sore. Cristiane agitated her father, and he chastised her for leaving early in the morning again and not spending more time with them. He had taken the week off from work to be with her and she'd barely been home, and now her mother lay injured on the sofa. To appease him, Cristiane agreed to have lunch with them tomorrow. Cristiane promised she'd be home.

Although she wanted to know what Isadora's research uncovered, Cristiane knew Isadora would want to know about David's findings, the dream, and then the male apparition in the kitchen. Cristiane didn't have all the photos from David, but she had a half-dozen clear shots for Isadora to analyze. Once she finished telling Isadora all the details, she slumped back into the chair and breathed a long, cleansing breath, letting it out slowly as she surveyed Isadora. "Why are you doing that thing with your face?"

Isadora stopped scrunching up her features from side to side and stared at Cristiane. "Oh, I'm stitching thoughts together, is all. Your discoveries have provided details that filled in the holes in my research, and, of course, created more questions." Isadora sipped at her drink. She offered nothing further in explanation to her companion for several minutes.

Cristiane fixed herself a drink and came back to sit opposite Isadora. "Is that mix in the refrigerator what you're drinking? It smelled yummy."

Isadora raised her glass, smiling. "One of my favorites, a Brandy Alexander. It's a wonderful dessert alternative. Wanna try a sip? You'd like it." She passed her martini glass to Cristiane and watched as Cris hesitated, sniffed the rim, and then put her lips to the edge. "At my age, I don't eat as much as I used to, but I enjoy my treats. Some drinks, like this one, take me back to particular people, times, and places in my life." She accepted the glass back from Cristiane. "This one and another favorite, Grasshoppers, remind me of years in New Orleans. A fascinating city full of culture and allure."

"It's delicious. I'll have to give it a go another time."

"Take this advice from an old crone. Tie experiences from places where you live or travel to activities, drinks, or food you can enjoy at any age. When you're well over ninety, like I am now, it is the small things, such as sipping a favorite drink, which carry you to the memories of years ago."

"That makes sense. What happened in New Orleans?"

"Another time. Let me get back to why you're here and discuss your gifts before we switch focus."

Cristiane nodded. Stories could wait. "You're right. What about my gifts, as you call it?"

"Witchcraft is like any other skill. Although given a magnificent gift or gifts, you must practice, hone, and study to become an expert. You have the gift of clairvoyance with the dreams. Sight and connection with the afterlife, perhaps as a medium. What we have yet to study is if you can manipulate your surroundings while in that dream state, but the spirit that manifested clearer to you was from your dream, and therefore a strong connection to this life."

"I realized he was from my dream, but couldn't that be my mind playing tricks on me?"

"Possibly, but as this mist and orb have manifested together frequently, I believe they are more associated with you and are attempting to communicate or warn you. The emerald talisman you have from your ancestors could play a residual part, but you are powerful in ways we are only now uncovering. The latest dream was a huge indicator. And you say you didn't recognize the home or the area? That is strange for such a vivid dream in which you were an active participant."

"The spirits have hovered around my mom much more than me. I don't think I've noticed either near my dad. Do you think Mom connects to the ghosts?" Cristiane sat on the couch's edge, intrigued by where the discussion was leading. "She's still closed off. I don't know how I could approach to ask about her past again or the club."

"I agree. I don't recommend asking her outright just yet. We're on the right track, I can feel it, but let's move on to Javier's. I sense it is all connected and leads to your mom, but you're the energy connection or these coincidences would have manifested long ago. Your powers drive the spirits' visibility, the issues surrounding the nightclub activity, and the concerns about your mother. I don't think she is having an affair, although that is possible. I didn't find any information to the contrary, but the activity under the nightclub is more sinister than an affair. I'd prefer an affair issue to what I believe is taking place."

"What is that exactly?"

"I believe your mother is involved in a cult." Isadora studied Cristiane, letting her words sink in before explaining her reasons.

"Hold on—a cult?"

"Yes, I'm quite certain. Based on the photos you and David provided, it's much worse than I imagined after leaving the initiation ceremony." Isadora took a breath and sipped her drink. The wrinkles across her brow deepened as worry enveloped her features. "With the Baphomet photo you sent, I thought the cult was a rather innocuous mix of satanic worshipers. Average people bent to contradict modern societal expectations, rebellious but harmless, nonetheless."

"What is a Baphomet?"

Isadora shuffled through the pile of photos and papers on the coffee table and handed Cristiane a photo. "I had prints made from the digital photos you sent from your mother's altar room. This one is the Sigil of Baphomet. The Baphomet is a symbol used by many occult groups and traditions. The most well-known these days being the Church of Satan, which has used this specific symbol, an upside-down pentagram and goat head, since the late 1960s. However, David's photos shed more light on the group, which is more concerning."

"What could be more concerning than worshipping Satan?" Cristiane's eyes widened with fright. She blinked several times and shook her head. She pulled at her mouth and then chewed on her stubby nails.

"Listen, please. The altar David found and the large wall tapestry are concerning. The group is not simply some attraction for bored urbanites. At the core, followers worship Lamashtu. However, the symbolism is conflicting. The members could be a mix of loyal followers, while local elitists join, bringing their money, looking for dark thrills. Troublesome, for certain. No one should pursue unleashing darkness on this scale. Lamashtu, the daughter of the sun god Anu in Mesopotamian mythology is a demon goddess. She is evil, full of bloodlust, chaos, and hatred."

"I've never heard of her. You make her sound worse than the devil."

"Perhaps, yes. Religion and mythology are fickle, particularly throughout the centuries. Think of Lamashtu akin to Lilith in Jewish theology. Some people further reason that Anu, a sky god, is like Christianity's God as the creator. Lamashtu is notorious for performing evil for her own enjoyment and no other reason other than she could. Her targets comprised unborn children, babies, pregnant women. She has also been associated with inflicting disease upon men. Unlike other deities who obey higher gods' rules and regulations, Lamashtu is divergent. She submits to no one and has her own set of laws."

"Why would anyone worship a deity so vile?" Cristiane shivered as goosebumps traveled up her arms. Although she had a tough time grasping what Isadora was saying, her intuition calmed her. She knew they were on the right trail. "What could my mother have to do with this group? I know we don't get along, but she's not evil. She's just, I don't know, bitchy."

Isadora chuckled at Cristiane's frankness. "That correlation is not clear to me. Individuals who follow these types of cults usually manifest behaviors outsiders see as troublesome and cause harm to others. Your mother hasn't been volatile or in trouble with the law, correct?"

"I don't think so, but I've been at college for three years. Growing up, she was an active parent until I was in middle school. She's never been physical or violent with me or my dad. If she's involved in this cult, she hides it well."

"There's an association with witches in some historical texts. Perhaps this cult developed that interpretation. However, there is as much likelihood that the group is a collective of vampires, demons, and humans. Whatever the case, it is dangerous."

"That we agree on." Cristiane gulped down the rest of her glass. "What do you think of the glowing eyed man from the nightclub?"

"I'm glad you brought it up. I almost forgot about him." Isadora dug through the papers on the table and retrieved a document. "I believe he's a demon called Xirnan, and because of the sling on one arm, I also think you hit him with your car when we were on our way to the initiation ceremony."

Cristiane dropped her jaw, wide-eyed, and took the paper from Isadora. She studied the worn newspaper article and photo. "Do you think this is him?"

"Maybe not, but it is possible. Demons live an extremely long time, unless decapitated or killed with specific skill. This clipping is over seventy years old."

"Seventy years? They look the same age."

"When I said they live a long time, I meant centuries, not decades. Seventy years to a demon is nothing. Their lifespan is more like what you would think of as a vampire's rather than human. They're walking death with skills far superior to mortals." Isadora waved off Cristiane's attempt to hand the article back. "Keep it. I want you to show it to your friends and see if anyone witnessed him lurking around your home or following you, your family. You need to be vigilant. Also, I want copies of the remaining photos as soon as possible. This situation needs coven attention."

Cristiane slid the document into her backpack. She stood, reaching for Isadora's glass.

"Bring me another, please. I believe I need a few more now that we're realizing the dangers we may face."

"Coming right up." Cristiane straightened but didn't budge, her chin quivering until she clenched her jaw. Thoughtful, she looked down at the floor, avoiding Isadora's gaze. "There's no way to turn back now, is there? I mean, we can't put the genie back in the bottle. I can't be a regular woman, no witchcraft, minding my own business. Life is more complicated. No job, kids, relationship, or future without this *gift* taking center stage. None of that is possible without watching over my shoulder, is it?"

Isadora's heart went out to her young pupil. Her frail arms encircled Cristiane as she stood and gave a firm hug. "Don't you worry. We'll get you through and without a scratch." Isadora pulled back and held tight to Cristiane's arms. Her eyes sparkled as she smiled. "Without a scratch might be a lie. I can't guarantee that, but we will get through this together. Sure, you've been thrown into the pit a bit more than most trainees. I know that is true. You're not alone. There's more firepower in this old woman, and the coven, than you can fathom. Your future will be whatever you decide to make of it."

Isadora took her glass and turned Cristiane toward the kitchen. They walked arm in arm. Cristiane let Isadora's words sink in. "Should we go to the police with what David found?"

"Eventually, yes. Right now, there isn't enough to illustrate a crime, other than David trespassing. The blood, if it is blood and not something else, may not be a concern unless it's proven to be human or from an illegal source, like animal cruelty-or ritualistic sacrifice." Isadora fixed herself another drink. "I will take everything to Sarah. We have a couple of police contacts in the coven. She can be discrete and share the photos with them before we provide an official report at the police station."

"Wow. That would be great." Cristiane felt better hearing that Isadora had a plan. "Okay. I think I've taken enough of your time tonight. I'll check with David and get the other pictures to you soon." She gave the old woman a hug. "Thanks for everything. I don't know what I'd do without you."

"You're never alone, remember that, but be cautious. Always wear the emerald necklace until we solve these questions and remember your training. Witchcraft is in your bones. You have the skills to defend yourself without conventional weapons, but it doesn't hurt to have a blade, particularly made of iron. Or if you're into guns, keep a handgun convenient for protection, if that eases your mind. Study the Book of Shadows, create your own spells, and practice. No matter what crosses your path, you have the power to control your destiny." Isadora had walked to the front door as she talked to Cristiane. They exchanged hugs again. Isadora kept the door open, silently watching Cristiane as she neared her car.

NINE

Nissa slammed her hand onto the table. The image of David's face froze on the computer screen in front of her. "How the hell did he get past the door?" She stretched fingers taut before balling her fists until her knuckles turned white. "Xirnan, where were you during this fiasco?"

"Forgive me, ma'am. I spent most of the evening in the office prepping for our next meeting with the board." Xirnan hung his head, expecting punishment for his folly. "I came out and faced the dance floor as the bloke passed us. I believed he came from the men's room."

Nissa glared at the two figures before her. Her heavy breathing did not abate, her anger palpable. Knox and Xirnan stood relaxed, with feet apart and hands behind their backs, awaiting orders. Only one person in her presence knew her deepest concern. Nissa looked at the ceiling, blew out an exasperated breath, and shook her head. "Knox, why were you in Malin's usual position?"

"Ma'am, Malin was escorting an unruly guest out the front door. He witnessed a patron assault a woman while he was at the bar. He took care of the matter rather than call me away from the dancefloor, so I backfilled his area until his return." Knox, who'd been hired as a bouncer and paid well for that service, didn't question his boss's anger or ask about what was in the basement. Whatever it was, he didn't need to understand more than Nissa offered to share.

Knox's demeanor was quiet, yet formidable because of years spent in the Marine Corps. Most of his service was embassy duty, protecting American dignitaries and the embassy grounds. After serving in several countries, the Corps offered him the opportunity to serve in special assignments with a related augmentation unit. Had it not been for early detection of kidney cancer and a medical discharge, he would be in uniform, rather than standing beside his current boss.

Nissa studied Knox, unsure if she could trust him with the club's other interests. "Xirnan, you stay with me. Knox, you may go, but tell Malin I want him in my office now."

"Yes, ma'am." Knox took a step back and turned to retreat. His military bearing was clear in each stride out of the office.

"My lady, if Malin is failing his duties, perhaps now is the time to grant my request," Xirnan asked matter-of-factly.

"Not this again, Xirnan." Nissa shook her head as she paced the floor, her heels generating crisp clicks with each step against the porcelain tiles.

A flicker of resentment swept across the demon's face. He lowered his head, silent.

A moment later, Malin stomped in. He acknowledged Nissa and continued to the accent table along the wall, grabbing the bourbon. "Anyone want a drink?" He poured three fingers, then plunked himself on the sofa. Nissa stopped walking and scowled until Malin acknowledged her with a not-so-sorrowful shrug.

Nissa studied him, more aware than ever of the differences in the two men, though they appeared so similar. Knox and Malin were of a similar build, and both had blond hair. Although Malin colored his gray, they both were wide-shouldered and wore their hair short. Other than having the same general features, they looked nothing alike up close. Malin had beady, dark hazel eyes over a pointed nose. His mouth, set in a grimace, portrayed him as ruthless and uncaring, which was his general personality. Although the men were around the same height, Malin was thickset and puffy from using anabolic steroids. Knox was broad, stealthy, and solid due to years of healthy living and military training. Knox carried a natural smile that reached his blue eyes. Nissa felt he was approachable yet could take care of issues around the club.

"Malin, you and Xirnan need to take care of this problem. I don't want to know how you do it. Find out what he knows." Nissa looked out the plate-glass window over Main Street as she barked the order. She trusted Xirnan with her life, but Malin could be unpredictable and aggressive. "It's been a long time since you've worked on a human's memories, Xirnan. Are you up to the task?"

Xirnan bowed acknowledgement with his cloaked head. His voice was a low, hollow vibration gliding through the room. "Madam Nissa, my skills are as sharp as whence I sprang from the mountains of Taurus. I assure you."

"Very well."

"Are we talking about the lad that made it into the chamber?" Malin popped up and walked around the office. "We don't need ancient snaggletooth to work on the guy. I can do that for ya." Malin turned and swaggered back toward them, gulping the last of his drink as he traveled. When within reach, he swatted Xirnan's shoulder with the back of his hand.

Not moving, Xirnan returned the gesture with a fiery glare.

"You will not 'work the guy' unless it is necessary." Nissa slid in front of Xirnan and pushed Malin. "That's enough posturing, Malin. You created this mess. We have enough concerns without you trying to kill yourself by Xirnan's hand."

"I'd like to see him try." Malin puffed out his chest for an instant, then smirked as he drew his hands up, acquiescing. "I'll leave your pet alone, Nissa."

Xirnan's eyes followed Malin back to the bourbon. As he observed another heavy pour, his mind conjured ways to torture and maim the man. Nissa would never allow such an action, but that didn't stop Xirnan from dreaming about the delectable deeds. He was sure an opportunity would reveal itself in due time. His mistress grew tired of Malin's arrogance and foolishness. After Malin's latest error, she would call upon Xirnan's services soon. He felt the uneasy energy brewing under her anger. The thought played in his mind, and he couldn't help letting a jagged-toothed smile creep across his hollow features.

"Malin, do not test me. I will end you myself if you don't pull your head out of your ass and take this seriously." Nissa remained cool, but there was an iciness to her tone. Malin nervously stretched his neck from side to side, aware that he was not in good favor. Nissa nodded briefly, noting her threat was well received. "Was anything stolen? Did we figure out how he got into the chamber?"

"Ma'am, if I may." Malin stood, buttoned his jacket, and locked his shoulders as he cleared his throat. "I completed an inventory this morning. He took nothing from the room. I'm not sure he made it down the stairs. There's one matter, but it may be a non-issue."

"I appreciate your candor, but I'll be the judge. What evidence?"

"The pocket-door. I am certain I closed it completely when I left, but it was ajar when you sent me to investigate. Like I said, no concern. I don't know if you or Xirnan went to the chamber before we saw the surveillance video, so I'm uncertain if he got down the stairs. He might have thought the door led to the restroom." Malin shrugged. "He wasn't a regular. We're having a challenging time trying to get a name."

"No name? What did the credit card receipt say?" Nissa tapped her nails against the mahogany wood desk.

"The girl paid cash. Charlene was their server and said she remembered little about them. They had some wine and ate, then danced for a while. The girl asked about singing at the club, so Charlene gave her a copy of the live music schedule and told her to come back to talk with you. She checked the table a few times because the fellow was gone for a time."

"You're right. That's nothing to go on. I've been in the chamber, and I may have left the slider open myself." Nissa sat behind her desk. She rubbed her forehead and temples, feeling a headache brewing. "Find out about this person but be casual. If he saw nothing, then no harm. We're to be more careful as we enter and exit, is all. Malin, you speak to him, for obvious reasons. But Xirnan, you must remain close in case the man's memory needs a cleanse. Do I make myself clear? No fighting or foul play, just a memory wipe."

"Yes, ma'am. As you wish." Xirnan gave a curt bow and turned to leave.

Malin turned to follow.

"Malin, stay behind for a moment." Nissa stood and came around the desk. She grabbed his hand and pressed her nails into the meat of his palm. Her eyes were full of fury as she glowered at Malin. "Remember your place and stop acting so smug. I will revel in tearing you apart limb from limb if it suits me. Do not screw this up."

"Yes, ma'am." Malin swallowed hard, his muscles contracting as his jaw clenched in fear. Not willing to say another word, he nodded understanding.

"Good, now get out."

TEN

Cristiane's next few days were uneventful. There wasn't even much caretaking to be done. Beatrice's injuries didn't keep her homebound for long. After two days of nursing assistance by her family, Beatrice was moving as if nothing happened. The incident didn't keep Christiane's parents from making plans to go out on Friday night.

Cristiane met her friends at Willie's and enjoyed being away from the house following two days couped up like she was a teenager. She needed to let off some steam. After meeting up with Jarvis a few nights ago, Cristiane hoped he would pop into the pub. She wanted the last two nights of spring break to be memorable.

Cristiane walked into the bar around eight o'clock. As she traveled to the back where she saw Tina and waved, she glanced to her left and noticed the ghost she and Robby had chatted about the previous weekend. She'd have to remind Isadora to stop over and help the poor soul cross over. Cristiane hadn't told Tina and Robby about the past few days. She was glad they were the first to arrive so they could talk.

After an hour, Tina and Robby stared at Cristiane in disbelief. "Wow, that's one way to spend your spring break." Robby raised his beer and gestured a toast before he chugged the last. He banged it on the table and pulled another bottle from the bucket sitting on the table. "How are you going to pull the truth from you mom? There's a lot she may be involved in that's dangerous. Have you thought about the police?"

"Briefly. I mean, Isadora thinks David would get in trouble because he trespassed. The photos are useless for an arrest. Unless the arrest was David's."

"Oh, man. You're right. That would suck." Robby looked at Tina, who was shaking her head.

"Yeah, Cris. I don't imagine the police are a clever idea. The only option you have is to ask your mom. You're going back to school on Sunday, right?" Tina nudged Robby to open a beer for her. "We can check on your parents when you are at school. Our engagement is a good excuse to visit. You know, in case your mom's fall wasn't really a fall."

"What? What do you mean?" Cristiane sat up straight. She hadn't given her mom's fall much attention.

"Didn't you find it weird that she was at an outdoor mall? The snow is finally clearing, but a few days ago, it would have been ugly at Mill Grove. They plowed the parking lot the day after your mom supposedly fell. And since when does she shop there? It's mostly baby furniture and toddler clothes these days." Tina took the beer offered by Robby and gave him a quick peck of thanks.

"Wow. I didn't think about it." Cristiane took a sip. The drink Isadora had the other night was quickly becoming a favorite. "I don't know why she would lie about a fall. She was scared after the woman stopped by the house. I remember her name was Nancy or Nessy. Oh, maybe Nissa. I think that's it." Cristiane stopped and pondered Tina's comments. *Had someone injured her mother?*

A group came through the door. Her senses tingled, and she smiled before looking up, happy to see many familiar faces in the crowd. Jarvis caught her eye as he strode quickly over to their table.

"Hey, I'm glad to see you." Jarvis rubbed her shoulder before he slid a chair next to Cristiane. Tina and Robby exchanged a quick glance.

"I was hoping I'd see you here, too." Cristiane beamed at Jarvis for half a beat longer than a usual greeting. After seconds, they chuckled and spotted Tina and Robby staring. "What? After seeing my mom at the club, we ran into each other. We talked for a bit." Cristiane shrugged and lifted her drink to hide her widening grin.

"Hmm. Okay." Tina winked at Jarvis.

He returned her wink with a dazzling smile. "I'm grabbing a round. Beers for you two, yes? What are you having, Cris?"

"It's a Brandy Alexander. It is chocolaty sweetness to die for—simply delicious."

"Can I try a sip?"

"Sure." She handed Jarvis her glass. "It's like dessert with a warm kick."

"Oh, that has a solid kick, but too sweet for me tonight." He placed the drink in her hand and slid his fingers across her hand before leaving. "I'll be right back."

Cristiane rubbed her hands, enjoying the warm trail his touch left on her skin. She watched him walk away and realized she was staring at his bum. She cleared her throat as she sat up in her seat.

"Spill." Tina tapped the table to get Cristiane's attention.

"There's nothing to tell. We talked for hours the other night. I believed there were a few sparks, but then with my mom's shit going on, I haven't been able to give Jarvis more thought until now." Cristiane's senses wandered back to the bar where she met Jarvis's eyes. He was smiling. "I'm open."

She shrugged and turned her attention to watching Jarvis as he waited for the bartender to fill his order.

Jarvis was a head taller than Cristiane. He had dark hair like hers, but with long layered waves that framed his face and reached for his collar. She bit her lip as she thought about his light brown eyes, hooded with thick brows, which reminded her of the sweet Rottweiler dog that lived next door. She caught herself eyeing Jarvis's shoulders, initially hoping he would turn again so she could see his eyes. But now she lingered, thinking about the muscles flowing down his back to a round rear and muscular thighs. Her head tilted slightly, and she raised an eyebrow as she wondered if he lifted weights. She liked how his pants fit, and they didn't slide halfway down his backside.

"Hello? Earth to Cris."

Cristiane jumped in her seat. Her face heated. "Tina!"

"Girl, you need to shift those eyes if you're not delivering the goods." Tina sipped her beer as Robby choked on his.

"Stop it."

"I'm just sayin'. He's gonna wonder what those eyes you're giving him mean." Tina clamped her lips, then turned to the oncoming group that included David, Joyce, Liam, and Zack. Jarvis trailed behind with their drinks. Tina smiled and hollered louder than necessary. "Hi, everybody! What's shaking?"

"Our booties!" Liam went and shook his butt at the group, with Zack joining him. They laughed and turned back to everyone, joining in laughter as greetings jumbled over one another while everyone settled around the table.

An hour passed by as the group joked and laughed together. Jarvis sat next to Cristiane and brushed a pinky along her hand. When he heard David mention a necklace David had given Cristiane, he pulled his hand away, wondering why David had given Cristiane such a meaningful gift.

"Cris, do you have it with you? I mentioned the necklace to Joyce, and she wondered what it looked like. Here's the photo Tina took of you wearing it to the Halloween party. I thought you might want it now. But the picture doesn't show the necklace well." David looked at Joyce and gave a goofy shrug and nudged the photo across the table at Cristiane.

Cristiane quickly squeezed Jarvis's fingers, that he'd pulled away a moment before, meeting his questioning eyes for a split second. "Yeah, I have it." She pulled loose a couple of buttons from her top and then reached around to undo the clasp. Not wanting Jarvis to wonder if there was still something between her and David, Cristiane turned to face Jarvis, her cleavage exposed as she pulled down at her shirt. His eyes followed down for a second. "Can you help undo the clasp, Jarvis?" Her green eyes waited for him to meet her gaze.

"Sure." Jarvis reached around while his face was within inches from hers, maintaining eye contact until she looked down. He felt her chin turn away, so his breath fell along her collar as his fingers searched for the hook. Her body pressed a fraction closer into his as her breasts brushed against his upper body. Her quick breath caught as he noticed goosebumps pop up below her collarbone and down to the swell of her chest. Jarvis knew it was mere seconds, but his senses picked up on every signal and so he pressed toward her in kind. As the clasp released, he caught the corner of her eye as his lips brushed against her ear. "Here ya go."

Cristiane skimmed her hand over his while he offered her the necklace. As she turned back, she leaned into him before adjusting forward and re-buttoned her shirt. Then she rose from her seat and handed the necklace to Joyce. "Here. It's quite gorgeous. I'm sure David told you about it. I guess it's the weirdest thing to change my life." As Cristiane slid back into her seat, she looked around the table to see if anyone noticed her interactions with Jarvis. The men didn't seem to notice. Liam and Zack had their shoulders close, whispering to each other. David and Joyce were looking at each other while Cristiane turned her attention to Robby and Tina.

Robby shot his chin down and giggled while Tina peered at Cristiane and then tipped her bottle toward her friend with a quick dip of her chin.

Cristiane looked down as she slipped one hand under the table and glided it over Jarvis's thigh and between his legs to rest above his knee. She turned her chin toward him a fraction and noticed the smile hinting at the corners of his lips. His hand slid under and covered hers as his other hand reached for Cristiane's photo. She peered at Jarvis. He seemed to notice everything in the picture. Her costume was of a provocative witch, dressed in a long black gown with a deep v neck that showed off the necklace. The dress hugged her curves, and the makeup made her look much older than she was.

"This is remarkable. And to think your ancestors specifically designed the locket to serve as a curse to whomever wore it or tried to get near." Joyce shivered as she turned the necklace over in her hands. "You all realize that could have gone in a bunch of wrong directions, don't you? That's some spooky stuff."

Cristiane tried to stay focused as Jarvis traced the top of her hand with his middle finger in little circles. "I know. We were all freaked out at first. Thankfully, Robby connected me with Isadora, and she helped banish the curse and free my ancestors. The ceremony was cool, right, guys?" Cristiane looked at her old friends as they nodded.

Joyce handed the necklace back to Cristiane. "I'm glad that everyone was safe. If anything had gone worse, I may not have this guy by my side." Joyce nuzzled into David as he wrapped an arm around her in return.

Robby added, "Seeing ghosts has been a part of my whole life. Isadora helped me make sense of that ability, and I'm glad the necklace brought us closer so I could share my experiences with my friends and my fiancée. I felt alone growing up. And then to meet the rest of you and be able to share my ghost-spotting weirdness has been another blessing." Robby nodded toward Jarvis, Liam, and Zack, then kissed Tina's hand. He raised his drink. "To unexpected forks in the road."

Everyone cheered and raised their glasses. "Here, here."

A short time later, Claire and Robyn walked in and waved to the group of friends in the back before reaching the bar. As they sat down, the bartender rang a bell over his head and hollered, "Closing in fifteen. Sorry folks, it's an early night."

Groans rang out through the pub in reply. Claire and Robyn shrugged and turned back toward the door before getting a chance to talk with anyone.

Waving as the two women stepped out, Robby said, "Well, I guess that's it." He downed the last of his beer and then offered to escort Tina out. The rest of the group quickly finished their drinks and said their farewells, then trickled toward the door. Cristiane and Jarvis, being sluggish, made their way out behind the others.

As they stood beside Cristiane's car and she dug inside her purse for her keys, Jarvis reached out, gently taking her hand. "I want to ask you something."

Cristiane looked up as Jarvis stepped closer. She dropped her bag at her feet and bent back against the car to face him. She regarded him for a second before tugging at his shirt to draw him in tighter. "What did you want to ask me?" Her heated breath formed miniature clouds in the frigid evening air as she studied his face.

Jarvis opened her jacket and slid his hands along her sides and around her back, stepping close and leaning into her. His eyes said everything as he licked his lips before bending his head to nuzzle into her hair. He felt her arms encircle his shoulders, pulling him until their bodies pressed hard against each other. His lips brushed across her scarred collarbone, leaving light kisses that sent shivers down her spine. Then his tongue trailed up along her neck until he took a slow breath near her ear, drinking in her scent. "Would you come to my place?" He pulled back, searching her face, waiting for an answer.

Cristiane didn't trust her voice. Her breathing was shallow as her heartbeat pounded along her pulse points. She didn't rush her answer. Of course, but she didn't want him to be a one-night stand. She liked him more than she was willing to admit. "On two conditions."

Confused but curious, he gave her a puzzled eye. "What conditions?"

"One, we will talk after I go back to school, and two, we go out on proper dates. No ghosting."

"Definitely, no ghosting. I'm not interested in one-nighters, especially with you." He kissed her and then picked up her bag from the ground. "We'll come back and get your car, if that's okay with you?"

"Perfect. Let's go." Cristiane took his outstretched hand as they turned together toward his truck.

ELEVEN

Cristiane poured a mug of coffee as Beatrice strolled into the kitchen dressed in leggings, a pullover jacket, and sneakers. "I wondered where you and Dad were this morning. Did you go out for a walk?" Cristiane raised a mug, to which Beatrice nodded in reply.

"I did. Your dad went to the office for a few hours. An emergency that couldn't wait." Beatrice took the coffee and sat at the counter. "So, what's up with sneaking in at the crack of dawn?"

"I didn't sneak anywhere." Cristiane's guard went up, ruffled by her mom's accusation. "I'm a grown woman and I was being polite by not making noise to wake you."

"I see." Beatrice sipped her coffee. "Were you careful at least? You know pregnancy in the middle of college would screw up—"

"Mom! What bug is up your ass this morning? If I want to share my sex life, if I'm having sex, I'll share when I'm damn well ready. What I do is my responsibility." Cristiane slammed her mug on the counter as she glared at Beatrice. "As we're going to get into each other's business, what's up with your lies, Mom? There is a lot to run through these days. First, why have you been doing witchcraft all these years under Dad's nose without at least telling him, or me?"

Beatrice had the mug midair and slowly placed it back on the counter. Her mouth remained agape as Cristiane threw the barrage of questions at her. She felt the heat rising from her neck through to her cheeks.

"You've been lying to us for years. Maybe your entire marriage with that warped version of an altar behind your closet. Oh, and then there's the damn club! Have you always been having an affair, or is that blond guy just the latest fling?" Cristiane's face was flush. Her hands were waving in the air as she pressed Beatrice with each accusation—the pent-up frustrations of the previous week let loose between them. She crossed her arms in front of her, waiting for her mother to answer. "Well, what do you have to say for yourself, Mother?"

Beatrice scowled at her daughter. Her fingers balled tight as fingernails dug into her palms, reminding her not to cast in anger. Her eyes darted as she processed the litany of questions. "When the hell did you see me at a club?" Beatrice's jaw clenched as she measured her words.

Still boiling, Cristiane sneered. "Last weekend when you said you were going to the book club. I knew it was a lie. I saw you outside Javier's with a woman and a man. His hands were all over your back when he escorted you out of the alley. So is book club code for when you want a side piece?" Cristiane spat the last statement out with venom, her face contorted in a menacing grimace. "And when the hell did you smoke? Jesus, Mom. Who are you?" Cristiane turned and pulled a paper towel from the roll and mopped up the coffee she'd spilled over the counter.

"The smoking is the least of your concerns." Through clenched jaws, her words were barely recognizable as Beatrice walked to the cabinet and pulled out two liquor bottles. She then walked back to her seat and carefully placed each bottle on the counter before sitting. Beatrice poured a generous portion of each into her mug. "You've said your piece. Now you're going to shut up and listen to me."

"I'm not—"

"For once, Cristiane Elizabeth, stop trying to argue with me and listen!" Beatrice stood and flung a pointed finger into Cristiane's face. Her hand shook with fury, and her face twisted with rage. She closed her eyes and took a deep breath in, long and slow, then let it out before opening her eyes again.

Cristiane stiffened. Her mother had been angry with her before, but nothing like this. The woman in front of Cristiane frightened her. She recognized nothing about this woman. Afraid to say a word, Cristiane nodded and slid onto a stool farthest from Beatrice.

"You're going to hear me out without a peep, do you understand?" Beatrice stirred her coffee and then took a long drink. She looked at the clock, sighed, and then dropped her head.

Cristiane didn't move.

"First, there are aspects of our lives as your parents that you're not privy to, period. Following me, searching through my personal space is unacceptable, no matter what you think you know. You say you're a grown woman, then act like it. If you have a question, then you ask like an adult. No more sneaking around and playing games."

Cristiane raised a finger as if to speak, but Beatrice waved her off.

"My turn." Beatrice shook her head and waved a finger no. "What you think you saw at the club is none of your business. My personal life does not need a stamp of approval by whomever shot out of my womb. Am I clear?" Beatrice did not wait for an answer. "I am not having an affair. That's all you need to know. You are not to go back to Javier's ever. Do you understand me? Never."

Cristiane placed her forearms on the table and laced her fingers. She felt the anger boiling up as her mother demanded she not to go to Javier's. As Beatrice spoke, Cristiane clenched her teeth and pursed lips, waiting until her mother finished barking orders.

"I am a witch. As I realized the other night, so are you. Don't think your toss of the door in Nissa's face went unnoticed. I had hoped you wouldn't learn of our family's gifts, but somehow you not only found out, but have been practicing and improving your skill set. You have no idea what is going on in the world around you, all I have done to keep you safe all these years. Your father and I have given you a wonderful life, to flourish, tucked away from the horrible events and people of the world so you could make something of yourself. Witchcraft does nothing more than allow the underbelly of the world to knock at your door repeatedly until it takes everything. I forbid you from continuing in the craft."

Cristiane jumped from her seat. "I will stop nothing just because you say so!" The words poured out of her, high and shaky because of her anger, but she would not listen to her mother. The lying, cheating stranger who stood in front of her, requiring she listen and fall in line like a child, was not her mom. Tears spilled over her cheeks as Cristiane paced the room with a finger pointing in the air. "I will continue as a witch. I will do as I damn well please. Thank you very much. The coven rejected me because they knew *you* were practicing dark magic. The one remarkable thing that has come my way in an incredibly long time is gone because of *you*, Mother. Why would I listen to you? You've lied, cheated, hidden things behind Dad's back, behind my back, my entire life! I'm done. Do you hear that, Mother? I'm done with you."

Cristiane didn't look at her mother. Instead, she stormed out and ran upstairs. Her bedroom door slammed behind her.

Beatrice sat at the kitchen counter. She didn't call or reach out to Cristiane. Instead, she stayed and drank coffee in silence. When the coffee was gone, she poured liquor into the empty mug and continued to drink.

Twenty minutes later, she heard Cristiane swing the bedroom door open and drag her bags down the stairs. Each bag made a thump as they slid on the staircase treads behind Cristiane. Beatrice listened as the front door opened and Cristiane hoisted each bag out onto the porch. The door slammed shut as Beatrice remained seated. A moment later, she heard a car's engine come to life, a car pull from the driveway, and then listened as the engine's rumble faded away in the distance.

Beatrice poured and drank, emptying both bottles. While running the argument through her head, she grew worried, and then frustrated with herself. She flung the empty bottles across the room, shattering glass, and watched as the debris cascaded to the floor. Beatrice cursed to herself. She lost her temper when she should have been transparent and explain the dangers. Instead, prideful as usual, she fought back and ruined everything.

Springfield was the safest place for Cristiane, now more than ever.

TWELVE

The fight with Beatrice left Cristiane outraged and upset. The stop to see her dad was useless, other than saying goodbye. He appeared to give his wife the benefit of the doubt over every topic his daughter raised. Cristiane didn't get the point of hiding anything from her dad and told him about their fight. He said little back to her, but she could tell that it bothered him. He asked a few questions about both of them being witches, which made Cristiane laugh. How did he not know his wife was practicing witchcraft for almost 25 years? The club unnerved him. Cristiane thought his unease had more to do with David's findings than his wife spotted with another man.

Cristiane left feeling disappointed and angry. Unable to reach Isadora, she called Tina on the drive to vent. By the time Cristiane reached Springfield, her anger had subdued. She'd leave contact up to her mother and concentrate on classwork.

Cristiane threw herself into her studies. Since returning to school, her dreams were full of darkness and left her feeling depressed and disconnected from the real world. The flaming eyes took shape several times in a grotesque child that did nothing but jeer and laugh as it tormented children or made Cristiane the target of its attacks in an immense home with hallways running in various directions. Cristiane woke after those nightmares wondering what it all meant. Was the creature coming after her?

It was an isolated time to deal with such awful visions on her own. Her roommate had not returned after spring break. Rumor around campus was that Lenor was pregnant and had dropped out of school. Cristiane didn't get along with her. They were cordial, but Lenor partied more than she attended classes and it had been a sore subject all year. Cristiane was thankful to have the dorm room to herself.

That said, the loneliness weighed on Cristiane. Over the following weeks, she didn't speak to her parents, and no one reached out to talk. Tina and Robby left messages and texted several times, but Cristiane refused to take their calls. The only exceptions had been a few calls with Isadora, and, to her delight and surprise, Jarvis. He'd been true to his word and stayed in touch, calling or sending texts often. Without him, she would have been depressed and heartbroken, yet they spoke almost every day. He drove to Springfield a few times so they could go out on proper dates and spend time together on the weekends. Her heart felt content whenever she thought of him, and that made her smile.

Isadora trained Cristiane with more difficult spells, which helped fill the time away from her college studies—teleportation being one oddity that Cristiane didn't seem to grasp. Isadora warned her of the dangers so often, she was too afraid to try it on her own. The incantation perplexed her and caused her anxiety even though the other teachings came so readily to her. Teleporting, although it was an amazing ability and sounded fancy, the thought of being torn into bits or having a brain hemorrhage if not performed properly terrified her. Isadora warned that the ability was to be used only in extreme circumstances because of its dangers. Cristiane was to practice on inanimate objects. There's no harm when a pencil doesn't reappear, but an animal or person obscurely disappearing for all eternity would be a problem. Starting slowly put Cristiane at ease. She would need the ability one day, so Isadora reiterated she had to practice often.

Even through the relative quiet since coming back to school, the time moved by fast. Ghosts seldom showed up in her room or in other campus buildings. The only remarkable notion was that ever since Cristiane saw the male figure in her parents' kitchen, he remained visible when he showed himself and was no longer a misty apparition behind the orb. Although the orb had not changed, the two entities appeared to be together, never one without the other. The apparitions lingered longer now that the male was visible, but she couldn't figure out how to communicate with them.

She nicknamed the male figure Henry, as his appearances reminded her of a haunting from her childhood. In her young eight-year-old mind, the haunting was real, even though she never saw a presence. Henry was the name she gave the flickering disturbance when she was a little girl. Her mother would tease her and yell whenever the bookcase lights flashed, "Grandpa Henry is calling you." Cristiane believed the haunting was from an old man and would huddle close to her mother, but eventually Beatrice confided the bookcase lights came on occasionally due to dust buildup on the touchpad and not because of an elderly ghost. Beatrice wiped the touch switch clean and then Henry didn't show for a long time. When the lights flickered again several weeks later, Cristiane looked at the dusty switch and blew on it, causing the lights to flicker again. Cristiane stopped believing in Henry after that. Now she smiled to herself at the irony of actual ghosts dropping in her space whenever they wanted to appear.

Cristiane had a few weeks before the semester was to end. She was getting anxious about what she'd do during the summer, either continue with the few remaining classes, or take a break so she could spend time with Jarvis. But going back to Andover would mean she'd have to stay at her parents' house. The thought made her uneasy, especially after she'd stormed out and hadn't spoken to her mother since. Without speaking to either of them for two months, she sent a text to her dad. He called back within seconds.

"Hi, sweet pea. I'm so glad to hear from you. How's school?"

"It's going well. Semester is almost over. I'm trying to decide if I should plow through another summer session or wait until the fall, since I have two classes to finish." Cristiane avoided their last discussion and remained upbeat. "So how's Mom? You two doing all right?" She heard a heavy sigh come through the phone.

"It's been a trying few months. We've had a run of bad luck with a few minor accidents, and we've been handling each one, but it's been hard. I don't want to discuss it on the phone." Jeffrey was tired and worn. "It'd be great to see you over the summer, but you must decide for yourself. Finishing your degree early is an enormous accomplishment."

"Dad, why didn't you call me about these accidents? Are you okay? What about Mom?" Cristiane was angry, but she didn't want her mother injured. If they needed help, then why didn't one of them call Cristiane? "I'll come by this weekend for a day trip, see you both, and test the waters with Mom. Have you talked things over since I left?"

"We did on some issues. She won't talk too much about the witch stuff except that it's all benign and I don't need to worry." Jeffrey was quiet for a minute before he spoke again. "Your mom says she's not having an affair and I believe her, so don't bring that up. It'll do her good to see you and maybe you can patch things up when you're here."

"That might be a tall order, Dad, but I'll come home Saturday. See you then." Cristiane hung up and then texted Jarvis about her plans. Although the opportunity to clear the air with Beatrice was welcome, she didn't want to be stuck in her parents' house overnight. Her dad's voice concerned Cristiane, so she sent Isadora a text, too.

Isadora didn't call but sent a series of texts. "Use your gift of sight. Beatrice is internally conflicted and whatever was shielding her is gone. Protect yourself and examine what might bother your father before you go home. Prepare."

Cristiane pondered Isadora's push for her to take control of her magic. She was right. Cristiane had not been pursuing her mystical powers as much as she did before the coven denied her initiation. Whatever was happening at home, she needed to have eyes on her parents before she walked into a room with her mother. It was a clever idea to look in on them through sight. Cristiane was frustrated with herself that she didn't think of it sooner.

Cristiane had conducted protection enchantments all week. After reading Isadora's text several times, she was concerned for her mother's welfare and took every precaution leading up to her weekend visit. Tonight Cristiane would attempt to astral project to her parents' home. She'd traveled around campus and the local area successfully as she practiced the art, but she was 150 miles away from her target. Cristiane wasn't sure if she'd be able to make the journey, so she took her time to prepare.

Cristiane slipped into bed. Her favorite music for projecting, binaural beats, played in the headphones as she took long slow breaths. She concentrated on relaxing her muscles, from toes to head, as the music lulled her physical body into a weightiness, dormant on the bed. At the same time, her mind and spirit soared through the subtle vibration radiating through her body. Her heart rate climbed as the recognizable ringing began in her ears. Cristiane rested her mind, allowing the buoyancy to envelop her soul until, after several minutes, she detected the familiar sense of her astral body easing out and standing up beside her physical form. Pleased with how quickly she could pull away from her physical form, Cristiane sought her target, the family home.

Cristiane remained outside her parents' house for a few moments, letting the strangeness of traveling so far from her body melt away from her mind. She didn't have to use the door, but simply thought of her destination and then was looking down the bedroom hallway. Happy with herself, she felt giddy with pride at her accomplishment. The emotion was short-lived as an ugly energy permeated from the end of the hall, her parents' bedroom.

Watchful of the unknown, Cristiane was thankful that she had taken precautions leading up to tonight. When she reached the door, she saw the oppressive force was like a heavy cloak surrounding Beatrice. A dull gray and red cloud appeared to slither around her mother, a pulsating wave that did not include her father. Jeffrey slept peacefully, hugging a pillow on the opposite side. Cristiane noticed a stitched contusion on his forehead and a few healing scratches on his arms. He seemed unaffected by the presence sharing their bedroom. The diabolical cocoon appeared to ensure it did not encompass anyone or anything other than her mother.

As Cristiane inched closer, the force gnawed at her psyche. How did her mother function if this energy followed her, enveloped her all the time? Cristiane concentrated on moving past the evil power and focused on her mother's aura. She had to know if it was permeating from Beatrice, which would indicate that her mother was the source, or if the presence was driven over her.

Beatrice contorted in a garbled fetal position, looking as if she'd fallen from a building rather than in a bed, her face in a sleepful scowl. She had lacerations on an arm and the side of her cheek. Her other arm was covered in a bright pink cast. Cristiane wondered what other injuries her mother had that she couldn't see.

Cristiane gazed at her mother's forehead, allowing the different aura colors to manifest. She noted an unusual blend radiating from Beatrice that concerned her. Although bright, Cristiane sensed the hellish gray blanket suppressing her mother's natural desires and energy. As she watched the evil move, Cristiane's heart went out to her mom. Something malevolent had a powerful hold and it wasn't going away without a struggle. As Cristiane pondered ideas, her intuition screamed that she reached the right conclusion. The murky wave encircling Beatrice stopped as a blackened branch jutted toward Cristiane's astral projection. Horrified, Cristiane moved back. Something or someone knew she was there. She must leave or risk never returning to her physical body.

THIRTEEN

Dawn cracked over the horizon as Cristiane dragged a bag over her shoulder and slogged through the dorm toward the parking lot. Cristiane had finished loading the car and slid into the driver's seat. She sent a quick text to Tina and Jarvis and then pulled the car into reverse when a tall man stopped behind her car, preventing Cristiane from backing out of the parking space. Dressed in a baseball cap, jeans, tee shirt, and zip-up hoodie, Cristiane couldn't gauge much else about the man through the rearview mirror. She honked the horn to get his attention. When he didn't respond, she pushed the window button to inch it open. "Hey, buddy. Ya mind moving your ass out of the way? You're holding me up."

"Aren't you polite, Ms. Bradford?"

Cristiane caught the deep condescension in his voice and sat motionless. She didn't know him, did she? Seconds ticked by and he didn't budge, so she turned the car engine off, pulled the pepper spray cartridge from her bag, and opened the door. She stood alongside the opening, ready to jump back inside if the situation turned south. The stranger took a few steps to his left and faced her. He wore a grin pressed across stiffened lips. Cristiane tightened her grip on the casing, her thumb poised at the trigger. "How do you know me? Are you a student?" Her cheerful tone belied the tumultuous somersaults of her belly. The guy oozed of cool disrespect and willful arrogance. She hated him and she didn't know who the hell he was.

His laugh was dull, like that of a boorish politician. "I'm not a student, but I am interested in asking you a few questions. Do you have a moment?"

Cristiane raised the hand, holding the pepper spray as a warning.

He replied by raising his hands. "Oh, I'm sorry if I frightened you. I am harmless, just an insurance adjuster. I have a few questions about the accident your parents had recently. My name is Malin." He pulled his pockets out, unzipped the hoodie, and then opened it while turning in a circle so Cristiane might see that he didn't have a weapon.

Cristiane relaxed and dropped her arm. An insurance adjuster. What the hell? "Fine. Sorry, it's just—you know, every girl's nightmare headline, *Student Found Strangled in Dorm Parking Lot.*" She shrugged as the gentleman walked a few steps closer.

"I understand." He used a slight southern accent, which worked to charm most ladies. Malin hoped it would lure Cristiane into speaking with him, or at least allow him in nearer. "Have you seen your parents since the accident? That was some doozy of a crash, if you ask me." He rubbed the back of his head while moving his baseball cap.

"Why would an insurance adjuster care if I have visited my parents?" Cristiane wasn't buying the fake southern charm. She studied Malin's face. He had grayish blond stubble across his chin and looked much older than she initially thought. She listened to her gut and it said he was an ass. "Do you have a business card?"

"Oh, sure. Of course, it's just a routine question. Hold a sec and let me pull one out." Malin stepped closer as he reached for his wallet. "Here, this is for you." Instead of handing her a business card, Malin reached out and clutched her hand with his massive fingers to envelop the spray cartridge and her thumb. Even if she squeezed the trigger, she would only dose her own hand. Malin pulled her toward the back of the vehicle and slammed the driver's door shut, then pinned her arms behind her with one hand. "Don't even think about screaming; no one can hear you. Look over my shoulder. Do you see the man under the tree?"

Cristiane did as he instructed, finding a person in a black hoodie. His face was down, but his stance was watchful, guarding, and ready to pounce if needed. She turned back to her assailant. He wore a musky cologne, which in any other situation might have smelled appealing, but it twisted her stomach tighter. She listened for anyone in the parking lot and heard nothing. Students should be getting into their cars or walking to class. Was a force masking their surroundings or making them invisible to others? Cristiane grew frightened when she thought of the potential answers. She could not move. "What the hell do you want?"

"That's much better. I like your tone, antagonistic yet accommodating, like your mother. I wonder what other ways you're like, dear old Mom." Malin ran his free hand up her thigh, trailing along her hip, and over her shoulder. He rested fingers behind her neck, cupping under her chin with his enormous thumb. He yanked her arms down, forcing her shoulders toward the back, and her chest and head jerked up as his eyes raked over her body. "I can take whatever I want. Right here. You look sweet, like your momma used to be." His thumb pressed across her bottom lip as the hooded figure in the distance took a step closer.

Cristiane rolled her head away from his touch and eyed the point of a thick broken tree branch resembling a javelin jutting out above their heads.

Malin grabbed at her face and pulled her head directly forward, his fingernails pushed into her cheeks, keeping her immobile.

Fury erupted as she concentrated her magic on freeing the sharp branch from the tree. She struggled to liberate a hand, but his grip only tightened. Cristiane winced under the intense pressure. The emerald pendant around her neck emanated a glowing warmth, fueling her magic and concentration onto the tree limb overhead.

"You like to fight. How encouraging." Malin's scruffy face descended toward Cristiane as the tree branch broke free and rocked through him, piercing Malin's cheeks like a skewer as she turned away. His lips gaped open like a fish while his mouth filled with blood.

Shocked by the spear through his cheeks, Malin tottered back. Fingers grabbed and clawed at his face as crimson trails escaped his mouth. He whimpered while he pulled at the branch, trying to dislodge it.

The drop in his attack was all Cristiane needed when his grip released. Her hands now free, she brought them together and pressed out away from herself, banishing him from her space. Malin flew away from her about twenty yards. The distance provided enough time for her to swing open the car door and lock herself inside. She started the car and backed out as fast as she could drive. When she faced forward to pull out of the parking lot, the hooded man stood in her way. She slammed her foot on the brake. "Shit!"

Frantically, Malin ran toward her, blood dripping from his chin as the branch remained transfixed on his flesh. The man blocking her path waved Malin to stay back. Who the hell was this guy? Can she catch a break and leave? This figure was much thinner, but as tall as her assailant. The over-sized hoodie draped as if it were covering a skeleton, dressed over chinos that hung from protruding hipbones. He didn't speak but raised his head to where Cristiane saw his sullied teeth through transparent, delicate lips, which appeared to hang above his skeletal jaw. The horrific, sallow skin covered bone, like cheesecloth over a plastic skeleton at Halloween.

Cristiane could not stop the shudder through her body. The man standing in front of her car was the scary creature outside of Javier's nightclub the night she followed her mother. Cristiane clenched the steering wheel, twisting her hands back and forth, pondering how to escape. While she looked through the rearview mirror contemplating retreat, the two men blocked her. Malin glared, wiping blood from the oozing punctures on his face. He stood with feet apart, stationed behind the vehicle. She had no way of escape without running over one of them. Her mind was spinning as she realized a voice was speaking inside her head.

Ah, there you are. Breathe, Cristiane. I am Xirnan. I won't harm you, and I won't allow Malin to either. Xirnan raised his head a smidge, so Cristiane could see his smoldering eyeballs under the black drape of his hood, unreadable other that the tiny flames festering within ice-cold violet eyes set deep in their sockets. His mouth remained in the same grotesque, void expression. *Go check on Mommy. We'll be in touch soon.*

She shook with a combination of fury and fear after releasing a held breath. "Get the hell out of my skull, you freak!" How did she understand him so clearly in her head? She wanted to leave as quickly as possible, but she couldn't drive the car through them.

Instead she clasped her hands and pressed out as she did to banish Malin a few minutes ago; however, her power had little effect on this target. Her spell shoved Xirnan's shoulders rather than expel him out of her way and his feet did not budge from their spot. Cristiane shook her head in frustration. What kind of monster stood in front of her?

Xirnan allowed a satisfied smirk to spread across the stiff parchment he had for a face. *This is going to be entertaining. Appreciate freedom while you still have it, young witch.* He bowed his emaciated head an inch or two toward Cristiane in farewell as he stepped to the side, allowing room for her to pass.

Cristiane glanced in the rearview mirror. Malin remained standing in the same position, arms crossed, unperturbed. She squared her shoulders, put a firm grip on the steering wheel to keep them from shaking, and sped past Xirnan without looking at him. The sooner she left, the better. She turned onto Wilbraham Avenue without checking traffic.

A mile down the road, she pulled over. Desperate for guidance, Cristiane called Isadora, but had to leave a message when she didn't answer. Convinced Isadora would return her call after hearing of the attack, Cristiane took a cleansing breath as her stomach growled in the car's silence. An older woman unlocked a café and propped the door open. Cristiane decided warm coffee and pastry were in order and went inside the café.

As she waited for her purchase, an SUV slowed as it passed her car.

Malin drove, blood oozing from the holes in his cheeks, while Xirnan leaned forward and grinned in her direction. "See you soon."

"Go to hell!" Cristiane screamed back in her head.

He answered her with a distant chuckle and invitation. "Happy to take you on a tour."

The barista handed Cristiane her coffee. "Have a lovely day."

"Not likely."

It wasn't until she merged onto the turnpike that Cristiane rummaged through her bag for her cell. Her hands were trembling, and the phone slid under her seat. She couldn't fight off tears as they bubbled over, streaming down her cheeks. Desperate to be with a friend, she pressed down on the gas pedal. Cristiane sensed the men were not far, and it terrified her. She didn't stop to retrieve the phone but pressed the gas pedal harder. She couldn't go straight to her parents. Cristiane needed guidance. She needed her patron, Isadora.

As Cristiane reached Worcester, her phone would ring and then stop, then ring again. Someone was trying to reach her but wasn't leaving a message. She pulled off near Union Station, retrieving her phone under the seat. There were four missed calls and several texts from her father. She didn't bother to read through the texts but called him.

"Dad, why are you blowing up my phone?"

Jeffrey didn't speak right away. Cristiane could hear him shuffling through the receiver. He cleared his throat. "Cris, it's your mom. She's at the hospital. You need to be here, please."

"I'm already on the road. I'll be there soon. What department, Dad?"

"Emergency. Trauma center." His voice quivered as he said the last two words.

"On my way. Love you." Cristiane hung up and tossed the phone in the passenger seat. She left Union Station and went back onto the highway without thinking of her assailants.

FOURTEEN

Cristiane rushed through the emergency room's automatic sliding doors and took in the scene, searching for her dad. A couple lingered in the far left corner, the lady rubbing at her swollen stomach while her partner chomped on potato chips. A man retching close by triggered Cristiane into stepping to the right. As she turned toward the noise, she not only saw the projectile vomit but received a heavy dose of the torturous scent of alcohol and seafood as it landed on the overflowing waste receptacle. Cristiane covered her nose and glanced over the crowd at a boy with a protruding bone being comforted by his mother, an elderly wife softly sobbing while holding a man's wedding ring, and finally her gaze followed to a young man reading a book next to a familiar older man, her father.

Jeffrey was talking to a man in a suit in the far right corner, near a set of swinging doors. The suited man had his head down, writing in a notebook. Cristiane waved as she caught her dad's eye and hurried over, giving her dad a hug. Jeffrey burst into tears as she held him tight. "Hey, Dad. It's okay. It's okay. I'm here." She pulled back after his sobs subsided to look at his face and then down his body for injuries. "Were you hurt?"

Jeffrey wiped at his face. "No, sweetie. I wasn't with your mom. Let's talk in a minute. I'm, uh, trying to answer this gentleman's questions." Jeffrey lightly held her upper arm and turned from Cristiane. "I'm sorry, Detective, your name again? This is our daughter, Cristiane."

"Jarvis, sir. Jarvis Morris." Unsure if Cristiane had mentioned him to her parents, Jarvis stretched out his hand for introductions.

"Oh, thank god you're here," Cristiane blurted as she gave him a tight embrace.

Jarvis returned her hug and pulled her close. "I am for as long as you need me." Jarvis kissed the top of her head and looked back at Mr. Bradford. "Sir, don't worry about my questions now. You and Cris can talk first. I can wait—"

"No, stay with us, please. Dad, I know Jarvis very well." Cristiane interrupted as she held Jarvis's hand and sought concurrence from her father. "Is there an area or somewhere we can talk?"

"Let me see if there is a private room available." Jarvis squeezed her hand and stepped over to the nurses' station.

Cristiane hated hospitals. The smell of antiseptic, blood, and an undercurrent of other bodily fluids unnerved her. All of it made her skin crawl. She looked through the square window of the swinging door, wondering where her mother was in the hospital. "Dad, where is Mom?"

"Surgery." Jeffrey pulled her to his side and wrapped an arm around her. "It's bad, Cris."

Jarvis turned back and motioned for them to follow him down the corridor to a windowless room. He flicked on the lights and drew the curtains facing the hallway closed. Then he motioned for the two to sit on the couch as he pulled a heavy plastic chair opposite them.

"Mr. Bradford. Would you like to tell Cristiane what happened before we get back to my questions, or would you prefer I go over what we've covered so far?" Jarvis was professional and patient. He had the smooth tone of a seasoned cop used to giving bad news to family while illustrating compassion during questioning. He ached to be sitting with Cristiane, but this was not the time. Jeffrey needed his daughter by his side.

"Would you?" Jeffrey answered quietly, defeated.

"Sure, Mr. Bradford." Jarvis shifted his gaze to Cristiane. He pulled the stiff plastic chair closer and reached across to take her hands. "Sweetie."

Jeffrey raised his eyebrows but didn't say a word.

"This will be hard." Jarvis noticed Jeffrey blink a few times and purse his lips, but he kept his focus on Cristiane. He knew Cristiane didn't get along with her mom, but the news would be painful for any child to hear, no matter how embittered they were with a parent. "Your mother is in critical condition. A woman who was hiking the trail found her earlier this morning near the Pond Loop. If the woman's dog hadn't been off leash and barked to alert his owner, your mother might not have been found in time. Beatrice has several knife wounds."

Jeffrey felt Cristiane stiffen, but he nodded to Jarvis to kept going.

"She lost a lot of blood and was barely breathing when Ms. Willard found her. A small bit of luck. Ms. Willard is a nurse and provided basic care, monitoring your mother's vitals until EMTs arrived. She's in awful shape, Cris. She's been in surgery for a few hours now."

Tears welled up and over her eyes as Cristiane brushed them away with her fingers. She took Jarvis's hand again while reaching for her father with the other. "Is she going to pull through?" She peered back and forth at both men, waiting for an answer. The minutes ticked by.

Jarvis hung his head and then looked at Jeffrey, waiting to see if he should continue.

Jeffrey sighed and finally answered his daughter. "We don't know." He leaned back against the sofa, lacing his fingers behind his head. "Someone cut her up a lot. I don't know how many stab wounds exactly, but her lungs were full of blood and the EMT said her spleen and maybe the liver too were damaged. The doctors rushed her into the operating room. The EMTs were cleaning the ambulance when I arrived. There was blood everywhere." Jeffrey wiped his eyebrows and tilted forward with his elbows on his knees. He wept again.

"Daddy." Cristiane rubbed his back. She cried along with him.

Jarvis sat back and let the two have a moment together. There was plenty of time to go through the routine questions and then delve into those that were more uncomfortable. He adored Cristiane, but the chief assigned him to the case and he had to work it by the book. Jarvis offered to get coffees and give them some time alone.

When he returned, Cristiane and her dad were calm and talking with ease. Jarvis was glad to see the two were not confrontational or assigning blame as he passed drinks around. "Here you go." He sat back in the uncomfortable chair and pulled out a notepad. "So, sir, if I may. I left word at the nurse's station that we were still here in case the doctor wanted to give you an update. Until then, I have a few questions I need to go over with you. And you as well, Cris."

"Okay, shoot." Cristiane gave a weak smile.

Jarvis asked all the usual questions, where they each were during the range of time Beatrice was out until Ms. Willard spotted her. He asked Jeffrey when Beatrice left the house that morning and how often she went to that trail. Cristiane answered along with her father, until Jarvis asked if they could think of anyone who had a gripe with Beatrice, or if anyone had threatened her recently.

Jeffrey looked at his daughter. Cristiane returned his gaze and scrunched up her brow. "Dad, the accidents lately. Were they accidents or could someone have been trying to intimidate you or Mom?"

"What do you mean? What accidents?" Jarvis wrote in his notepad.

"We've had a bout of bad luck the past several weeks. I'm sure it's not related, but Beatrice has come home banged up a few times and then we had a car accident a few weeks ago. The mechanic said the axel snapped or something. Beatrice just had her cast removed two days ago for the hairline fracture. It healed quickly, in record time. This morning was the first time she'd been out to walk or run since the doctor removed the cast." Jeffrey shrugged, not seeing a correlation to the stabbing.

"I'll circle back with more questions about each of the incidents you mentioned. It could be nothing or it could be a lead." Jarvis finished writing and then looked up. He noticed Cristiane working something out in her head. "Cris, did you think of something else?"

"I'm not sure. It's possible. Do you remember the lady who came by the house a few months ago, Dad? She and Mom had a heated argument in the front yard. I know Mom said Nissa was notifying her about a book club member's death, but that woman was pissed at Mom." Cristiane glanced at Jarvis and joggled her head. "There's more than what Mom let on. She was frightened when she came up to my room to talk. Like really terrified."

"You think so? She said nothing more about it to me. You and she came downstairs for ice cream, and we had a great night after that. Are you sure they were arguing?" Jeffrey was confused, thinking back on that night. "Nothing sticks out except her yelling at you before she rushed out the door."

"I'm positive, Dad. Something isn't right with that woman." Cristiane looked at Jarvis. "I can tell you more about it later."

They heard a brief knock on the door before two people came in wearing fresh scrubs. The older woman stepped forward as a man about Jarvis's age stayed back from the group. She reached out to shake Jarvis's hand. "Detective, Mr. Bradford, Ms. Bradford, I'm Dr. Maria Torres, and this is my surgical resident, Nathan Larson." Dr. Torres gestured toward her resident and then turned, clasping her hands in front of herself. "Detective, do you mind hanging outside as I talk with the Bradfords privately?"

"Of course." Jarvis followed Nathan out of the exit.

"Please, sit." Dr. Torres smoothed her white jacket and took the seat Jarvis left and crossed her legs. "First, Mrs. Bradford is out of surgery and stable in the ICU. She suffered multiple lacerations to her lungs, spleen, liver, and stomach, as well as a severe concussion due to a blow to the head."

Cristiane and her father nodded, both jittering in their seats. He gestured with one hand raised and then slid back into the couch, crossing his legs and hands. "Please continue."

"We had to remove your wife's spleen." Dr. Torres saw the surprise on both their faces and quickly raised her hands up. "Don't worry. People can live a normal life without a spleen. Our biggest concern at this point is proper healing without infection. Her lungs took a heavy hit because of the shortage of oxygen and filling with blood. We patched one stab wound to the right lung and removed a small portion of her left lung. The bottom of her left was too mangled to repair, but again, she has most of it, approximately 80 percent remains. She has sutures along the left side of her liver and the top of her stomach. We will monitor her for three to four days for infection, but otherwise, we are optimistic that she will have a full recovery."

In unison, Cristiane and Jeffrey blew out a deep breath.

"You both process stress the same." Dr. Torres smiled at the two in front of her.

Cristiane leaned back and crossed fingers behind her head and closed her eyes. She took a few cleansing breaths before she opened her eyes again. "When can we see her?"

"You can peek in on her now, but she won't wake for a while. Once she's awake, we'll do some cognitive testing due to the blood loss, lack of oxygen, and the concussion. But you should be able to talk with her once she comes around. We'll keep her sedated until tomorrow morning." Dr. Torres stood, indicating her notification was complete.

Jeffrey rose and followed Dr. Torres to the door. "Thank you for everything." He shook her hand.

Cristiane shook the doctor's hand and followed the others out of the room. They turned the corner, and the doctor continued through a set of double doors as Cristiane and Jeffrey met Jarvis midway down the hall. Jarvis was leaning back with one knee raised, his dress shoe braced against the beige hospital wall while flipping through his notes. As soon as he saw Cristiane, he jumped up and studied her facial expressions as she grew near.

"The doctor thinks she's going to be okay." A smile of relief spread up to her eyes. "I'm going with my dad to visit Mom for a few minutes. Do you mind waiting?" Cristiane took his hand as they walked toward the ICU.

"Not at all. I have questions for her if she's up for it." Jarvis squeezed Cristiane's hand; happy they didn't receive unpleasant news.

"She won't be awake until tomorrow. They're keeping her sedated overnight." Cristiane stopped outside the ICU doors as Jeffrey continued without waiting for her. "I'll be right back. We need to talk about a few things away from my dad."

"Sure. No problem. I'll be here." Jarvis leaned against the wall and propped up his leg again.

"Thanks" Cristiane kissed him and turned toward her father.

FIFTEEN

With Jeffrey staying at the hospital, Cristiane and Jarvis went to his home. Cristiane had pent-up anxiety and angst over the day, her nerves frayed. She needed to run or let off some steam. She'd journeyed through a roller coaster of emotions, and it was still early afternoon.

When she pulled up to the apartment, Cristiane knew exactly what she needed and knew Jarvis would happily agree.

After an awkward but satisfying reunion, Jarvis spread a picnic out on his bed. He'd been at the crime scene and then the hospital all morning. He enjoyed watching Cristiane eat. And he loved that she had an appetite and was not afraid to appreciate a meal with someone. Once they satiated their grumbling bellies, Jarvis directed their attention to her mother's case.

While Jarvis retrieved his notebook, Cristiane pulled on one of his t-shirts. She crumpled the fabric and drew in a slow, deep breath as her head pushed through the neckline. Jeez, even his clothes lying around the room smelled like him. She plunked back onto the bed and grinned as she watched Jarvis fumble to stick a leg through a pair of shorts and remain upright.

Jarvis snatched at his notepad and pen. "What's so funny?"

"Oh, nothing. I thought you might be a dancer with all that footwork."

"Dancer, me? I'm as graceful as a two-headed giraffe with eight legs." Jarvis shot a truncated curtsy to Cristiane before plopping onto the bed. "So, what did you want to share without your dad?"

Cristiane spent the next hour telling Jarvis about the night Nissa came to the house and argued with her mother in the freezing snow. Even though she'd vented to him about some of the fight during one of his visits to Springfield, Jarvis asked her to share it again for his case notes.

Cristiane hashed out every detail, including going through her mom's altar room, following her mom to Javier's, and then David's findings of Javier's underground chambers. She told him about sharing the photos with her sponsor, Isadora, to find out what type of witchcraft her mother had been practicing over the years. Cristiane explained everything except the coven's refusal to induct her into the group. The rejection hurt too much and she'd pushed her feelings down deeply the past few months. When she thought about it again, the hurt boiled up.

"I'm glad you spoke with Isadora about much of this, as these details wouldn't be suitable for a police report. But I can talk with her and the coven. We—"

"What? You mean you're in the Sacred Pillars Coven?" Cristiane dropped the neckline of the t-shirt she'd been holding to her nose. She was shocked Jarvis hadn't mentioned he was a witch or in the coven before now.

"Well, yes. It's not like we go around advertising we're a witch any more than the fact we're members of an organization that manifests magic and works to weed out evil." Jarvis looked at Cristiane, perplexed. "I thought you knew."

"How the hell would I know?" Cristiane jumped from the bed and poured a glass of wine. "Who would have told me?"

"We don't share outside of the coven. It's not like we talk about witch matters with David and Joyce at the bar, but Tina knows a lot more since they live together. With how long you've known Isadora, Robby, and Tina. I thought— well, I thought one of them would have said something." Jarvis reached to pull Cristiane into his arms, but she twisted her shoulder out of reach and walked out of the room toward the kitchen.

She stopped midway and twirled around to face him. "Wait a minute. You mean Robby is in the coven?"

"Yes. Of course. About two years now. Isadora was his sponsor as well. That's how we've all become friends: Liam, Zack, Claire, Robyn, and me. We didn't know Robby before he joined the coven." Jarvis knew he shouldn't be giving out the news, but his head was spinning at the thought of her long-time magic connections keeping their involvement secret for so long. He'd known Cristiane for a couple of months. It wasn't his place to disclose those details when she wasn't a member.

He trailed behind as she downed the wine and put the glass on the counter, grabbed her bag, and started jamming things into it while haphazardly flinging on clothes. Jarvis followed like a lost puppy. "I'm sorry. Cris, I assumed you knew. I shouldn't be the one. We swear to uphold the sanctity of the coven." He rubbed the back of his head. "Hell, Cris, how are you dealing with all this stuff on your own?"

"Well, clearly, I didn't have a damn clue about either of you." Cristiane turned on him, tears streaming down as the anger shone across her face. "I've been on my own forever and come to find out my closest friends aren't really my friends at all. Tina, Isadora, Robby, and now you. They have been hiding this huge truth from me for years when everyone knew I was struggling."

"Cris, come on. It's not like that. I thought you'd be joining after you finished college. Tina and Robby thought the same." Jarvis felt terrible for giving more news that hurt her. He tried once more to pull her close and again she rebuffed him.

Cristiane made it to the entryway, bag overflowing, and her shoes on but not tied as she opened the door and swung around to Jarvis. "No. No, I won't be joining the damn coven because, like I said, I'm on my own." Cristiane spat her words like daggers shooting across the room. "Sarah refused to initiate me because of my mother. No one cares what I'm up against. As always, I'll take care of it myself." She slammed the door behind her.

Jarvis followed and ran down the hall after her.

"Don't, Jarvis. Leave me alone." Cristiane banged on the elevator button until the doors opened. Jarvis attempted to follow her inside, but she shoved him back into the hall. "I mean it. Stay away from me."

Cristiane sat in her car for a long time before leaving the apartment complex. At least Jarvis hadn't come running after her, so she could cry in peace. The more she ran the conversation over in her head, the angrier she became. She drove, not knowing what to do, in case Jarvis came looking for her. As soon as she pulled out to the street, her phone rang several times. She looked briefly in case it was her father, but every call was from Jarvis. She put it on silent at the nearest stop sign and drove to her parents' house.

Once inside, Cristiane couldn't help but think back to the last time she saw her mother. Over two months had passed since the horrible fight, which ended with Cristiane raging back to Springfield. None of Beatrice's behavior over spring break made sense. Her mother could be difficult, but it's like she was leading an entirely separate life. A life

Beatrice didn't want her family to be involved with in the least bit.

Cristiane threw her overnight bag in her old bedroom and then walked around the empty upstairs. Other than her bedroom, which her parents had kept the same since she was in high school, the space felt foreign. The guest room used to be her entertainment room, complete with a large television, mini fridge, and a couple of monstrous fluffy bean bag chairs. A daybed used to be against the far wall out of the way, but available if anyone came to visit or a friend, usually Tina, stayed overnight. Now the room, painted a creamy yellow, contained a queen bed and matching furniture, and color-coordinated artwork on the walls. Cristiane didn't walk in. Instead she worried her lip and turned back to the hallway.

The room across the hall used to be full of toys, sports equipment, and trophies from Cristiane's youth lining the shelves. This room also underwent a transformation. No sign of Cristiane to be seen, but now there was a sewing machine, a dress form, and an artist's easel. Was her mother designing clothes? Cristiane warily stepped into the room and surveyed the shelves and drawers. There were binders full of designer clothes and catalog photos cut out and placed on the pages. The binders were labeled with her parents' names and then a few with special occasions, then Cristiane came across her own name. She pulled down the binder and found tabs for graduation, first job, wedding, among others. Cristiane glanced through the pages and found dozens of catalog pictures and sketches. The sketches were drawn and colored in, and some had other color markings next to the sketches for an alternative color choice. She opened the closet doors and found fabric hanging neatly on hangers and rolls stacked on shelves. Cristiane realized her mother had spent hours on the designs while Cristiane had given little thought to life events yet to come.

Cristiane felt it was impossible to understand her mother. The sewing room and clothing designs were the latest in a series of pursuits Cristiane found out of character and downright bizarre. She had missed so many chances to connect with Beatrice growing up, and now the void between them felt so vast, Cristiane couldn't imagine them coming back together. But her mother must have thought of Cristiane often, to gather and create the stunning clothing designs for major events in her future. Why then, was she so difficult to forge a relationship with this past decade?

As Cristiane pondered the mismatched thoughts and events leading up to her mother's stabbing, an idea, not of her mother, but of Isadora, sprang up. Isadora reminded Cristiane many times to trust her intuition, to trust her gut. So, she wandered toward her parents' room, where last night she witnessed the vile darkness swirling around her mother. Cristiane sensed it was true as soon as the thought struck her—the stabbing was not random. Whatever presence was in their room, it knew Cristiane's astral projection was there and took revenge on her mother.

Cristiane's heart sank. Did she cause the stabbing, almost killing her mother, by invading her parents' room while they slept? It didn't make sense. If an entity sensed Cristiane in the room, why didn't it come after her? Before the question took root, Cristiane knew the answer. Not it, but they. They came after her this morning in the parking lot at school. Whatever or whomever was behind Beatrice's stabbing knew where Cristiane went to school, probably knew her friends, everything.

With renewed conviction, Cristiane glanced around her parents' room. Everything was in its place except for her dad's clothes. Cristiane's eyes roamed the room and landed on her mother's closet door. Compelled to follow her instincts, Cristiane hopped off the bed and worked her way through the hidden door into the modest space Beatrice used as an altar room.

Without regard for hiding her presence, Cristiane flipped the light switch and then pulled open drawers, rummaging through every shelf, book, and a pile of trinkets. In the back of a drawer, she found a box enclosed in a velvet bag and pulled it into the light. The bag was dust-covered and the drawstring dry and brittle. Cristiane pulled at the string and watched the rope disintegrate from the tension. The box looked new, with a crisp white bow on top. As she opened the box, the hinge creaked defiance at being disturbed after years of abandonment. There was tissue inside, folded over with an embossed foil seal in place. Cristiane pulled the seal and peeled away the wrapping to find a heart-shaped gold locket embellished with the letter M. Why would her mother keep a locket hidden away in her altar room? She rolled it in her hand and opened it to find no pictures or other engravings inside. Without more to go on, she placed it on the table and stubbed her foot again on the trunk she'd found during her last search.

Cristiane pulled the trunk out and quickly dispelled of the padlock with an unlatching spell. The bolt dropped to the floor with a thud. With no time to waste, Cristiane kicked it away and kneeled down to investigate the contents. Cristiane lifted out a robe and set it aside. There were several journals and video tapes on the side tray. Curiosity piqued, Cristiane pulled the four items out and placed the journals with the locket. The old-fashioned tube television in the corner now made sense as she went over to find an outdated VHS player on the TV cart. Dates inscribed on the curled-up labels showed the videos were over 25 years old, if the dates were accurate. Cristiane turned on the television, hoping it would spring to life, and nodded to herself when the light gray static filled the screen.

She slid the oldest tape into the player and crossed her fingers to press the play button. She pushed the lid down and sat waiting for the initial recording static to clear into decipherable images. A younger version of her mother's face filled the screen. Cristiane couldn't hear and gave the old sound dial a heavy turn as her mother's voice boomed, 'found, give this tape to the Sacred Pillars Coven.' Her mother's face left the camera and a darkened room illuminated by torches and full of robed people came into view. Alarmed, Cristiane rewound the tape to hear her mother's entire statement. As she watched and listened, Cristiane realized she could be her mother's twin. Her mother's voice, in a hurried whisper, filled the room.

"Trust no one and safeguard this with your life. If I go missing, or my body is found, give this tape to the Sacred Pillars Coven."

The scene was difficult to decipher. Beatrice must have had a small camera hidden as she circled the murkiness. Thirteen people dressed in black robes gathered around a theater stage in the spacious room, chanting something undiscernible. Beatrice, not aligned in the circle, stood behind two people as she faced the stage. Low humming music echoed from the walls as footfalls traipsed across the stage, muffled by another robe-wearer. The circle grew silent as the lone figure on the stage raised their arms out wide.

"Witch, are you here?"

"Yes, ma'am."

"Have you completed the protections for our meeting?"

"Yes, ma'am. I have cloaked the chamber from outsiders' senses and prohibited entry from anyone without your mark. Protections are complete." The camera shook as Beatrice tugged at her robe and ran her hands down her sides. A heavy sigh blew from her lips.

"Ladies and gentlemen, my Craze of Chaos family, welcome once more to our gathering. Tonight is a special treat as we carry out this splendid sacrifice, celebrating worship and thanks to our goddess. As the original seven declared, so shall we. She is the divine madness, the queen of freedom. May she look kindly upon this flock as we embrace her gifts of chaos."

"Still not joining the festivities, Beatrice?"

Beatrice froze as the prickly voice grated near her ear. "Xirnan, I am not a member, as you are aware." Beatrice brought her feet together and stood tall.

Xirnan stood just out of view. "Not yet, but soon. Nissa made sure you had no choice."

"Go away, demon." Beatrice trembled with rage. Her focus remained on the stage as the man's chuckle grew distant.

"Very good." Nissa lowered her billowing arms and peered out toward her congregation. Nights like this charged her spirit and filled her with anticipation and elation. Once she unleashed the goddess's blessings on her devout followers, the celebration would take over the rest of the evening. Many in the group, Nissa knew, were mere participants for the drink and folly, but a chosen few had experienced the glorious rewards of their goddess. The mystical gifts were plentiful after ceremonies, such as the one this evening. "I present to you our sacrifice."

Cristiane moved closer to the screen, her elbows on her knees, head cradled in her palms as she was transfixed to the images. She bolted upright as the stage lit up with lights and flames illuminating the space to include an enormous table draped with a black cloth. Nissa lifted the covering seconds after the lights came on to reveal a naked man chained and shackled to an ornate altar table. Cristiane recognized it from David's photos. She bit at her nails as the spectacle played out on the screen.

Nissa bent over and removed the blindfold and ear coverings from the man secured to the table. His head and shoulders shifted as if he were waking from a deep sleep. The crowd whispered and cheered as they transfixed their eyes on the stage. The room's energy increased to a palpable level. Nissa gazed at her cult followers, feeding off their energy. A slow-growing smirk played at her lips as she saw the same eager anticipation from those gathered. And then she swung her arm at the prisoner on the table, giving a crisp, hard slap that answered back across the room in a twangy, distorted sound.

A muffled scream penetrated the chamber a moment later, followed by a roar of laughter from the crowd. Beatrice muttered something, but Cristiane couldn't make out the words. She watched Nissa turn to receive two glass goblets from another robed figure and then held the chalices over the man for the crowd to see. She waited for the volume to lower from the room. Her head bowed to her chest as she continued to hold the two chalices over the squirming, whimpering figure.

Nissa's voice grew loud as she chanted in an unrecognizable language. Participants quieted their laughter and replaced it with a low four-beat cadenced purr. The combination of Nissa's chant and the crowd's humming unnerved Cristiane, but she couldn't pull her eyes away. As the group continued its feverish chant, a cloaked figure returned to the stage, moving about the table, placing cords around the man.

Cristiane's eyes widened, and her hand moved to cover her gaping mouth. The cloaked figure pulled off his hood as he bent down. Cristiane saw he was the same ghostly man who stood in the way of her car in Springfield and spoke to her telepathically. She remained dumbstruck as she watched Xirnan flick a finger repeatedly at the flesh before inserting a butterfly needle into the man's neck, another in an arm facing the crowd, and then another at the top of a foot.

"No. No. No." Cristiane couldn't believe what she was seeing as Xirnan took one goblet from Nissa and held it below the table near the man's head and lifted the line coming from the needle in the prisoner's neck.

They were draining his blood.

Cristiane jumped from the trunk and rocked back and forth, her palms cupping her cheeks. She watched as Xirnan filled the goblets and handed them back to Nissa with a nod.

He then placed three bowls on the floor and opened what Cristiane believed were venous catheter valves. Within seconds, she watched as the lines filled with blood, running the length of tubing to drip into the pans. Cristiane blew out a sigh as she noticed the blood didn't spurt out. Perhaps the man would survive the cruel torture.

"May the goddess, Lamashtu, accept this humble sacrifice and bestow her gifts on us in return." Nissa raised the blood-filled goblets high in the air to her right and turned to the left, ensuring the congregation's eyes followed along until she brought the containers back to her front. "Our demon goddess, as you drank man's life-force millennia ago, we sing your praise and drink this freshly drawn blood to show our respect and adoration for you. Accept this sacrifice as our pledge." Nissa pulled a chalice to her lips and drank. She handed the glasses to Xirnan, who walked to the edge of the stage and handed one to the participants on either side of the stage.

A shudder rolled through Cristiane as she peered at the screen. This woman was drinking the blood of a man lying on the table, watching as she consumed him. It was revolting to Cristiane as she stopped the tape and closed her eyes. How could her mother be involved in such horrific crimes? She shook her head, took a few deep breaths, and tapped the play button again.

The hooded figures each took a sip and then passed the chalice to the next member in the circle until they met near the two figures where Beatrice stood. Beatrice waved off the offer from each to drink from the chalices but took the cups and walked around the circle up to the stage and placed them at the edge of the altar, near the man's feet. The bowl nearest to her was nearly full of blood. As Beatrice stood straight, the camera captured the man's body from his feet to his head. His eyes fluttered in weak bursts and his skin was pale and moist with beads of perspiration. His breathing was short and rapid. Beatrice jumped as Nissa barked in her ear.

"Witch. Unless you're ready to join us, you may leave the altar." Nissa's face was inches away.

Beatrice cowered, taking two steps back. "No, ma'am."

"Then get out of my way."

"Yes, ma'am." The camera captured feet and floor as Beatrice stooped and turned away.

Beatrice stood off to the side of the gathering, allowing the camera to capture the gruesome festivities. Gothic music, lending to images of old temples and ancient ruins, filled the chamber. Blood pooled into the bowls until crimson waves spilled over the edges and flowed down to the room floor. No one regarded the man who lay dead on the altar. Three men gathered the bowls and met Nissa in the center of the crowd. She let the robe slip from her shoulders and fall to the floor. She kicked the material aside, exposing her nakedness to the group. The men converged and began painting markings along her face and body.

As the men circled around Nissa, Cristiane recognized one of the three men, Malin. He had grabbed her in Springfield. She curled her hands into tight fists as her jaw clenched and released over and over. Nissa and Malin had been in her mother's life for too long.

On screen, the men turned and stood shoulder to shoulder, peering out to the now hoodless crowd. The members revealing elated, enthusiastic faces, their robes dropped one by one to the floor. Naked bodies surrounded the men and received blood markings on their faces and along their torsos, arms, and legs. As each finished receiving the markings, they moved to the far corner of the room, where food and drinks spread along a rolling table. Xirnan set out liquor and wine and pulled a cooler out and raised the lid.

As the three men finished marking themselves with the blood, the crowd was feasting and drinking at the far corner. After a few minutes, some wandered out of the center and began dancing and writhing to the somber music. As participants touched and pulled close, they smeared blood on each other. Beatrice turned away, her footfalls shifting toward the back of the stage.

Cristiane had her finger on the stop button when Nissa's back came into view. She pulled her hand away, waiting as Nissa stepped back into a robe and zipped it, covering her blood-stained body.

Beatrice stepped back into the shadow as Xirnan came around to Nissa's side. "Nissa, I closed the altar curtain. Shall I retrieve Malin now?"

"Yes."

Again, the view went dark. Footfalls told Cristiane that her mother was on the move until the altar came into view. Beatrice didn't join the others but remained far off from her previous position. Nissa, Malin, and Xirnan joined hands at the head and either side of the prisoner's torso. They spoke in tongues, barely above a whisper. Cristiane realized this part of the proceedings was not for the other members. The incantation, repeated a half-dozen times, stopped at the same time they dropped their hands. Malin stepped back as Nissa moved in front of him.

She and Xirnan bent over the man for a minute or two, muttering over each other as their hands darted around the man's abdomen. As fast as they started, they stopped and said something at the same time. Then they rose together and Nissa moved back toward the man's head. The three grasped each other's hands and chanted the same as before, but after each repetition, they said a different word before the phrase was repeated. This time Cristiane counted how many rounds they spoke the chant, seven times. At the end of the last, Cristiane heard a vibrating hum, almost inaudible, from their direction. Cristiane couldn't tell whether the threesome was humming, or the sound was coming from another source.

After a minute, the three figures rose. Cristiane sat down on the trunk and leaned forward, kneading her hands together. Her mouth hung open. The screen now showed the three levitated over the man, stopping about three feet above the stage floor. Their eyes were open and glowing red. The hum grew louder to Cristiane, although the source was yet undetermined. She noticed the man's torso was also glowing a dark crimson, gaining brightness as the vibration grew louder. How did the crowd on the other side of the curtain not hear the loud humming? Cristiane covered her ears with her hands, as her eyes stayed transfixed on the television.

Cerise bubbling appeared on the prisoner's torso, slow at the beginning, then gaining height as if blood were boiling out of him. The vibrating hum grew incessant. Cristiane pressed hard against her ears, closing her eyes tight for a split second as she shook the sound away. Her eyes opened to see blood shooting skyward in three streams to their open mouths. The crimson liquid spilled over lips and ran down their faces. Three sets of eyes that a moment ago were glowing bright red abated to darkness as the stream ran its course. The trio drifted back to the floor, and the hum softened until the only sound was the backdrop of party music coming from the main chamber.

"Excellent. Lamashtu is pleased." Nissa wiped at her face with a robe sleeve. "Xirnan, you know what to do. Malin, see to our guests."

Once the three were out of sight. Beatrice rushed toward the altar table, ensuring the camera captured the man's carved torso and face before she rushed back to her hiding place. Within a minute, Xirnan returned with a large bag over one arm and a bucket in the other.

The screen went black. Cristiane blinked a few times and took a couple of cleansing breaths. She made sure the tape had stopped before pulling it out of the player and slipped it back into the cover. Her mental state was not ready to review the second tape or read the journals, so she placed them with the other items she'd gathered from the room. She turned to place the robe back in the chest when she noticed a bundle in the bottom and pulled it out. The object was heavy as Cristiane cradled it in one hand and unwrapped the delicate flax fabric with the other.

She studied the strange figurine and turned it under the light. It looked familiar, but she couldn't place where she would have seen such a thing. Cristiane pushed the thought aside as she looked at the etching on the underside of the sculpture. The etching was like the carving on the poor man's body in the video. Unable to process anything more, Cristiane turned the object in her hand to wrap it. The object slipped, and she grabbed it close with her free hand. As a sharp edge pierced her finger, causing it to ooze blood, a vision burst into her mind.

A guttural, piercing voice filled her head. "What is this intrusion? You are not the child promised to me."

Cristiane dropped the figurine and the vision disappeared. "Holy shit—what the hell was that?" She spun around the room, looking for whatever spoke to her, but she was alone. Shaken, Cristiane took the piece of linen and wrapped the object, being careful not to touch it or get more blood on it. She ran out of the room and came back with a small duffle bag and threw the other items she'd placed on the table earlier into the bag. Cristiane looked at the strange figurine, hesitant to take it but also afraid to leave it open where her father could stumble upon it. With a sigh, she placed it in the trunk and tossed the bag on top.

SIXTEEN

Cristiane hoisted the trunk to her bedroom, plunked it down on the bed, and stared at the wall. What could she do now? Furious with everyone who could help her, what could she do? Unwilling to speak to Jarvis or Robby, she pulled her cell phone from her pocket, ignored the dozens of texts sent from Jarvis, Robby, and Tina, and sent a brief text to Tina: "I need to talk, just you. Call when you can." She tossed the phone on the nightstand and laid back.

It had grown dark since Cristiane had ventured into the house. A waning crescent moon illuminated a cloudless sky. The bright points of the moon seemed to reach out to touch the stars, like giant talons in the night. Cristiane opened the starlight app on her phone, finding Gemini, Venus, and Mercury high in the heavens. She wondered what magical worlds lay beyond her sight. She pondered if something ominous complicated magic across the universe, or if it only felt that way to her.

Cristiane's phone rang. It was Tina.

"Hey, girl. How are you? I'm so glad you reached out." Tina waited for Cristiane to say something.

"I haven't read messages. I just need to know why. Why didn't anyone tell me?" Cristiane choked on the last words, swallowing hard. Her eyes were tearing, but the last thing she wanted to do was cry over the phone.

"I wanted to tell you as soon as they gave Robby an invitation. You realize I would have, but the coven has rules, binding, a bunch of stuff I don't understand. The coven would have banished Robby if I said anything. I'm so sorry."

Cristiane could hear Tina sniffling over the phone. Tina was a fighter, but she fell apart if she hurt a friend. "I'm not mad at you. Well, maybe a bit." Cristiane laughed and smiled to herself. "But I can't believe Robby or Isadora didn't say a word. It's been two years. I'm struggling to figure this stuff out about my mom and I feel abandoned." Cristiane grew silent.

Tina let the silence persist for a minute. Her heart went out to Cristiane, her best friend before she'd started dating Robby was alone. She hated herself for not pushing Robby or Isadora to say something. "I don't blame you, Cris. I'd be pissed, too. Especially with how close you and Jarvis have become. But they're bound by a code to protect everyone. I only know bits and pieces—as a friend of the coven—a non-magical who is married to a coven member or in a committed, close relationship. Robby wouldn't have been able to keep it from me. I'm sure Isadora realized that with how long we've been together, but I had to swear to hold myself to the same rules as Robby. But Isadora could have told you. She was once the high priestess, so she wouldn't have suffered repercussions."

"Isadora used to be the high priestess? I never knew." Cristiane stood up straight, shocked at this latest bit of news.

"Wow. I don't see why she wouldn't tell you. She was the leader about twenty years ago. You understand she's older than dirt."

Cristiane chuckled, remembering she had made the same statements a few times to Robby after meeting Isadora during high school. She felt better talking with Tina. It'd been ages since the two of them hung out without the guys. "Hey, wanna come over and keep me company? Dad's at the hospital with Mom. He won't leave her side tonight. I could use an old-fashioned sleepover with my best friend."

"I'd love to. On my way in ten."

"Thank you!" Cristiane smiled, relieved she still had Tina's friendship without the mystical headaches.

While Cristiane waited for Tina to visit, she looked over the liquor cabinet and refrigerator—happy to see someone had stocked it well with food and drink. She needed an escape. Tonight, hanging out with Tina would be a great distraction.

Cristiane busied herself with fixing a drink. Her spirit companions were around again, but she'd become so used to their presence at her parent's house, she thought of them as accessories. She passed by them as she moved into the living room, looking for movies. The man hadn't tried to communicate with her since she'd gone back to school weeks ago, and her dreams had settled down as well. She wondered if there was a connection between the two.

Her last frightening dream was of the large estate with the nearby car accident. The thought of kicking the skull gave her goosebumps. After the dream, the man's apparition became clearer, as if her dream and the ghosts were linked, but she couldn't put her finger on what it meant. She pulled out a couple of horror movies, then settled into her dad's recliner, waiting for Tina to arrive. As time crept, she gazed at the spirit and orb wafting in the corner. Why didn't the orb appear clearer after the dream? Was it a person, or perhaps an animal or a pet? As Cristiane pondered the possibilities, the man looked down at the orb as if he read Cristiane's mind, and he swung his head from side to side. She noticed and sat up. "Are you trying to tell me something?"

The spirit turned toward Cristiane and nodded, and he moved several feet closer.

"Oh, my god! Umm—okay then." Cristiane set her drink on the coffee table and interlaced her fingers, thinking. "If I ask you a question, can you answer yes or no?"

Another nod.

"Can you speak to me?"

A shake of his hazy head. No.

"Okay, got it. Were you the man driving the car?"

A nod.

Cristiane grew excited. Why hadn't she tried to talk to the spirit more in the past? Her eyes settled on the orb, which was by the man's right side. But it remained hovering without additional detail. It looked the same as it always had, a hovering ball of ashen gases. "Is the orb the dead boy from the car?"

The spirit didn't nod or shake his head, confusing Cristiane.

"Uh, what does that mean?" Cristiane stared, full of random thoughts, at the apparition. She took a sip of her drink, then pursed her lips. She needed to ask better questions. After a moment, she let out a heavy sigh as her eyes landed on a picture of her parents. "Did you know my mother, Beatrice?"

The spirit bowed.

"Great! We're getting somewhere." She drew her legs up and sat cross-legged in the recliner, leaning forward, deep in thought. "Were you involved with Nissa Marth?"

The apparition shook.

"Damn it. It's like playing poker with a ghost. I don't know where to start with questions or determine what is meaningful." She stretched her arms above her head and then circled her head around, stretching her neck. It was frustrating as she ran through her mind what she'd learned. The man knew Beatrice and he was the dead guy from her dream. So, he must have been by the home from her dream, too. Although the orb was confusing Cristiane, she didn't dwell on it. The man's spirit could communicate with her. Yes or no was better than nothing. "Before you died, had you been to a large estate by the water?"

A thumbs up. At least he was creative with his ability to reply.

Cristiane's mouth hung agape as her stomach tightened. Intuition was working through her and sending her senses into overdrive. Evil lurked in his answers. But was he the cause of evil or its recipient? Did she have a choice? She had to push on and ask questions. "Were you murdered, or was it an accident?"

No response.

"Right, only yes or no. Was—"

The front door burst open, with Tina banging her bags against the doorjamb as she turned about, trying to close it after rushing in. "Hi! I knew you probably had little here, so I stopped and picked up snacks." Tina walked past her shocked friend and dropped the bags on the kitchen island.

"You scared the crap out of me!" Cristiane unwrapped her legs and stood up to greet her friend.

Tina came back into the room and wrapped her arms around Cristiane. "It's so good to see you. I've missed girls' night."

Cristiane returned the embrace with a tight squeeze. "Me, too. It's fun to see the guys, but we haven't hung out in ages." She looked around after letting her friend go. The apparitions were gone.

"What are you looking for? That ghost pair still giving you the heebie-jeebies?"

"They were here a minute ago." Cristiane shrugged as she pulled Tina into the kitchen and started removing items from the bags. "They don't freak me out anymore, but I can communicate with one of them. Well, sort of. He was answering yes and no questions before you showed up. I imagine my dreams link to the two spirits, but I don't have a clear idea of how yet."

"Wow. That's crazy." Tina took the soda and juice from Cristiane and put the items in the refrigerator. "You mentioned that some of your dreams since becoming a witch have been about actual events. I wonder what else you have as an innate ability."

"I'm sure I'll find out eventually, but I still feel lost most days. It's not like I can practice magic at school. There's always a cost and I can't risk it in my dorm. I had hoped the coven would provide a safe space for me, but that's not happening, so…" Cristiane let the statement linger in the air. She didn't want to explain the rejection to Tina. Not yet anyway.

"Hey, before I forget to ask. Have you heard from David? Joyce texted as I was leaving the house. He skipped out on her this afternoon, and she hasn't been able to reach him." Cristiane shook her head no. Tina pulled her phone from her purse and checked her messages. "I'll tell her you haven't."

"It's not like David to bail on Joyce. He adores her." Cristiane dragged out a bar stool and sat down. She took a long pull on her drink to finish it while Tina texted back and forth with Joyce. "Why does she think he's avoiding her?"

"Not avoiding, exactly." Tina looked up from her phone. "He left Joyce's this morning for the gym, then he was supposed to go home—shower, change, whatever—and then meet back at her place to go shopping for climbing gear. She hasn't seen him since this morning and he's not answering his phone. It goes straight to voicemail."

"His mom hasn't been in touch with him either. They're both worried, but when Joyce called the police, the station said they won't do a missing person's report until the morning. The cop said David could be sleeping off a hangover or something and she'd hear from him by tomorrow. It's not like him to not respond, especially if he and Joyce made plans." Tina frowned and looked askance. "What do you think?

"I believe you're right. Ask Joyce if she wants to come over. She shouldn't be alone, worrying by herself."

"Great idea!" Tina bent over, her thumbs gliding over the phone.

"Want a drink?" Cristiane shook her empty glass and stood, waiting for Tina's answer.

"Please. Whatever you're drinking is fine. Thanks." Tina glanced at her phone. "She says yes, but David's mom is with her. Okay if they both come over?"

"Absolutely. David's mom is a hoot, but her anxiety is worse than mine. She shouldn't be alone either." Cristiane walked over to the bar as Tina's thumbs drifted across the phone's keyboard.

"Agreed. They're on their way." Tina put her phone down and walked over to Cristiane, making their drinks. "I sent Robby a text asking if he's heard from David, too. You, um, wanna text Jarvis and the others, or do you want me to text them?"

"Can you?" Cristiane handed Tina her drink. Not wanting to think about Jarvis, she glanced away. "Jarvis might get a rush on the police looking for David. I don't know any of the others' phone numbers, and I-I just can't talk to Jarvis yet."

"I got you. No worries." Tina sent the message to the others. Then she slid the phone in her pocket. "Let's chat about my wedding before Joyce and Mrs. Howson arrive. There's something I want to ask you."

SEVENTEEN

Two days later, Beatrice folded the post-op instructions the nurse, Judy, had reviewed with her. Beatrice insisted on a few hours in the sunshine and Judy helped her patient from the wheelchair to the bench in the courtyard. Judy warned her to be extremely careful. The doctor insisted Beatrice thoroughly understand the self-care directions. Also, Judy was to ensure Jeffrey understood what Beatrice needed for care before the doctor would sign discharge papers.

Nissa sauntered toward Beatrice with two athletic-looking companions, dressed in black clothes and boots, following behind. As she smiled to Beatrice, she stopped Judy with a gentle pat on the forearm and a look of concern that could win an Oscar as she peered at the medic's nametag. "Excuse me, Judy. I'm so worried about my dear friend, Mrs. Bradford. Will she be okay?"

"Of course, Ms.?"

"Ms. Marth. Please, everyone calls me Nissa." She smiled at Judy, leaned in and held her hand on the nurse's forearm. It was a marvelous performance to anyone in the yard watching the exchange.

Judy stared down at Nissa's hand on her arm and pulled back from the touch. Although Judy was short and stocky, she didn't tolerate handsy people. She was a power lifter and strong, despite appearing overweight under the scrubs. Nursing required immense strength. The infirm or weak needed someone with muscle to help turn them in bed or lifted off the floor from a fall. Few women could lift a man by themselves, but Judy could handle it, just as she could handle anyone who gave her trouble. "Ms. Marth. She will be fine after resting and allowing her wounds to heal. She is an incredibly lucky woman."

"Beatrice and I have been friends for decades. Isn't that right, Bea?" Nissa turned her gaze, while flapping her eyelashes, expecting Beatrice to corroborate the statement. Beatrice nodded as Nissa turned back to Judy. "The book club has been so worried. We can't wait to have her back in the fold."

"Not for a while, I'm afraid. She'll go home soon, but she'll need to recuperate for some time to come. I have to go. You may visit your friend for a few minutes before the orderly comes to retrieve her." Judy looked at the two accompanying Nissa. As she passed by them, she turned back to Beatrice. "You going to be okay with these folks?"

Beatrice pursed her lips and nodded. Judy was a no-nonsense nurse, but she had a heart of gold. She would twist the arm of anyone upsetting a patient and not think twice. But Nissa wasn't a force to mess with either. "I'll be fine. Thank you, Judy."

Nissa clasped her hands behind her back, waiting for Judy to retreat into the confines of the hospital. Calculating eyes turned to Beatrice while Nissa rubbed her lips together as if she were forcefully smoothing out lip balm, and then lowered her gaze. "Xirnan must be slipping. You shouldn't be breathing, Beatrice. But as you are, I hope you realize you cannot renege on our deal any longer. I expect you to join us, and bring your daughter with you, or you both will suffer the fate you should have a few days ago. Am I making myself clear?" Nissa leaned in close to Beatrice's ear. "If you resist again, I will let Xirnan contend with you however the demon wishes. He does enjoy torturing witches."

Beatrice shook as she peered around the courtyard and wrung her hands. Unable to cast without patients or visitors noticing, she was cornered, powerless to retreat. "I hear you, Nissa. Our deal was never for Cristiane. She has free will. You and your family can't make her do anything."

Nissa's nostrils flared as her jaw clenched as she rose. Her eyes darted around the well-manicured lawn, counting a dozen or more people. Too many witnesses that she couldn't contain without Xirnan. "I'm aware. But you can and will persuade her, or you both will suffer the consequences."

"Do whatever you choose with me, but my daughter will not become involved with you." Beatrice saw Cristiane and Jeffrey come through the double doors Nissa had walked through a few moments ago. "Now leave before I do something all will regret."

Cristiane noticed her mother before Jeffrey did. Nissa was leaning down to her mother's ear, while two individuals faced out toward other patients and the surroundings. In a protective stance, they looked to be on guard. She quickly took in the scene and evaluated the threat of those surrounding her mother. Cristiane leaned toward her father as their pace slowed on approach. "Dad, do you know who those people are with Mom?"

"I don't think so. Maybe they're staff."

Annoyed with her father's ability to be so naïve, Cristiane rolled her eyes and released a slow breath as they continued to get closer to the group. Her gut tightened with each step; her fingers fidgeting as she sensed the danger.

"Go home, Dad." Cristiane turned to stand in his way. "I will tell you more when I get home, but you need to leave."

"I'm not going anywhere. What has gotten into you?" His pace abruptly halted as he studied his daughter with disbelief. Choosing not to confront her, he stepped around and pushed lightly on his daughter's arm as he passed her, then suddenly halted.

"Where?" Jeffrey searched about, bewildered, as he looked from his daughter to his wife and back.

Cristiane followed her father's gaze. Nissa and her companions were nowhere in sight. Rushing to her mother, Cristiane whispered in her ear before her father caught up to her. "What did she want?"

Shaken, Beatrice replied, on the verge of tears as she pulled her coat up tight around her throat, "Not here, Cris. We'll talk about it when I get home."

"Not here?" Cristiane's voice raised with anger. The residents in the square turned in their direction. Aware that others were watching, she lowered her voice. "This is an excellent place to discuss someone trying to kill you."

Jeffrey caught the last few words.

"Who is killing? What is happening with you two? Beatrice, who came to see you?" Jeffrey prattled off the questions without awaiting a reply. Instead, he bent down next to his wife's side and studied her face. She was shivering quietly, her eyes darting back and forth. Something had scared her and his wife did not scare easily. Seeing a tear slide down her cheek, he wiped it off with the back of his gloved hand as he stood. With a cool, stern tone, he pushed. "Why did you want me to leave, Cris? What's going on? One of you had better tell me what the fuck is going on right now."

"Honey, please." Beatrice's voice was passive and shy as she reached for his hand.

Jeffrey pulled away and blew out a puff of air. He rubbed his head and paced in front of Beatrice for a minute. Abruptly, he stopped and turned toward his wife. With a flat voice, he continued, "Just answer me two things. Is someone trying to kill you and were or are you having an affair?"

Shocked by his accusation, Beatrice's mouth stood agape as her shoulders slumped down. Quietly, she busied her hands by tugging at her gloves, then pulling the coat collar tight again. She didn't respond for a long time but held his eye.

"First, I've been stabbed repeatedly. Yes, someone tried to kill me. Second, no, darling. I am not, nor have I ever, had an affair. You are the love of my life." Her gaze didn't waiver as she stared him in the eye. "You and our daughter are the light in what was, and sometimes still is, a gloomy life. I am so thankful for you." She watched as her words softened his features. She spoke with truth and felt the hardness of so many secretive years falling away. "But there is a lot you don't know, either of you, that I'll share when home."

"That's not for two days," Cristiane and Jeffrey said at the same time.

"I know, but I can't discuss it here. Especially after seeing Nissa visit. I don't trust speaking about anything personal. We'll have plenty of time to talk and I promise to tell you everything." Beatrice pulled her husband down to her level and kissed his cheek. "Be a love and get us coffees from the gift shop to warm us up. I want to talk with Cristiane for a minute."

"Fine. It is freezing, but we're not done." Jeffrey relaxed as he reached for his wallet and checked its contents.

"No coffee for me, Dad. I'm going to run to a friend's house before I meet you back home." Cristiane kept her eyes on Beatrice as her dad walked toward the building.

Beatrice motioned for Cristiane to sit next to her on the bench. "Cristiane, I know you are practicing magic. I saw you when Nissa showed up at the house. It is dangerous."

"Mom, of course it's dangerous! David is missing and now look at what she's done to you. She did this, right? No one would stab you unless they were evil." Cristiane spat the words out through a curt whisper so others couldn't hear them. "We need to talk about more than what you're revealing to Dad."

"You're right. It's gotten out of hand. I kept you a secret from everyone, and it is time for me to pay the price of that secret. I'm sorry I've caused so much trouble and heartache." Beatrice's voice weak and defeated, she clasped Cristiane's hand with her eyes hung low as she continued. "David is missing?"

Cristiane sat back on the bench next to her mother. "Yes, Joyce called two nights ago. He was to meet her after going to the gym, but he never showed. She called and texted all day—nothing. Of course, the police didn't want to investigate right away, but we have a friend in the district who pushed the department into action. David's mom and Joyce went out with search parties this morning." She pulled at a loose coat button thread with her free hand, not wanting Beatrice to see the tears in her eyes.

"I'm so sorry. Harm should not have come to anyone. I wanted to keep my family separate from the hold Nissa and her cult had on me." Beatrice squeezed Cristiane's hand and tried to put her arm around, but Cristiane jerked back.

"Hold. What hold?" Cristiane pulled her hand away, glaring at her mother.

"It's a long story. We need support from other witches, powerful witches, and I burned too many bridges to ask for help." Beatrice glanced up at her daughter with hopeful eyes. She looked back and forth around them before continuing, "Are you with a coven? We'll need their help fighting Nissa and her group."

"No. I'm not with a coven. The high priestess denied me because of you." The bitterness in her voice was palpable.

"Oh no! I'm so sorry," Beatrice turned her face down. "Who is the high priestess?"

"Sarah. She knows you from college." Cristiane shook her head. "I've been an apprentice to an older woman, Isadora, since senior year. She's in the coven. I was going to see her after visiting you."

Beatrice whipped her head up, hope beaming from her eyes. "Isadora, I remember the name from long ago. She can help smooth things over with Sarah, I'm sure."

"What happened between you and Sarah, Mom? When she found out you were my mother, the entire group reacted with disdain to the news. There was no discussion. She at once denied me at what was to be my initiation ceremony."

"There's a lot to unpack regarding Sarah, but there's one thing I can share now." Beatrice shrugged her shoulders as if to say what she was about to share was of little importance.

"What's that?" Cristiane, eager to gain any insight, waited for her mother to continue.

The mood lighter, Beatrice uttered a soft chuckle. "She and I were close friends in college. There were several reasons our friendship fell apart, but one of the biggest reasons was that she thought I stole her boyfriend, Luke, from her. Of course, he and I had been seeing each other long before Sarah put eyes on him, but she was so infatuated with him I didn't have the heart to introduce them when she found out I was seeing someone. Long story short, of course. Eventually, she saw us together and hated me for stealing him. Other extremely notable events happened that relate to why the coven denied you initiation, but that's enough about Sarah for the moment. The rest will have to wait until I am home. I hope she can forget about the past and help us."

"I don't know, Mom. It was clear Sarah does not care for you." Cristiane glanced around and leaned in closer to Beatrice. "She said you practice with a sinister group. Is that true?"

"Shh, we will not talk about that here, Cris. That's enough about this problem." Beatrice reached out to grab her daughter's shoulder but abruptly stopped and grimaced. Instead, she embraced her torso, cradling her injuries.

The movement startling Cristiane and she reached for her mother's hand. "Are you okay?"

Beatrice held Cristiane's grip tightly for a moment then let it soften as she continued in a faint whisper, "Yes, it is true. Don't ask me any more questions. Not now."

Cristiane, staring back at Beatrice, finally acquiesced after a long pause. "Fine, Mother, but you better tell Dad and me everything soon. At least tell me you're not staying with that awful group."

Relieved, Beatrice let go of her daughter's shoulder. Her head bent down as she took in a deep breath and slowly let it out. "I'll need help, but yes, I have wanted to escape for a long time."

"Promise?"

"Yes. One hundred percent, yes."

Cristiane stood to go. "That's all I need to hear. I should see Isadora if we're to round up help before you leave this place."

"Thank you." Beatrice grasped the bench arm to help herself up, then opened her arms for a hug. "I love you, sweetie. You know that, don't you?"

"We've had some rough times, but yes, Mom. I know." Cristiane returned her mother's embrace. "I love you, too."

Cristiane released her mother. "Dad's coming back. I'll see you later."

Beatrice nodded and then watched as Cristiane paused to give her dad a quick peck on the cheek. Cristiane waved to her parents before she continued toward the parking lot.

Once in her car, Cristiane waited for the air to warm by texting Isadora that she wanted to stop by as soon as possible. Putting the shifter in reverse as she turned to look behind her, she noticed an envelope stuck under the windshield wiper. Shifting back to park, Cristiane jerked the door open and snatched the parcel before the cold made its way back into the warming vehicle.

Cristiane noticed her name scribbled on the envelope. *Not an advertisement.* She jerked the paper out of the envelope. It read

> *Cristiane (what a lovely name),*
> *Our first meeting was quite a surprise for both of us. I'm sure there is much your dear mum has not mentioned and I am eager to get*

to know you. Meet me at Javier's Hideout tomorrow night, at 9 pm.
        Nissa

EIGHTEEN

Cristiane sat cross-legged on Isadora's couch, holding her drink as she watched Isadora walk back and forth over a worn path in the rug. *This isn't the first time that rug has seen Isadora flustered,* Cristiane mused as she took another sip.

"Cris, she's going to try every trick she can think of to pull you into the fold, even coercion or misrepresenting facts. Especially after Malin and Xirnan's visit to your school, there's no telling what they'll do next. Although I don't think it's smart for someone from the coven to go with you when you meet Nissa, you shouldn't go without help. Javier's is going to be full of her people, demons, and who knows what else is part of her warped group. You can't go alone." Isadora grumbled as she paced. "I wish Sarah would hurry and get here."

"Isadora, calm down. It'll be okay. I can handle myself," Cristiane said with confidence.

Isadora stopped and glared at Cristiane. "I trained you well, but you are not ready to face a cult of dark magic by yourself, young lady. Not even an experienced witch like myself or Sarah would walk in without a substantial defensive position. You never meet on the other party's turf."

"Well, I wouldn't be surprised if she took David, and we know she's behind the attempt to kill my mom." Cristiane shrugged. She knew the drinks were going to her head, but she couldn't stop herself from talking as she waved her arms over her head. "I'm just saying, I don't think she knows I'm a witch, unless Xirnan has reported back to her. He looked at me strangely when he realized I was a witch, like it was his delightful secret to keep. I believe Nissa's mad at Mom for hiding me all these years. My instincts say she thinks I'm some naïve girl. It might work to our advantage if she continues to think I'm non-magical." Cristiane finished with a big swallow, draining her glass for the second time that evening. She noticed Isadora was still glaring and had her hands folded across her chest.

"You're drunk."

"Not yet, but I'm working on it." Cristiane chuckled as she rose to mix herself another drink. "If I'm going to meet my mother's arch-nemesis tomorrow night, I think I earned the drinks tonight and the hangover in the morning. You want another?"

Isadora handed her half-empty wineglass to Cristiane. "Just top it off. One of us must be sober when Sarah arrives. And by the way, Sarah is your mother's arch-nemesis. I don't know what we call Nissa yet."

"Touché!" Cristiane bellowed from the kitchen. "I can't wait to hear Sarah's side. Mom said they fought over a guy in college. There is more to the story. I'm sure of it."

The doorbell rang.

"More how?"

"I don't know. Maybe we're about to find out," Cristiane hollered back.

After checking the peephole, Isadora opened the door and greeted Sarah. "Thank you for coming out to see us so quickly, High Priestess. There is much to discuss."

"Isadora, call me Sarah. There is no need for pretense when we're alone." Sarah hugged her old friend before stepping into the home she'd known for decades.

"We're not a—"

"Here's your wine." Cristiane handed Isadora her glass. "Oh, where are my manners? What would you like to drink, High Priestess Sarah?" Cristiane gave a short curtsy. "We have wine, and we have some hard stuff if you're up for it." She sipped at her full drink while peering over the glass rim.

Sarah raised an eyebrow, then looked at Isadora.

Isadora quickly replied, "She's blowing off some steam after seeing Nissa."

"Seeing Nissa? When did that happen?" Sarah's voice echoed her concern.

"Cristiane, tell the high priestess what happened today." Isadora picked up her wine and took a sip. She pointed to it, asking Sarah if she also wanted a glass.

"What are you drinking, Cristiane?" Sarah asked, while taking a seat on the couch.

Cristiane smiled and answered where she stood. "A tequila sunrise—heavy on tequila."

"Sounds perfect. Make mine exactly like yours." Sarah returned a genuine smile.

"Are you sure?" The request clearly surprised Cristiane.

"Absolutely."

"All righty, just hope Isadora has room for both of us to crash here tonight," Cristiane muttered and then turned back toward the kitchen while taking another sip of her drink.

When Cristiane was out of earshot, Sarah asked Isadora, "You haven't taught her the sober spell?"

Laughing, Isadora offered, "She needs to learn the consequences of drinking too much before she's granted such a quick fix. Otherwise, she will not value the lesson. She recently turned 21. I don't want to give it away too soon."

"I forgot how much of a gem you are, Isadora. Isn't she in college?"

"Yes, third year. She'll graduate early if she continues so well in her coursework." The pride Isadora had for Cristiane was unmistakable.

"You think of her as your own, don't you? You once thought of me that way, too." Sarah looked at Isadora with love as she quickly reminisced over the years spent learning the craft in this very house around Cristiane's age.

Isadora nodded, as speaking would reveal too much emotion. She loved Cristiane as if she were her own grandchild.

"She may be legal now to drink, but I'd bet she has been stumbling drunk many times since her freshman year, or even earlier. Instruct the girl before she tries to cast a spell while intoxicated, which causes a problem. The opposing lesson is much more dangerous."

Cristiane came around the corner as Sarah finished her statement.

"What lesson?" Cristiane asked as she handed Sarah the drink and remained standing, watching as Sarah took a sip. She smiled, waiting to see the high priestess's reaction to the potent cocktail.

"Hmm—this brings back memories. You've learned to make a powerful drink without the usual terrible taste. I like it!" Sarah sat back, smiling as she watched Cristiane beam and sit in the over-sized recliner opposite her, cross-legged, as she herself used to do at Isadora's as a young pupil.

"You two were talking about a lesson?" Cristiane persisted in knowing what she missed out on while in the kitchen. Her tongue was thick in her mouth as the last word mangled out her lips.

"Oh yes, that." Isadora cleared her throat. "I guess it's best to cover it now before you get too drunk to remember it. There's a spell that prevents hangovers and can clear your head quickly, no matter how much you've had to drink."

"What!" Cristiane slapped the chair arm and sported her best childish pout, with lower lip flipped out, toward Isadora. She spoke after seeing Isadora shake her head and grin. "Do you know how useful that would have been?"

"Forgive an old woman. I have forgotten how spirited college can be, but Sarah reminded me it is much more useful for you to know the spell than for you to go without. However, don't abuse it. Alcohol will still damage your body. Use the spell sparingly, child." Isadora preached as if she were teaching a substance abuse class.

"Buzz kill, huh?" Sarah cut in, smiling at Cristiane. She glanced at her old teacher with heartfelt gratitude. "Isadora, why don't I teach Cristiane the spell? Do you have some snacks we can have while we talk about the issues ahead of us? We will do the lesson quickly."

"Why didn't I think of it? Of course, you two carry on while I put a tray together for us to enjoy." Isadora gave the two ladies time to get to know one another.

Fifteen minutes later, Isadora set down a huge charcuterie board full of meats, cheeses, olives, and fruit on the coffee table. She rushed back into the kitchen and came back with a split bowl full of crackers and chips.

"Wow, this looks delicious," Cristiane said as she stacked a few morsels and popped it in her mouth.

Minx, Isadora's cat, purred as she rubbed against her owner with a nose in the air, smelling the tantalizing treats within reach.

"Shoo away, Minx. Your food is in the kitchen." Isadora lifted her pet and turned her away.

"So, Cristiane and I have become sufficiently acquainted while she learned the sober spell." Sarah nodded toward Cristiane and gave her a wink. "How are you feeling?"

"I feel great! I wish I'd known about this a long time ago. Isadora, you've been holding out on me." Cristiane gave her mentor a playful sour face.

"Okay, ladies. Let's get down to business. I understand your friend David is missing. He's the one who provided the photos of the ritual chamber under the club, correct?" Sarah glanced at Isadora for confirmation.

Cristiane nodded. "Yes, that's right. David was at the gym yesterday morning but hasn't been heard from since. The police completed a missing person's report today."

"And Isadora told me about Beatrice's stabbing and hospital stay. Are you sure Nissa caused her injuries? She visited your mother today, I understand. I believed they were friends?" Sarah asked, careful to watch Cristiane's body language. Still concerned about Beatrice's involvement in Nissa's sect, she needed to know if she and her coven could trust Beatrice and Cristiane.

"Not friends. At least that is the impression Mom left me with today. She is scared and she wants out, but I guess you can't walk away." Cristiane looked at Isadora and Sarah for confirmation. "Maybe she tried to leave, and that's why they went after her. I haven't been able to talk to Mom about it. However, I doubt Nissa did the work herself. Someone from her coven attacked my mother and left her for dead. And when you add their visit today to the hospital, I'm certain my mother continues to be in danger." Cristiane was sober. She sat up straight, leaning toward the other ladies, ready to work out a plan.

"What do you mean, *their* visit?" Sarah shot Isadora a glance. "I thought Nissa visited Beatrice today. Who else was there?"

"I'm sorry. I meant to tell Isadora when I arrived, but we were discussing your visit, and I forgot to mention the others." Cristiane leaned back in the seat as she continued her tale. "When my dad and I arrived in the courtyard, we saw Nissa leaning in, talking to Mom. But two others guarded them—a man and a woman. They stood facing outward, watching everyone in the area. My skin tingled; I knew we were in danger.

"My dad knew nothing about Mom's witchcraft or the cult. He suspected she was having an affair until today. I tried to stop him before we got closer and have him leave, but when he refused and walked around me, Nissa and her two goons were gone. My mother was sitting alone, looking haggard and rattled by the visit. Mom never cries, but she had tears rolling down her face. She was terrified.

"I had already planned to come over and see Isadora about other issues, but then when I got to my car, I found this note under the wiper blade." Cristiane handed Sarah the note as she continued. "Nissa wants me to go to Javier's tomorrow night. My mom won't be released until the next day. But she's still healing and getting therapy at home after that. I don't know what to do. Should I go alone, ignore it?"

"You cannot ignore the note. I'm sure they fixed the paper with a reading spell, so she knew you read it as soon as you opened the fold. She may know that we have read it, too. That is hard to say." Sarah flipped the note over in her hand as she thought about the situation.

"Sarah, Cris knows how to protect herself from simple threats, but we have not covered the dark arts. As is your rule, we do not teach such ways without your awareness and the support of the coven." Isadora gently reminded Sarah as she watched her leader think through the situation.

"Yes. Thank you, Isadora. I understand and appreciate that you kept to our practices," Sarah assured her old friend. "I do not worry about your teaching methods. In this instance, it might have served us better if you had branched out from my confines, but that too would have unknown consequences. No worries, you did the right thing."

Sarah stood and paced in the same area of the rug as Isadora had before Sarah arrived.

"Remind me to get you a new rug, Isadora. You two wear this one out with your pacing."

Isadora laughed at Cristiane's offer. "Yes, this old rug has seen better days, but I assure you, the path is worn with thoughtful contemplations that have protected the coven for decades. My path as coven leader, and those who followed me, including Sarah, is etched into the weave as part of the burden of leadership. I couldn't part with it."

"You were high priestess?" Cristiane showed mock surprise as she had learned Isadora used to be the high priestess from Tina. She waited for Isadora to share more.

Instead, Sarah continued the history lesson as she looked on her wise teacher. She placed a hand on Isadora's shoulder and gave a loving squeeze. "Yes, Isadora was my mentor, just as she has been yours. She was high priestess then and shared her knowledge and guidance with a select few trainees, including me. The rules of the coven are her rules. I simply have followed a superb example."

"So many questions—I had no idea." Cristiane was intrigued, but it was getting late. She looked at the wall clock and realized they weren't any closer to a decision. "But that can wait. What should I do about meeting Nissa?"

Sarah sat down at the edge of the sofa. She pulled a long draw on her drink, emptying it before continuing. "I have a plan. I believe you only know Isadora from the coven, but that won't do for her to accompany you, or I. Either of us would draw too much attent—"

Cristiane glanced at Isadora, then Sarah.

"Actually—I know others."

Isadora avoided Cristiane's gaze.

"I won't side-step this conversation asking how you know coven members. Who else do you know?" Sarah noticed Isadora was not meeting Cristiane's eyes. "That may be helpful."

"My old friend Robby. He doesn't know that I know he's in the coven, but I guess Isadora also didn't tell me because you rejected me." With emphasis on the last three words, Cristiane addressed Sarah but continued to look at Isadora, waiting for Isadora to acknowledge her assumption.

Isadora looked up with a weak smile. She crossed her hands over her chest. "Yes, dear. That is true. I'm sorry. I didn't want to upset you more. I was going to tell you soon, but I held off because you were so devastated."

"Fine, fine. Who else? I suppose this person shared that Robby is a member." Sarah asked, ignoring the sensitive exchange between the two women. Waving her hand in the air, she was eager to move the conversation along.

"Yes. Detective Morris, Jarvis Morris. He didn't mean to tell me. It kinda slipped and then I got mad and stormed out. He didn't have a chance to explain more," Cristiane answered while fidgeting with a string from the hole in her jeans. She didn't want to get him in trouble with the coven.

"You know Jarvis? Splendid!" Relieved, Sarah slumped back in her seat. "That is better than I had hoped. I will discuss both issues with him tomorrow. If I can get a personal item of David's, Isadora and I may be able to help with the search. But Jarvis will be your escort to meet Nissa."

"Um—can I mention it to him first? He, well—he and I have been seeing each other the past few months, but we had that bit of a row about the coven and I should talk to him." Cristiane pulled the string she'd been toying with from her jeans. She kept her eyes on the hole in her jeans as she waited, hopeful, to hear if Sarah would grant her request. The seconds ticked by without a sound.

In unison, both women began chuckling, continuing until they each gasped for air.

Confused, Cristiane waited for someone to speak. The longer they laughed, she grew annoyed, then angry. "What is so funny?"

Sarah cleared her throat and sighed. "Oh, nothing really. You looked so innocent as you asked, and—well, we know Jarvis. It seemed such a contradiction I couldn't help myself." Sarah looked at Isadora, who was nodding her head in agreement.

"Contradiction? What do you mean?"

"Don't fret. Jarvis is a wonderful man. He has seen more than his share of darkness." Isadora reassured Cristiane. "That is all we mean. He is more of a worldly person than you or many of the other witches in the coven.

I'm sure you'll learn more as you get to know him. It isn't our place to tell you. Let him have that opportunity."

"Isadora is correct. Pardon our jest, but he is perfect to accompany you. I will have coven members outside the club in case of an altercation. The club will be full of patrons. Nissa won't make a scene. At least, nothing too alarming to outsiders, but she is dangerous.

"Nissa will try to trick you, pull you in, tell you lies, anything to get you to join her side. Protect yourself before you show up. At the club, call upon your ancestors with your talisman, if you must. What once contained a powerful curse woven with dark magic is now a powerful amulet—a charm with untapped potential and the ability to summon your ancestors when you face great peril. Rachel and Prudence can aid in an emergency, but they may not linger on this side of the veil for long.

"As I said, the coven will provide support outside of the club. You and Jarvis should show up about thirty minutes early, so that you can position yourselves with the best vantage point and learn your surroundings. There will be four of us, including me. Isadora will not be going. Of course, Jarvis will be with you, and he is a knowledgeable senior member. We won't be visible, but you will know we're present, and I'll be close enough to monitor and provide you with an extra layer of protection. Do you have questions for me? Think about it. I'm going to get another drink. Do you want one?" Sarah got up from the couch. She grabbed Cristiane's glass.

Isadora shook her head.

Cristiane pondered what she would say to Nissa the following night. She wanted to speak to her mother before the meeting but knew that was probably impossible until they released Beatrice from the hospital. All things considered, she felt good about the upcoming meeting, especially since Jarvis could accompany her. Other than Jarvis keeping the coven secret, she was really enjoying her time with him. She couldn't blame him now for keeping the coven rules and not sharing his involvement or that Robby was a member. He made a promise and kept it. She should admire him for being so trustworthy. With Jarvis by her side, Cristiane was more at ease about the impending appointment.

Isadora watched Cristiane. They didn't speak while Cristiane worked out in her mind the plan Sarah devised for her meeting. But was her young pupil ready for such a task? Isadora worried and fretted that she hadn't taught her well over the years. The overwhelming task of convening with Nissa, a dark leader with at least one demon by her side, would frighten a much more seasoned witch. "We'll make the gathering as safe as possible. Do you think your training has been adequate to meet Nissa face to face?"

"I think so. It's hard for me to say. I don't know what I'm getting into with any of this, but after everything that's happened lately, with David's disappearance and then someone trying to kill my mom, someone needs to stand up to Nissa. If I'm not doing it alone, I can do it."

Sarah came back to the living room and handed Cristiane her drink. "I'm glad you feel at ease. Jarvis is a wonderful witch and a fabulous young man. I'm happy to hear that you and he know each other. Now that we have the meeting taken care of, tell me a little more about growing up and your relationship with your mother."

They spent the rest of the evening talking about Cristiane's relationship with Beatrice and how controversial it was—notably through Cristiane's high school years. Although their clashes were always more difficult than typical adolescent battles, Cristiane realized Beatrice had changed since the stabbing. Cristiane felt a shift in her mother. Beatrice wasn't as confrontational or stand-offish but was now more protective and defenseless. "Oh, don't misunderstand me. My mother has been keeping many secrets for an awfully long time. But after today, I am convinced she is afraid for her life, maybe for all of us in the family. She can no longer have two distinct lives without the secrets interfering with her daily habits and her family. She said she has wanted out for years. I don't know why she hadn't left earlier, but now she needs help. She's vulnerable and doesn't have the strength to go it alone."

Sarah left an hour later. She was disappointed with herself. Her judgment of Cristiane was premature. The girl was innocent to the darkness surrounding the Bradford family. But no matter the circumstances, Sarah needed to understand Beatrice's involvement in the cult as Sarah's predecessor Roberta had lost her life to a sinister occult. The rune markings and horrific gashes on Roberta's body indicated dark magic. Sarah had thought of Beatrice when she took over as high priestess, not realizing her intuition might have been pointing her toward Nissa's cult. She let their old rift cloud her judgment. Time muddled the details, but she would not let the situation slip by without aiding Cristiane. The future of her coven and the lives of many innocent people could depend on how she resolved the problem.

She'd assign Joe, her second-longest serving member, and Liam to research her old friend's history while she had a conversation with Beatrice alone. Maybe she'd get lucky and Beatrice would share her involvement and how the situation began. But if not, she'd have the two witches flush out Beatrice's past. It had been over two decades since their college friendship ended. Sarah needed to understand more of Beatrice's life during that time to ensure no threat remained for Cristiane or other witches.

Once Cris was in the guest room, she called Jarvis. He picked up after the first ring.

"I'm sorry. Please forgive me." Jarvis rambled into the phone.

Cristiane grinned despite herself. She'd been mad at him for being a witch and not telling her, but he had no reason to apologize for keeping his word to the coven. She felt terrible for walking out on him. "No. It's me who should apologize. I shouldn't have targeted you with my pent-up hurt and frustration. I'm sorry I took it out on you." A tremendous weight lifted from her spirit. She didn't realize how much the argument had weighed on her until that moment. Excited to share the details of her evening, she slid down into the covers.

"Phew. I thought I'd blown it. Are you sure you're okay? I've been worried sick."

She heard him blow out a deep breath.

"I think so. You have time to talk? I have so much to tell you."

"I can talk all night."

They started sharing their theories about David. Jarvis agreed Cristiane might be right about Nissa's involvement in David's disappearance. A traffic cam had caught him driving north with two others in the car. The camera shot was fuzzy, but the man in the passenger seat could be a guy from Javier's nightclub. The other person was unidentifiable. David didn't look pleased in the photo, but he didn't appear harmed, either.

Cristiane shared what she'd learned the past few days. With everything happening so fast, she started with the visit from Malin and Xirnan at school, then hearing about her mother's stabbing. She told him about seeing Nissa with her mom at the hospital, the note on her car, and then spending the rest of the day at Isadora's, speaking with Sarah. "Oh, not only do Sarah and Isadora know we're seeing each other, but the high priestess was happy to hear the news. She's much cooler than I imagined, especially after the first time I met her. I thought she was awful."

"She's great with everyone in the coven. I'm sure you'll feel the same in no time. That's great news, Cris." Jared replied. "I've been looking forward to seeing you. Although it is under such circumstances, I'm glad I get to see you tomorrow. I'll be by your side. We can handle her, I promise."

Cristiane smiled, "Me, too. I'm nervous, of course, but I'm so glad that you're going to be with me. Sarah is going to call you tomorrow about the meeting." Cristiane tried to stifle a yawn but failed.

"You should get some sleep. You may feel sober in your head, but your body still needs to recover. Magic isn't free."

She could feel his smile and warmth come through the phone. "I know."

"Great. See you tomorrow. Text when you're ready for company. Goodnight, Cris. Sweet dreams."

"Good night." Cristiane closed her eyes and cradled the phone to her chest. She was happy. Surprised by the revelation amid her troubles, she took in the moment of quiet and relished the foreign feeling. A few days ago, she felt more alone than ever. Now she and Tina were closer. Cristiane had Jarvis back in her life, and Isadora and Sarah were by her side. With their help, she was resolved to face a demon-worshipping crazy woman. Her mother was open and wanted to share her secrets with the family. Today everything was changing for the better. Now if only David would turn up, she could breathe easy.

NINETEEN

Cris and Jarvis arrived at 8:30 in the evening as the rays of the sun in its leisurely descent etched out a kaleidoscope of colors through the skyline. Once inside the club, the couple found a table and waited for their host. Cristiane settled into her surroundings. If the meeting went sideways, the music and noise from the crowd would provide adequate cover. She felt comfortable and appreciated the lack of bright lights. The nightclub was mysterious, with a few low-level lights giving a romantic ambiance. She hadn't been inside before, and she suddenly remembered David had been there on her behalf. Cristiane tapped her leg up and down while biting at a nail.

"Cris, what's wrong? Why are you shaking?"

"It's nothing. It's just in my head. I was thinking David had been here recently, and now he's been missing for days."

Jarvis scooted his chair closer to Cris and put his arm around her. "I'm so sorry. It's hard to think about, but right now we need to stay focused. If Nissa has powers, she can sense weakness. Sarah is convinced this cult is more threatening than what we've uncovered so far. We must stay sharp."

Jarvis lifted Cristiane's face and looked into her eyes. "It's going to be okay. I will be right here, beside you."

"You're right. You're right. I know you are, and I appreciate you being here more than you know."

"Well, that's good to hear." He smiled as he peered around to see if anyone was looking. He eased in, within an inch of Cristiane's lips. "I'm going to kiss you now."

Cristiane smirked as she tilted her head so her eyes could catch his expression. "Are you asking or telling?"

"Oh, may I kiss you? Consent is of utmost importance." His breath caressed her cheek.

"I wondered when you were going to ask." She met his lips softly at first, scarcely touching. The electricity was rising between them. She slid nails through the back of his hair and pulled him in tight as she kissed him harder.

"Wow! Where did that come from?"

She chuckled. "I heard you were worldly. So before you wander off, I wanted to say, I hope you stick around for a while."

"Worldly, huh? Who told you that?"

"Is it true? It quite intrigued Sarah and Isadora when I mentioned we had dated the past few months."

The two had their faces close together and Cris's hands locked around Jarvis' neck when someone from behind cleared their throat, breaking their moment.

"Ahem. I thought we were meeting alone."

Nissa stood a few feet away from their table. Cris didn't answer her for a long moment.

A daunting figure, Nissa's energy emanated confidence. She was taller than Cristiane remembered. Not thin, but also not thick. Cristiane mused she was like a mythical creature, an Amazonian woman ready for war with broad shoulders and muscular legs. She wasn't ugly—she was even attractive if Cris were to describe her physical appearance without considering how Nissa made her feel. Each time she had encountered Nissa her gut clenched. Tonight was no exception. Cris knew it was her intuition attuning her to the dangers lurking beneath the surface. On heightened alert, her skin prickled, ready to strike.

As she straightened and held Jarvis's hand, Cristiane looked Nissa in the eye. "You didn't ask to meet alone, so I thought I'd bring a friend and enjoy the club. I don't know you. Did you think I would come by myself?" Cris spoke in a firm, cordial voice. She didn't want Nissa to sense her fighting instincts, and she didn't want to start the conversation. It was up to Nissa to reveal her intentions. Cris would not help her.

Nissa looked around her club and realized that there were several people within earshot. She wanted a more intimate conversation. "Shall we go in the back where it is quiet?"

"No, thank you. We'll sit here at the table and talk." Cris smiled and pulled out a chair. She patted the seat.

Nissa looked at Jarvis. "Why don't you be a dear and get us a few drinks? On me. Margaritas."

Cris agreed with a nod and a wink at her boyfriend. "It's okay. I'll be fine." Cristiane nodded to her adversary, Ms. Marth, as the woman sat at their table.

Jarvis walked a few steps, stopped and turned, assessing how the two women at the table were interacting. With nothing to indicate an immediate danger, he continued to the bar.

Nissa leaned toward Cristiane with a warm smile. "Ms. Bradford, your mother and I have been dear friends for many years. She is a valued member of an association that I lead. Our members enjoy an elite benefit package, one that is so private, membership remains a valued secret. Our executive-level membership is quite exclusive and selectively chosen by me. Your mother promised to elevate her membership many times but has yet to do so. Since meeting you, I thought perhaps you could join with her, and I would elevate both your memberships simultaneously. With you by her side, I believe Beatrice would commit to the club while appreciating the top-tier perks even more."

Cristiane returned Nissa's smile with her own smirk. "You're creative with the sales pitch, I'll give you that. Where are the details? What benefits? What are the perks of this exclusive club? If it's so wonderful, why hasn't my mother mentioned it to me or my father before?"

"Like I said, it is a bit of a secret. Your mother didn't come to the group as many of the regular members do, by pledging a great deal of money but because of her unique talents, which she has supplied limitedly over the years. I'm sure you understand society's wealthy wish to remain anonymous when giving their funds and time to such an organization. If publicized, everyone would want to be a member."

"I think I'll talk to my mother about this club and hear what she has to say." Cristiane leaned back in her chair with her hands at the table's edge.

"Trust me, your mother would want you to be a part of this as soon as possible. We can go to my office and take care of your dues now, and then we can bring your mom by another night to do the same. It's a simple matter for the executive-level. Unorthodox perhaps, but a simple gesture."

"What *gesture?*"

"Before we get into that, promise that you'll bring your mother to me. She owes me this much. She's agreed to take the oath many times over the years but has yet to follow through." Nissa reached out to grasp Cristiane's hand but was unsuccessful as Cristiane pushed back from the table.

"I don't know what games you're playing, Ms. Marth, but none of this makes sense. I'm not joining your private club or paying for a mysterious membership. My mother is her own woman. She doesn't owe you or anyone else a damn thing." Cristiane crossed her arms over her chest, watching the heat flush over Nissa's cheeks.

Nissa cracked her neck before leveling her gaze. "Child, you react in haste. Your mother owes me more than you can fathom. I implore you, for your own good, to join me now."

As Jarvis approached the table juggling three drinks in hand, he heard the women's voices rising.

"I will not join you. I owe you nothing. My mother owes you nothing."

Her words hissed through gritted teeth, Nissa charged. "Your mother owes—us, *me*—her life after I opened my home to her. She had no one. She made a promise, and there is no withdrawing from that pledge without sacrifice."

"Ladies, voices." After setting the drinks on the table, he peered at the women. He smiled and put an arm on each woman's shoulder, then said, "You're making a scene."

Nissa leaned in close to Cristiane. "You do not know what your mother has done. You shouldn't exist. But since you do, I will ensure not only your mother keeps her commitment, but you join in the obligation with her."

Cris stood up, ready to attack Nissa, "I'd die first. Fuck off."

Nissa slid the chair out and stood without a word. She tugged at the bottom of her dress, smoothing out the wrinkles from sitting, then quietly stepped back and slid the chair into the table's edge.

With a side glance and a tilt of her head toward Jarvis, a note of realization traversed Nissa's eyes. She grasped at something in her pocket and pulled out an ornate token. Her hands opened, palms outward as she breathed in, her head moving ever so slightly as her senses scanned the area, then she closed her hands into fists.

Cristiane gestured toward the coin in Nissa's palm and realized what the vile woman was doing. Nissa was exploring if witches or other magical creatures were nearby. Cristiane stepped back, knocking the chair over, and took a defensive stance. Fingers touched her emerald talisman, ready to call on her family's power at a moment's notice. The hand movement caught Nissa's attention.

"Oh, you are a crafty girl." Nissa planted her weight on one heel and placed fists on her hips while eyeing Cristiane from toe to head. "Perhaps the maiden's arcane forces don't fall far from the mother. You are cleverly hidden. I thought you were ignorant of your powers, so I didn't run a perimeter check before I came to see you. Don't fret—I won't make that mistake again. Careful, young lady, your dead body might be exactly what I require in the end."

Cristiane raised her hands, ready to cast. Jarvis grabbed them in his hands and pulled her to him. Nissa smiled as she turned and walked away. She reached the back of the club and continued down a dimly lit corridor as Cristiane glared at her back.

"Cris, don't let her get to you. Sit down and breathe. Let's act as if nothing happened and enjoy our drinks. Don't show her she got under your skin. There are cameras in every corner. She's watching."

Cristiane scanned the walls, quickly noting the cameras that she should have noticed. Jarvis touched her chin with his fingertips and gently nudged her to face him.

Cris couldn't resist after looking into his cocoa-colored eyes. "You're right. You're right. I know." She gave him a slight smile, followed with a quick kiss, then sat back at the table. Cristiane scanned the room and found three cameras that were within view. A camera high on the wall near the ceiling held her attention. Cristiane smiled, raising both hands, and flipped off the camera.

Jarvis choked on his drink, coughed, then laughed between attempts to clear his throat. He slid his arm around her. "You're feisty." He nuzzled into her neck. "There's nothing more going to happen tonight. We'll meet with Sarah tomorrow and tell her everything. Let's enjoy the rest of the night."

Cris pulled back a little and examined Jarvis, wondering if their thoughts were aligned. But then he turned away, putting his hands on the table, leaving her confused.

As Jarvis thought about their fight, he licked his lips as the nerve endings sprang to attention. Cristiane needed to set the pace of their relationship. He kept his eyes on the table and said, "Whatever you want to do. If that's us starting again from scratch or taking it slow after the past few days. Whatever you want me to be, I'm here for you. I don't want to take this for granted."

Jarvis was nervous. He didn't want to screw up her trust and lose her again. His drink had water dripping down the side of the glass and he ran a finger along the bottom, catching droplets before they hit the table. He cupped the glass and took a sip of his drink. When he looked back at Cris, she was staring at him.

"Whatever, huh? I didn't realize you were so adventurous—or trusting." With an eyebrow raised, Cris pursed her lips and batted her eyelashes. They both laughed.

"Whatever you want to do." He bent down, waiting for her lips to meet his own. When they did, he pulled her in for a deep kiss.

Nissa watched the couple from the security room. How did Beatrice conceal this powerful daughter for years? Did Xirnan know of this young witch's active powers and keep it to himself? If so, why? The questions fueled more questions and enraged Nissa, her fists balling at her sides. She slammed one fist into the control desk, causing the guard to jump.

"Ma'am, did you want to review the tape from when you left the table? Umm-you won't be happy. But she's got moxie, for sure." Forney, one of Nissa's close guards, manned the control room. By Nissa's side at the hospital, Fortney recognized Cristiane when the couple arrived, and then monitored the two throughout the night.

"What? Show me." Nissa leaned onto the desk with her fists. Her face blank, she watched as Cristiane examined the room and found the camera, then gave a one-finger salute with not one hand, but both. *The girl had moxie. Fortney was right.* As Nissa asked for the video to repeat a few times, she shook her head and laughed.

Amused by the girl, Nissa reasoned Cristiane was a lot like her mother at that age, full of promise and courage. Somewhere along the line, Beatrice withered, cowered away—or did she? To have hidden Cristiane for over two decades took strength and audacity. Character traits that Nissa thought she'd stomped out of Beatrice long ago, molding her to join as one of the seven. Her elite, dedicated to the dark occult.

Perhaps leaving Beatrice alone for so long was a mistake.

"Fortney, bring Beatrice Bradford's file from my safe. I'll be in the chamber for the evening."

"Yes, ma'am." Forney nodded and stepped out of the room.

Her fingers tapped on the desk as Nissa watched the couple cuddling and kissing. *If Beatrice is beyond conversion to the cause, her daughter and her lover may serve our purpose. Two witches of prime age would please our goddess and complete the required pledges. Draigh would finally realize all I have worked toward is real—is significant—is serious.*

TWENTY

Cristiane and Jarvis spent the following morning with Isadora and Sarah. Cristiane reiterated what Nissa said about Beatrice owing her for help given long ago. To Cristiane's surprise, Nissa didn't realize she was a witch until last night. The revelation shocked the club owner. Xirnan must have kept the information to himself because he and Malin knew she was a witch in Springfield. Neither of the men were at the club last night. Nissa hadn't suspected members outside until after their heated exchange. She'd made no precautions or surveillance before Jarvis and Cristiane came to the club.

"How did Nissa not know you were a witch if Beatrice has been part of her group? There is something wrong with this relationship." Sarah mused as she furrowed her brow. "Your mother has the answers. Any chance she'll open to you?"

"I think so." Cristiane nodded. "She's coming home this afternoon, and she's promised to tell Dad and me everything."

"Is your father magical?"

"No. He couldn't hide it from me."

"If he's not magical, he needs protection. Jarvis, stand guard until we know Jeffrey is out of harm's way." Sarah turned to see Jarvis bow his head in agreement. She glanced back at Cristiane. "Do you trust that your mother will tell you the truth?"

"I do now. I can sense it. The atmosphere in the house has changed, lifted, where it no longer feels ominous." Cristiane tilted her head and pursed her lips. "I suppose the weight of protecting us gave the house a heavy sensation all these years, but now that I understand my instincts and magic, I can feel the burden my mother carried all this time peeling away from the house. Does that make sense?"

"It does. And it also suggests that the blanket of darkness around your mother is gone. However, since she's not been in the house for some time, it may return this evening. Be on guard."

"I will." Cristiane met the high priestess's eyes.

"Cristiane, Isadora and I could not sense David's presence. Nissa could be holding him somewhere, cloaked by magic, or his disappearance isn't related to her. But I want you to know we're trying to locate him."

"I appreciate your help." She sat in Isadora's living room, pensive but optimistic. Sarah had come to her aid and asked for nothing in return the past few days. She turned out to be the exact opposite of what Cristiane imagined after the rejection at the initiation ceremony. As the thoughts ran through Cristiane's mind, she realized Sarah remained transfixed on her.

"Cristiane, I hope you will forgive me. I owe you an enormous apology. You, too, Isadora." Sarah looked to her wise crone, her source of wisdom and sage advice, and bowed while displaying a weak smile. "I am sorry that I turned you both away at the initiation ceremony a few months ago. I am terribly sorry."

Jarvis swiveled to Cristiane, his brows raised and eyes bulging. "What?"

"Ah, Jarvis, now you understand why Cristiane was so sensitive to the news of Robby's initiation. I am to blame for her not being a member of the coven. I turned her away because I knew her mother was involved with Nissa. None of us has a complete understanding of that group, but I have suspicions I will share soon." Sarah turned her attention back to Cristiane, watching as the young lady's eyes welled with tears. "The information Cristiane has provided, with the help of her missing friend David, has shed light on the group's activities. I'll get into that later. Right now, I have amends to make with this young lady."

Cristiane returned Sarah's continuous scrutiny with a shaky smile. "Apology accepted." A tear spilled over, and she wiped it away as fast as it had fallen. She felt their eyes on her, making her nervous.

"Cristiane, if you would, please stand with me." Sarah pulled back the worn rug, revealing a circle design in the wood brandished with a pentagram. She stood and offered her hand, waiting for Cristiane to rise and join her. Once Cristiane stood, Sarah glanced at the others, nodding to Isadora.

Isadora rose, lit a candle that had crystal chunks imbedded in it, along with flower petals and other tiny items Cristiane couldn't decipher. Isadora then sprinkled herbs over it and placed it within the circle before she stood next to Sarah.

"Jarvis, you may remain seated or witness along Cristiane's side." Sarah showed no preference as she waited to see what Jarvis would do. Once he moved to rise, she beamed with approval.

Confusion marked the younger witches' faces, but Jarvis rose and stood next to Cristiane without question. Cristiane bit her lip, unsure what was happening.

Isadora raised her hands over Cristiane's head and muttered a rhythmic chant that sounded like humming to the others in the area. As she did so, the etching on the floor shimmered brightly. "Is it still your desire to join the Sacred Pillars Coven and continue your magical journey with us?"

Cristiane blinked at the two women standing in front of her, a smile radiating across her face. "Absolutely. Yes."

Sarah reached out and took Cristiane's hands between her own. Isadora's arms dropped and her fingers came to rest over the other two women's hands. Sarah smiled back at Cristiane. "I cannot initiate you this day, but we may offer you the coven's protection if you give us permission to do so, and the goddess wills it. You may find this evening more special than your future initiation ceremony. We stand in one of the coven's first circles of trust, etched into the floor in the home now owned by the former High Priestess Isadora. Through the grace of the Mother Goddess, we offer you all the power, magic, and support of the Sacred Pillars Coven as you embark on the journey to discover truth, unveil the darkness from the shadows, and dispel evil from your home and family. Do you give us permission?"

Isadora resumed her cadenced hum. Jarvis, realizing that Sarah was offering the coven's protection and energy to Cristiane, placed his hand on Cristiane's shoulder.

"Yes." Cristiane stood taller as the three witches surrounded her.

Sarah slid one hand out and offered it to Jarvis. He accepted, and Sarah guided his hand to the bundle of hands clasped together. "I appeal to the Horned God and Mother Goddess in this hour of need to provide Cristiane with all the earthly elemental energies: earth, air, fire, water, and spirit. If it is your divine will to embolden her magic, we ask that you surround our newborn witch with your love, power, and light, along with the influence of our coven members to strengthen her on her journey. Until we initiate her into our coven during the light of the full moon, we ask for your blessings to be bestowed upon Cristiane. For the greater good of all involved."

The air within the room stirred, creating a breeze that encapsulated the four. Cristiane looked to the three seasoned witches for guidance, but all three had their eyes closed, humming the same rhythmic tone Isadora began moments ago. Jarvis had moved his other hand from Cristiane's shoulder and added it, too. Sarah's right hand provided the foundation while her left rested atop the other six, cocooning the trio, as they were her responsibility as the high priestess. The wind spun more quickly as a mist gathered, forming a chest and head crowned with horns. And another stunning face, crowned with a crescent moon surrounded by long, flowing hair—the Mother Goddess emerged from the mist.

The Horned God raised a staff. His voice was deep. "High Priestess, we grant your request. I imbue this young witch with the influence of the sun and the strength to sustain her against the demonic entities in her path. The Blessed Mother and I are pleased to see her magical lineage restored and prospering within a wholesome soul. Blessed be." With Cristiane's mouth agape, the Horned God extended his staff over Cristiane's head as an infused shard of light fell from it and shattered, dropping delicate ribbons of illumination over Cristiane. The light tendrils soaked into her skin, giving a golden shimmer to her face and body.

The Mother Goddess moved closer to the circle of witches as the Horned God slid back into her shadow. Her long hair and billowing gown flowed behind her. The crescent moon hovered over her head like a halo, glistening with a silver sheen. The color matched the icy blue silver of her eyes. "My lovely witches, it pleases me so much that you have found Cristiane and welcomed her in this burdensome time of need to receive the coven's support. She has wandered alone too long without her mother's guidance.

"It pleases me. Sarah and Isadora have fulfilled the mother's role to bring Cristiane into her own as a young witch. With my blessing, may Cristiane bring Beatrice back to us, to a righteous path and reinforce her family's magical bond. With the power of the five elements to guide her journey, I enable Cristiane to call upon and utilize the many gifts of those within the coven as the moment requires it, and whether the gift is natural to her magical abilities or not, she will, until the coven initiation, have use of all their arcane magic. Sarah, are you willing to be responsible for this young witch's survival?"

"Yes, Blessed Mother, I am. For the higher good of all involved."

"Blessed be. So it shall be." The Mother Goddess raised her hands, palms facing skyward. Soon tiny strands of gold appeared in the air from each direction, shifting toward her hands. As the last three golden tendrils rose from within the circle, the threads twisted into five braided curls. Finally, five silver threads lifted from the goddess's hair and wrapped around each braid. As each weave was complete, the braids hovered above the witches' heads.

Mesmerized by the spectacle before her, Cristiane followed with her eyes the gold strings as they landed in the goddess's hand and braided into thicker strands, then leaped back into the air. She wondered why the goddess would need to pull magic from outside herself, but then realized the gold strands were from the coven members' magic as the last three gold fibers came from Jarvis, Sarah, and Isadora. The finished braids sparkled as a rainbow of colors danced through them. It was as if they were alive, colors gliding back and forth along the length.

The Mother Goddess extended her arms out. The braids continued to hover over the heads of the four witches gathered in the circle, their eyes raised to their deities. "Sarah, I give you the power to observe through Cristiane's eyes and speak with her telepathically."

Sarah bowed her head and closed her eyes, acknowledging the Mother Goddess's miracle. "Blessed be."

"Cristiane, with each braid you will call upon the powers of the coven to aid in your journey. Be specific and clear in your incantation, as they have not yet connected you to the other members through the coven's initiation and binding ritual, which would normally help solidify this bond. That is why I have woven myself into the braids. May your spirit be true and righteous, guiding your spells and casting. With my blessing, may each element bend to your need, so long as the magic be for the greater good."

Mother Goddess spoke each of the five elements as a braid drifted down and wrapped around Cristiane's wrists, bonding with a bright glow of color to Cristiane before disappearing. Cristiane sensed a warmth radiate through her body, growing stronger with each braid as it touched her skin.

"How is your mood, child?" The Mother Goddess smiled down, watching the young witch.

"Amazing! Thank you, Blessed Mother." Cristiane had her eyes closed as the sensation of the five braids of magic melded into her body. She felt as if her skin were humming as the magic ebbed and flowed through her. Her head swayed back and forth as if she were listening to music. Soon she realized the rhythm of the mystical flow matched the humming beat Isadora had been doing at the beginning of the calling. She took in a long breath and opened her eyes. "Simply incredible."

"Blessed be." The three witches holding her hands in the circle called together.

"It is wonderful. Had your heart proven to be dark, you would have experienced a painful illness. You are a blessed soul, young witch. The binding remains until the high priestess anoints you at initiation to her coven. Sarah, do not forget your duty." Once Sarah nodded to the goddess, the deity returned next to the Horned God.

In unison, the deities raised their arms. "Blessings we bestow upon thee for the greater good. By all that is sacred, so it shall be." The wind whirled about three times, then vanished. The only indication that the deities had been there was Cristiane shimmering with a golden glow and smiling from ear to ear.

"Wow!" Cristiane fell back into the recliner and inspected her skin. She rubbed at her forearms and wrists with a fingertip.

Jarvis appeared as enamored as Cristiane. "Incredible. I've never experienced the god and goddess so intimately before."

"Yes. It is a rare sight. Many witches never experience such a grand event. I, too, did not expect such a presence at our request." Sarah looked at Cristiane, still mesmerized by the magic glowing off her skin. The shine would gradually recede, but the immediate effects were rather dazzling. "Unfortunately, that means the situation is more serious than I had predicted. Whatever Nissa is involved in, there is great power, perhaps even ancient magic. The Mother Goddess would not offer such a gift as her own hair woven into the braids without an awareness of evil within Cristiane's path."

Cristiane rose as the shimmer to her skin faded. "I believe I know what that is about."

"What do you mean?" Sarah had moved the rug back into place.

"After I ran from Jarvis's apartment the other day, I was alone at home and gave my mother's altar room a complete run through. I turned over everything and found old video tapes and journals. Most I haven't been able to go through yet, but I played one video. It was super creepy. My mom had recorded it in secret in case anything happened to her."

Cristiane explained what she had gathered from the room and viewed on the video while the four ate lunch at Isadora's. She told them about the man strapped to the altar and drained of blood until he was dead. When Cristiane described the markings carved into the body, Sarah and Jarvis shared a glance and then both peered over at Isadora.

"What? Do you know what I'm talking about?" Cristiane asked all three.

"Perhaps. I'd need to see the tape first, to be sure." Sarah noticed the wall clock. "What time is your mother being released from the hospital?"

Cristiane looked up. "Oh shit. I need to go now. I'm supposed to pick up Dad at home so we can go together."

She pushed up from the table and pulled her phone from a back pocket. As she texted her father, she apologized to the group. "I'm sorry. I gotta go. Can we talk about this tomorrow?"

"Cristiane, I'd like to review the contents of the trunk, along with the videos and journals as soon as possible. Is it all right with you if Jarvis picks up the trunk from your house and brings it back to me?" Sarah rose from the table and walked with Cristiane to the door. "I'm afraid we're running out of time. The more we know about Nissa and her group, the better we can help you and Beatrice."

"Yes, that's a great idea. Just be careful of the wrapped figurine. It's possessed or something. The evil made me sick." Cristiane gave Sarah and Isadora a quick hug and ran out the door, with Jarvis trailing.

Isadora looked at Sarah. "I have a terrible sense of foreboding. Do you know what she meant by a possessed figurine?"

Sarah shook her head. "I don't, but I imagine your feeling is spot on. If the video is as old as Cristiane said, then we both know part of this story." Isadora scrunched up her wrinkled brow, to which Sarah replied. "Your protégé, Roberta, was killed with etched markings on her body."

"Why didn't I know?"

"You had retired. It wasn't your responsibility anymore. If I'd told you, would you have left it alone?"

"Of course not. I would have turned everything upside down to find her killer."

"Exactly my point. At 71 years old, you would have been the next victim. We appreciate your wisdom and tutelage, but you must realize even now, at 96 years of age, you cannot be on the front lines any longer. These events are connected. I am sure of it. Beatrice is involved, willingly or not."

"Oh no! You don't think-oh, that can't be." Isadora's crooked fingers covered her mouth. "If Beatrice is engaged in that mess, we can't let Cristiane go home."

Sarah wrapped an arm around her old mentor and guided Isadora back to the living room. "The gods themselves arm her. We can't put the coven in further danger without understanding the enemy. I promise I'll do everything I can to protect her."

When Cristiane and Jarvis arrived at the Bradford house, Jeffrey was pacing on the porch. They looked at each other as Jeffrey sprang along the steps toward the driveway.

"Where have you been? We're going to be late." Jeffrey met the couple as Cristiane climbed out of the truck and closed her door.

"Sorry, Dad. I'll be ready in just a second. I need to give Jarvis something before we leave."

"Cris, let him grab it on his own. He can lock up on his way out." Jeffrey was beside his car with the driver's door open.

Cristiane shook her head and reached for Jarvis' hand. "Do you mind? I'll text you when we're back home and have Mom settled."

"No problem. The trunk is in your room, right?" Jarvis kissed her and turned to walk up the porch to the front door.

"Yep. In the corner. You can't miss it." Cristiane gave Jarvis a thumbs up before dashing to her father's car and hopping into the passenger's seat.

Jeffrey maneuvered the sedan around Jarvis's truck in seconds and onto the road toward the hospital.

Xirnan pressed another layer of salve over the long red gouge across its abdomen. It laid back on Nissa's office couch with a heavy sigh. Healing embers rose from the balm and darted over the laceration as magic stitched the pieces of delicate skin together. Breath labored, it longed for a youthful physique.

Clicking heels announced his mistress entering her office.

Nissa stopped and scowled at the demon. "What are you doing here? Where is Malin?"

With difficulty, Xirnan said, "Malin will not be joining us."

"What did you do?" Nissa squatted and jabbed a finger into Xirnan's wound, drawing fresh blood. The scurrying glimmers rushed toward the new opening to repair it. Nissa huffed, stood, and then walked to the bar table.

Xirnan grunted in agony. "Exactly what was necessary and quite overdue."

TWENTY-ONE

A few hours later, Beatrice walked into the house with Jeffrey and Cristiane. As she crossed the threshold, Beatrice stopped and looked around the room. The energy felt different, the air lighter, than when she'd left for her walk a few days ago. She turned to her family before they could get through the door. "Did you do a cleanse on the house, Cris? A weight has lifted." Beatrice noticed Cristiane shake her head. "We need to talk about things now, before I lose my nerve. I promised you both answers."

Cristiane and Jeffrey looked at each other and then back at Beatrice. Jeffrey shrugged and walked past his wife. "Fine, but at least let me put your stuff in our bedroom first."

Beatrice mumbled an 'okay' as Cristiane came up beside her. "That's good, Mom." Cristiane peered around the space just as her mother had a moment ago. "You're right. The energy is better now, lighter." She put a hand on her mother's shoulder, giving it a light tap before moving farther into the house and up the stairs.

Once both had returned, Beatrice asked Cristiane to make her a drink. Cristiane agreed and came back with a beer for her dad and handed her mother a tequila sunrise, same as hers. Jeffrey and Cristiane sat facing Beatrice, waiting for her to start the conversation. After a minute, Cristiane cleared her throat.

"Mom, maybe if I speak first, it will help you fill in the gaps," Cristiane offered. Beatrice bobbed her head and gave a quick jerk to her lips. "Okay. Umm—Dad, some of this may sound out there, but just go with it for now. Unless—are you a witch, too?"

"Goodness, no."

Cristiane gave her hand a shake and bobbed her head. "Okay, then. Well, like I said, I'll explain what I know, and then you can ask anything you want after Mom speaks. Sound good?" She witnessed her father nod, but his distorted face said he was confused. "So, Mom, we're certain Nissa is involved in dark occult shit. I mean demon, devil worship-type stuff. We've also come to realize you're not a willing participant, but somehow stuck in the middle. Am I close?"

Beatrice nodded and took a long draw on her drink.

"We've been working behind the scenes, making our own conclusions, but I'll be brief. Last night, I met Nissa at Javier's club with Jarvis. She had left a note on my car at the hospital requesting to meet. After discussing the note with Isadora and Sarah, we came up with a plan. Sarah and other coven members waited outside the club in case I needed help. Thankfully, the argument didn't escalate. Nissa insisted I join her elitist club or suffer the consequences—not only myself, but you, too. She practically admitted to your attempted murder and said you were of no use to her unless you took part in the blood oath. But since you haven't solidified your pact over many years associated with her, she wants me. She almost begged for me to join last night but talked in riddles. She insisted you owe her your life. Not sure what that meant." Cristiane watched as the color drained from Beatrice's face.

As Cristiane remembered the trunk full of videos, journals, and the cursed totem, she said, "Oh, and I ransacked that pit you called an altar room and took a bunch of items out for Sarah to investigate. By the way, what does the locket mean? It looked new."

Beatrice rose from her seat as she threw out a hand, gesturing Cristiane to stop. "Thanks, but I think I've heard enough and need to put this situation into context before you go much farther." She finished the drink in two big gulps. "Can you make me another? I'm going to need it."

"Sure." Cristiane left her parents alone as she wandered into the kitchen.

Jeffrey, dumbstruck into silence, gave Beatrice a look that gave her chills. She lowered her chin to her chest. "Sweetie, I realize it sounds awful, and it is, but you understand that everything I have done is to protect Cristiane and you."

"I don't know who you are, Bea." Jeffrey clenched his teeth, glaring at his wife. The shock eventually wore on him. His chest caved as his shoulders slumped and his forlorn face fell. After a moment, he turned away and stared out the window.

Cristiane returned with fresh drinks for everyone. She placed another beer on the table next to her dad. He guzzled the first, which he had barely touched before, then slammed the empty bottle on the table. He grabbed the other, almost taking Cristiane's fingers with it.

"Whoa." Cristiane's eyes went back and forth between the two.

"We'll get through this, I promise." Beatrice continued to stand as she waited for Cristiane to sit back down so she could tell her story. "So you both understand, I need to take you back 26 years, my junior year in college, the same age you are now, Cristiane. Remember the man I told you about a few days ago, Luke? All of this started around that relationship." Beatrice sipped her drink and then sat down.

Beatrice spent the next hour explaining how Sarah and she had fought over Luke. "No matter what I said, Sarah was convinced that I ran after Luke out of spite and dated him to irritate her. However, we'd been seeing each other for months and didn't know how to tell Sarah once I realized he had captivated her. When she found out we'd been dating, Sarah retaliated out of anger. Soon, none of my friends at school, friends also to Sarah, would associate with me. Luke and I became inseparable and, because of spending so much time together, I got pregnant."

Jeffrey stopped gazing out the window and turned to glare at his wife.

Beatrice raised a finger and stood again. She paced as she spoke of the past. "Once I found out, I had no one to confide in. Sarah and my other college friends had exiled me. It mortified my mother that her daughter was pregnant out of wedlock and a junior in college. We argued, and I ran into town. I wandered into Javier's, although it wasn't called that years ago. I forget the name now, but I met Nissa. She said her father owned the club, but I'm not sure if that's true. His name is Draigh Vossen. I've never met him, saw him once from a distance, but she talked of him as if he were a god. At first, I thought it was sweet that she thought so much of her father, but strange that he didn't check on her or the business. She was sweet at first—friendly—and listened to my troubles. It was much later when I suspected her of interfering in my relationship with Luke. I didn't piece it together right away.

"Anyway, Luke didn't know about the pregnancy. I went to meet him one night to tell him and saw him cozying up with Sarah in the restaurant by school. My hormones were all over the place and I was so angry and alone. My mother refused to have anything to do with me until I introduced her to Luke. She expected us to marry, of course. After I saw Luke with Sarah, my world fell apart. My magic wasn't as good as it is now, but I knew if I was angry, it would be catastrophic. That night when I saw my future, everything I'd hoped for, disappear, I unleashed my rage at the restaurant, blowing out the front windows. Glass flew everywhere, chairs and anything near the front jetted through the air. I ran away terrified and angry. Nissa offered me respite. I stayed with her in Andover for a brief time.

"I left school without a word to anyone and then spent the rest of my pregnancy in New York at one of her family's estates. It was a lovely home by the water and offered a peaceful break from the chaos in which I found myself. While I lived there, Nissa became an even closer friend and confidante. I felt I owed her my life. I was vulnerable and alone. Because of her generosity and support, I promised to use my abilities to protect her gatherings and one day, after I'd had the baby, I would take the oath and join her sect. But as time wore on, her narcissistic tendencies grew troublesome. She'd twist things I said or did to make it appear I was ungrateful and she threatened to throw me out. Desperate, I clung to the small bits of pleasantness she offered when it suited her."

Jeffrey kept his chin tucked, staring at his feet as a thumb silently tapped the beer bottle in his hand. He felt Cristiane's eyes boring into him, but he refused to meet her gaze.

"Eventually, I wound up joining the gatherings at the house, held in the basement, providing entertainment and protection for the attendees. Then Nissa would reinforce that her wealth and everything she had offered was because of their faith, that I should embrace the cult completely and reap the rewards for myself. If I would only take the blood oath, my life would be more magical than I could imagine. The monthly gatherings were harmless, or so I thought at first. But every few months, there would be more visitors, more security, more secrecy, and she wanted me to protect those gatherings. At first, she was killing small animals. She said after the baby, I'd join the proceedings, but there's no way I could ever concede to such brutality and chaos.

"I used the pregnancy as an excuse for a while, but when I lost Michael at birth, I was hysterical. He lived only a few hours. I held him, but he had trouble breathing, and the midwife took him away. A moment later, Nissa handed him back to me, saying he was gone. She insisted I stay in New York, and she'd nurse me back to health. I'm certain she drugged me for a few days, pressuring me to take the blood oath. And once I belonged to her goddess, I would want for nothing. Her goal was to gather seven magical beings for Lamashtu and their future path would be nothing less than spectacular. The pressure was too much."

Dumbstruck, Jeffrey turned to Cristiane. His face scrunched as he shook his head. He peered forward again, his shoulders slumped while he rubbed his brow, refusing to meet Beatrice's eyes.

"Soon after losing the baby, my instincts were getting back to normal, and I felt the evil lurking on the property. It was something more fiendish than I had imagined as I stumbled across one of the actual ceremonies, one unlike anything I had attended before. They were sacrificing people, drinking the blood, dancing in a fountain, and eating flesh. It was diabolical. Nissa spotted me, of course, and threatened my life. Caught, I swore I wouldn't expose them, that I had wandered into the ceremony delirious from crying over the loss of Michael.

"As I shook and sobbed, I professed I wasn't doing well and needed help for severe depression, that I didn't trust myself or my magic any longer. I kept up the ruse and acted out for several weeks. I pretended to be distraught and unruly, Nissa left me alone to get over the loss of my son. Nissa remained out of touch and after a few more days, she had me transported back here.

"She thought I would join her cult because I was so isolated from friends and family. She tried to immerse me into the elite gatherings, with wealthy locals, thinking a new man would help lure me into the fold. But after witnessing the ceremony in New York, I kept a hidden camera, knowing she would hold a deadly ceremony in the chamber below the club. I realized I had to leave. That's when I took the video.

It was vile, but she threated me over and over. I needed evidence—leverage in case she acted on her warnings. After seeing a newborn in the club one evening, I fell back on the distress ruse to stay out of her vengeful path. Shortly after, I left and lived with my mother for a few months until I could get back into classes and finish college. Nissa never reached out after she thought I'd relapsed."

Beatrice stopped pacing and looked at her family. Jeffrey refused to meet her gaze.

Cristiane shrugged as she met her mother's eyes while silently mouthing, "Sorry."

Beatrice sighed and closed her eyes. After a deep breath, she looked up. "As soon as I felt that your father and I were getting serious, I used alchemy to hide and protect us from Nissa and her demon goon, Xirnan. My instincts were tingling all the time, sensing that she had people looking for me. When Cristiane was born, I knew the family magic flowed through her veins, and I continued to hide and protect her from Nissa and Xirnan. The protection spells became more intricate. To hide dormant magic in a child took great care and energy. Over the years, it took more power than I could manage, and I became overtired and bitter.

"As Cristiane reached her teen years, I had to suppress her inherent magic to protect her. Although it seemed counterintuitive to be near Nissa, I reconnected with her. I believed it was beneficial to keep Nissa from searching for me and then discover my family. So as Cristiane matured, I reached out to Nissa and began my previous duties of protecting the gatherings at the club and providing magical subterfuge whenever Nissa asked for it.

"Although I'm not proud of my part, the energy from the gatherings helped support my mystic needs to protect our family. Until David discovered and gave you the pendant, my actions were manageable. But once Cristiane had the family talisman, I have worked non-stop to divert attention, point toward other magical creatures, anything to keep Nissa and her demons from noticing Cristiane's potential. One blessing, her arrogance is a weakness. We can fool her.

"That mysterious scar on your collarbone—I deduced that you received it from banishing the curse on the pendant. It works like a calling card and required more energy to suppress it and your gifts from Xirnan's senses. Our ancestors mixed dark magic into their abilities, which attracts creatures like Xirnan. Nissa's power waxes and wanes with the ceremonies she conducts. She has no power for long stretches, but directly after a sacrifice, a human sacrifice, she is hell on earth.

"But Xirnan is darkness like no other. His powers come from evil that is centuries old, and he has cast a heavy cloak over me for far too long. I fear I can no longer hold it at bay." Beatrice paced as she spoke, not looking at her family, but kept her head down. She was afraid to see the expressions on their faces as she spoke about the various aspects of her checkered past. If they abandoned her, she might as well not have been saved from the stabbing. Trying to beat Nissa, Xirnan, and the others was an unwinnable battle. She wouldn't survive. After Beatrice sat, she put her elbows on her knees and rested her head in her hands.

Jeffrey's shock had bled away as Beatrice spoke, or he remained flabbergasted. She couldn't tell. He didn't say a word and it frightened her. He was her rock. Regardless of whether he knew what she was involved in, she relied on his quiet strength to get through each day.

Cristiane saw the fear in her mother's eyes as Beatrice waited for Jeffrey to say something. "Mom, I understand Dad's going to have a tough time, but I heard you and I understand." The two women let the silence seep in as Jeffrey processed his wife's history. Once or twice, he looked like he was going to say something, then he'd slump back in his seat, worrying his lips.

Distracted, it took a few minutes for Cristiane to acknowledge the apparitions behind her mother. The man was awfully close as the orb remained by his side. "Mom, do you have the ability to see ghosts, spirits?"

"No. Why do you ask?"

"Well, I do, ever since I've worn the emerald locket." Cristiane reached into her shirt collar and pulled the pendant out so it was visible. "There are two that have been with me on and off for years, and they're both behind you."

Beatrice popped up and spun around. "Here? Now?"

Her father jumped out of his seat and shook as he stepped away from the chair. "That is creepy. Who are they?"

"I'm uncertain, but I think one is Luke and the other is their baby." Cristiane stood and walked to within inches of the ghost.

"What are they doing? Don't go near them."

"Dad, it's okay. They can't hurt me." Her focus remained on the male apparition, his features sharpening, coming into focus in front of her eyes. "Am I right? Are you Luke with the baby, Michael?"

No response.

"What did he say?" Beatrice crossed her arms.

"Nothing."

"What do you mean, nothing?"

Cristiane sighed and turned to her mother with a blank expression. She noticed her father watching the exchange with interest from a safe distance. Was that a crooked grin on his face? "Just what I said. Nothing. He can answer yes or no questions. That's it. I thought for certain he was Luke, but I guess—wait a minute. Did you say yes?"

The spirit continued to nod.

"Okay. So let's see. You're Luke, right?"

Another affirmative gesture.

"Mom, the ghost is saying he's Luke. Um, he has a square jaw with dimples and close-set eyes. He's giving me a Johnny Depp vibe, but more rugged. I can't tell his hair color. Oh wait, from my dream, I remember he has chestnut brown hair. Is that him?"

"You're freaking me out, Cris. There's no way Luke's ghost is in our living room. Is he dead? I mean, obviously if his spirit is here, he's dead, but I guess I never looked for him after everything happened." Beatrice walked around the area Cristiane was looking. She swept out with an arm, like she was clearing through fog as she took cautious steps in various directions.

"Mom, stop acting weird. You're a witch, for crying out loud! You can pass right through and it doesn't bother him, or he can simply drift to another spot." Cristiane flung her wrist toward the spot a few paces to her right. "Like he did now. He's over here next to Dad. But stop it. Seriously."

Jeffrey rushed to the opposite side of the room, clutching the beer bottle like a pirate scurrying with his loot.

Cristiane rolled her eyes at her father. As her face turned toward her mother, she found Beatrice squinting with eyes darting about the room, looking for Luke's apparition.

Luke paused in front of his former lover, chuckling, with a finger on the tip of Beatrice's nose.

Cristiane whispered in her father's ear, then burst out laughing.

"Why are you laughing?" Beatrice put her hands on her hips, leaning her weight on one leg as she eyed her daughter. Behind Cristiane, Jeffrey tucked his chin, darted his eyes between the two women, and covered his mouth to hide his own amusement. "So everyone thinks this is funny, huh?"

Jeffrey couldn't contain himself any longer and joined Cristiane, and the ghost he couldn't see, in a good belly laugh at Beatrice's expense. After ten or fifteen seconds, the laughter quieted down.

As Beatrice crossed her arms over her chest and let out a huff, she rolled her eyes, smiling. "Well, at least we're all in a better mood."

"Can we move on now?" Cristiane turned her attention to Luke. "So we've established that you're Luke. What about the orb that is always by your side?"

Luke looked to his side and scrunched up his face in disgust.

"Oh! I didn't expect that."

"What?"

"He's not fond of the sidekick."

"That's his child! Oh, if I could see him, I'd give him a piece of my m—"

"Mom! He's shaking his head no. I don't think the orb is Michael."

Luke nodded, then pointed at the floating sphere by his side and shook his head.

"Hmm. I'm confused. Normally, if a couple of spirits roam together, there is a familiar connection."

"Cristiane, we have more pressing issues than Luke's spirit floating around the room."

Luke nodded.

Cristiane shrugged. "Luke seems to concur."

"Isn't that nice?" Beatrice twisted her mouth.

No longer as angry, Jeffrey appeared amused by the two women in his life and his wife's former lover. "Looks like Luke and I agree on something. Can we move on to what's going on in real life?"

Luke faded away with the orb lingering for a few seconds longer, then it, too, disappeared.

"They're gone now." Cristiane peered around the room, then plopped back onto the couch, tucking her legs underneath herself. "I think we need to talk about a battle plan. Nissa will not give up without a fight. I think Dad should leave town until things settle down and he's out of danger."

"Listen to me, sweet pea." Jeffrey turned to Cristiane. "I may not see ghosts or shoot laser beams out of my fingertips, but I'll be damned if my wife and daughter think they're going to hide me away while they fight some demon bitch. I can hold my own."

"Dad, I didn't mean you couldn't, but it's dangerous." Cristiane tilted her head toward Beatrice, expecting support.

"Jeffrey may be quiet and steadfast, but there's much you don't realize about your father, dear." Beatrice smiled at her husband. "Still waters run deep."

"I don't know if I get what that means, but Dad can't stay here. This house has been swarming with dark magic for months, maybe years."

"I agree, but a hotel isn't a promising idea. Innocent people could get hurt."

Cristiane reached for her phone. "Jarvis. Dad, stay with Jarvis. He's a witch and a cop. No one would look for you at his place. I'm sure he wouldn't mind."

"Oh, right. Who's Jarvis?" Confusion was written on Beatrice's face.

"He's the cop looking into your stabbing and, apparently, our daughter's new boyfriend." Jeffrey offered in explanation. "That would work. I'm sure he won't mind me taking over a few weapons, just in case."

"Weapons?" Cristiane stared at her father like he was a stranger. "What weapons?"

"Sweetie, there are things about both of us you never knew. I'll tell you about my life before I married your mother after all this blows over." Jeffrey patted Cristiane's knee.

Cristiane's phone rang before she could respond. It was Jarvis. Jarvis was speaking a mile a minute. She couldn't get a word in to talk about Jeffrey's idea.

Cristiane held the phone away for a second. "It's about David." She grew quiet and put her head down as Jarvis spoke on the other end. She shook her head as tears spilled over and dripped onto her jeans. "No, no, no." Her words were soft, muffled through sniffles and tears she didn't bother to wipe away.

When the call ended, she stared at the phone in her hand.

Beatrice knelt down in front of Cristiane. "What did Jarvis say?"

Cristiane took a deep breath. "David is dead."

The next day was full of anguish as Mrs. Carol Howson went through the agonizing tasks of officially identifying David's body, speaking to the police, and then deciding how to bury her son. Trying to raise a teenage boy without his father had been full of challenges. How she wished she had someone with her now. David liked to tease and joke, his coping mechanisms that used to drive her crazy after his father passed away. If only now she could hear one of his jests about her inability to reach a glass or put towels away on the upper shelves.

She and David had become so close to Joyce. They had learned so much about the environment that Carol's previous beliefs about traditional burial no longer made sense. With Joyce's help, Mrs. Howson decided on an intimate service in the Berkshires later in the summer. She felt the decision was right, even though it would take a bit of time to plan.

Two days after learning of David's death, Joyce and Carol joined the Bradfords at Jarvis's apartment. Robby and Tina came by to offer condolences and support. Jarvis asked them all to meet so he could discuss the case. He had the unique position to offer not only information from a police investigation angle but also the mystical, and he couldn't offer both at the precinct.

"David loved everyone in this room." Carol wiped at her tears as she spoke. "He'd grown up so much the past few years and it's because of your friendship and support. After his father passed, he got through that loss with your help. Thank you all for being here. I don't know how I'm going to live in that big house, knowing neither is going to walk through the door again."

Joyce pulled David's mother close as the sobs took over.

"Mrs. Howson, I can't imagine the pain you're going through, but I promise to do everything I can to find who did this to David." Jarvis kneeled in front of Carol, rubbing her shoulder. He rose and glanced around his living room. "A quick overview. As many of you know the police are not releasing details to the public, but out of respect for Mrs. Howson, I won't be too specific. Someone murdered David in a very brutal and unorthodox manner. A local fisherman found David and another body nearby, but we won't discuss that too much as authorities work to locate the other person's next of kin. I can say that an exclusive group of agents is assisting in the investigation and we're confident we will succeed in justice for David."

"Thank you, Jarvis." Carol stood and squeezed his hand. "We appreciate everything you're doing. I guess I need to go. I'll be at Joyce's if you need to reach me."

"Of course. Don't hesitate to call if you have questions or want to talk." Jarvis hugged her and escorted her and Joyce to the front door.

Once they left, Jarvis turned his consideration to those remaining to share what he knew about the investigation. "A fisherman spotted David's car, partially covered with tree branches, several yards off the dirt road leading to the boat ramp. He noticed as he drove by blood smeared across the car's hood and stopped. Otherwise, he wouldn't have thought to stop as people park all over the area to fish. The man ran to see if anyone needed help. He found carnage and what he thought were two bodies. Both of which took a few days to identify."

"Why did it take so long for them to be identified?" Tina asked.

"Well, that's why I said it was brutal and unorthodox. We suspect the killer initially fought with David. But— there's no easy way to say this. The killer also beheaded David. They found his body several feet from his head." Jarvis let the shock of the details settle with everyone for a minute. "The other body was even more gruesome. The detectives wrote it up as a grenade-type explosion, which blasted the body to pieces. There was no evidence of explosives in or near the vicinity. I have a theory, which Sarah and Isadora are helping me to clarify."

"What's your theory?" Cristiane walked over from where she had sat near the kitchen and stood next to Jarvis.

Jarvis put his arm around her. "I think Nissa took David. A couple of her thugs, anyway, who were to scare him or rough him up, but it went sideways. There was blood from a third in the underbrush and on some remains, but not on David's. I assume the third person was Nissa's demon, Xirnan, but I'm waiting for the DNA to come back."

"How can a demon have DNA?" Jeffrey asked from his spot on the couch.

"Demons use humans to move around in our world. From what Cristiane has told me about Xirnan, he's occupying an incredibly old meatsuit. I hope the DNA will lead to a missing person's report, but even if we don't get a hit, I'm sure the other dead body is Nissa's cocky nightclub manager, Malin Hobbs. That man's DNA was under David's nails and on his face. Sarah is confirming if he's been at the club the past week."

Cristiane looked up at Jarvis. "So you think Malin fought with and then killed David? Xirnan then got pissed because Malin took things too far, so he killed Malin. Is that it?"

"Exactly. You said yourself that Malin was a cocky son of a bitch." Jarvis nodded and looked around. "Xirnan was the serene one when they showed up in Springfield, right?"

"Yes. Freaky, but definitely in control."

"I think Xirnan is still alive, but he couldn't risk Malin doing or saying something that would jeopardize the cult. No matter the external pressures, I don't know if we'll ever find out what exactly happened out there. But I'd bet Xirnan used his powers to blow Malin to smithereens. If Xirnan was harmed, it means his meatsuit is failing, and his powers are weakening."

Beatrice raised a finger. "You're right, Jarvis. I won't get into the history, but I've known Xirnan for a long time. His current form is not how he appeared when we first met. The elderly man was not his intended target, but an emergency replacement because of a botched attempt to possess a more youthful body. He is ancient for a demon, over 1600 years old. Although some powers are extraordinary at his age, others must have the perfect scenario to remain strong. The body he possesses is failing, therefore the demon is in a weakened position."

Jarvis raised a brow, deep in thought. "That gives us an advantage. All along, I thought Nissa might work for Xirnan. Do you know their relationship?"

"Xirnan is sworn to obey Nissa, not the other way around." Beatrice stood and poured a glass of red wine. "Her father, if he is actually her father, Draigh Vossen, bound Xirnan to Nissa decades ago. Had it not been for Nissa's threats to unleash her father's other demons on me and Xirnan's thirst for blood—mine especially—I would have been able to leave that shitshow she calls a cult long ago."

All eyes were on Beatrice as she gulped down the glass and then refilled it. Cristiane cleared her throat. "Um— everyone, Mom has some history we can talk about later."

"Sorry." Beatrice shook her head and sat back next to her husband.

"Okay." Jarvis ruffled his brows and shrugged at Cristiane, to which she mouthed 'later,' in reply. "That's helpful, Mrs. Bradford. There was a lot of blood at the scene, the third party's blood. If it is Xirnan's, then it shows he's more vulnerable."

"Oh, I almost forgot. I hit him with my car and damaged his shoulder a few months ago, too."

"That was you?" Beatrice asked Cristiane. "He needs another host. This one will not heal under his power any longer. Time is running short, but his duty to Nissa is not yet fulfilled. Xirnan is obligated to Draigh or a high-ranking demon under Draigh's charge. If the vessel fails, Xirnan will be condemned as a disappointment. I believe the arrangement forcing an aged host was intentional—that Draigh wanted Xirnan to fail. Xirnan, I feel, believes this as well, and it has enraged him for a long time. Once he asked Nissa if he could take Malin's body because he annoyed everyone, but Draigh wouldn't allow it. There's no love lost between those two men."

"Maybe that contributed to the situation when they took David." Robby added.

"Could be. Malin is an asshole, but he keeps the club running and Nissa likes to use his assets whenever she's in the mood."

"What assets? Does he have any abilities?" The questions came from Jarvis.

"If being a horn dog is an ability, then yes. Otherwise, he's just a cocky jackass that she's fond of using." Beatrice laced her words with sarcastic venom.

Everyone laughed.

Jarvis raised a hand to get the group's attention. "This conversation tells you there's more to this situation than the police department can handle. The local coven has already supported Cristiane in the challenges facing the Bradford family, but Sarah Killian is assisting me in the mystical aspects surrounding this case. We'll draw whatever resources we need from the coven to help in the matter."

Tina and Robby had been chatting between themselves for a minute before Robby stood. "Is Nissa aware that the coven is helping Cristiane? Should we be concerned about our safety?" He looked at Tina and Jeffrey. "Or the safety of our non-magical family members until this is resolved?"

"Great questions, Robby." Jarvis walked around his living room in thought. "I think it's important for everyone to be watchful and take extra precautions. Mr. Bradford is staying with me, but he has combat experience. I'd suggest Tina stay with other family. It's up to you, but we don't know the extent of the threat yet."

"Understood. Thanks, Jarvis." Robby turned his attention to Tina. "We should probably have you stay out of town with your aunt or another relative."

Jarvis nodded and turned to the Bradfords.

Cristiane excused herself to call Joyce and check on her and Mrs. Howson. She stepped out of the apartment as Robby and Tina walked together into the kitchen.

After ten minutes, Jarvis looked around his apartment. "Anyone see Cristiane come back inside?" They each looked at each other, shaking their heads.

Beatrice stood, calling to Cristiane as she wandered into the bedroom and looked in the master bath. She returned to the living room. "She's not in the apartment."

Robby shrugged and offered, "She's probably still talking with Joyce."

Jarvis opened the door and peered into the hallway. He hollered before the door slammed shut behind him, "I'm going to look for her."

Beatrice paced, her stomach turning. "I don't feel her near anymore."

Robby closed his eyes. "Me either."

Tina and Jeffrey asked what that meant.

Neither answered, afraid to speak, making their suppositions real.

Fifteen minutes later, Jarvis barged through the door. "She's gone."

TWENTY-THREE

Cristiane's eyes felt like weights dangled from her lids. Her mind whirled as her eyes flickered, fighting against the desire to sleep. She took a deep breath and choked on the stench filling her nostrils. As she forced her sleep-blurred and unreliable eyes to open, the surrounding blackness made her question if she was awake. However, her bladder told her it was ready to explode.

She turned over and pressed her hands against the padding underneath as she shuddered against the putrid air filling her lungs. Death clung to the air. Her heels landed with a thud, as she expected to swing her feet over the side of a bed. Sharp pain shot up her legs, causing her head to clear. While she drew her knees up to inspect her feet, the pressure on her bladder was intense. *Where the hell am I?*

"Let me out of here!" Her scream rang back to her, raucous and crisp, in the darkness. Cristiane listened for a response. Nothing but hollow silence answered her.

Barefoot, the stone floor felt cool against the throbbing in her feet. She took a few wobbly steps and reached out to find a wall to hold her steady. Her body ached as she contorted her neck, arms, and legs, registering the level of grievances to each area. Other than the probable gash in her foot from slamming her heels on the rough, jagged floor, she had no other physical injuries. She searched her pockets for her mojo bag, coming up empty, and then remembered it was at Jarvis's apartment.

The scuff of her feet irritated her ears, the sound magnifying with each step as she was cautious to not bang her foot against another object in the room. She tried to lift her feet to reduce the noise they made across the rocky floor. That and the sound of her own breath as her fingers felt along the walls—both disturbances annoyed her.

The wall to her left was sticky and reeked of decades-old rust. She continued to pat the walls as her feet shuffled across the unknown terrain. Discovering a door, she turned the handle only to find it locked. Cristiane finished canvassing the room and found nothing—no way out and no toilet. She shivered and rubbed her arms.

Without an exit, she had no choice and made toward the door as far away from the mattress as she could get. She might need to sleep there again. She slid down her pants, squatted by the door frame, and relieved her aching, protruding bladder. Dehydrated, the stench of ammonia struck her nostrils. As she waited to finish her business, her witch senses, her intuition, reached out to discover what was beyond her rudimentary accommodations. Surprised by the sensation of several people in the area, she quickly stood and covered herself.

A distant rattle of chains seemed to come from behind the entrance. Cristiane stepped away as the door creaked open with a jolt. Light spilled into the room, blinding Cristiane. She raised her arm, shielding her eyes from the glare.

"My apologies, Ms. Bradford. I didn't realize you were awake." Xirnan, dressed in a long cloak, stepped into the doorway, hands clasped behind his back. He sniffed the air and looked down before letting his next step land and back peddled to avoid the fresh urine snaking along the juts in the rock floor. A grin slithered across his sallow lips. "Oh my, I left you down here a wee too long, didn't I? Let's get you cleaned up before you join Ms. Marth. Come with me, please." Xirnan gestured with a whip of his bony hand for Cristiane to exit in front of him.

"I'm not going anywhere with you."

His jutting eyes meandered from her bloodied feet, up her mundane, conventional clothes, pausing a fraction of a second at her gleaming emerald eyes, and then continued until they rested at the scraggly, tousled, chestnut hair atop her grimy face. "I assure you; the alternative is to stay here and die in this cell. Your choice." Xirnan waved a hand into the room she had occupied the past several hours.

Her gaze followed his skeletal fingers as the illumination shed light on blood stains splattered from floor to ceiling. Bits of bone littered the floor like tiny chips of wood from a hatchet. Her eyes traveled to the shackles high on the wall, holding snippets of dried flesh dangling from steel chains. She shuddered as the thought of remaining in the hellhole churned her stomach.

Xirnan's hands returned to rest behind his back. His expression was empty as he waited for Cristiane to move. "Do not waste your young magic on me, dear. I would hate to cause you harm so soon."

Cristiane contemplated using the arcane arsenal provided by the coven, but she'd not attempted any new powers since receiving them. She could wield fire, but against an old demon, the outcome was questionable. She'd been without food or water for an unknown period. What effect that would have on her stamina or effectiveness in casting was uncertain. She wasn't willing to risk it, especially not knowing where she was. Best to play along for now and, at the very least, get out of the death room. Cristiane turned back to Xirnan. "A shower would be nice."

As Xirnan's looked down at the urine near his feet, his wrinkled, gaunt nose and jagged teeth sneering at the floor, he nodded. "Indeed."

Cristiane stepped beside Xirnan; her hands out front as she passed through the foot-thick, impenetrable cell walls.

The door was like a bank vault, deep with a massive spindle to slide the enormous bolt into place. A modern key code and thumb-print lock employed a second mechanism deadbolt under the first. "A bit of overkill on the dungeon master tricks, isn't it?"

Xirnan left the cell door open as he stepped away. The two walked side-by-side. Although Xirnan made no move to indicate he planned to force her way through the cavernous dwelling, Cristiane remained on guard. His hands stayed clasped behind his back as they journeyed through the lighted area. Large black sconces lined the great hall, bathing the stone walls in light. Cristiane kept an arms-length between them, one eye on Xirnan and the other on the floor, careful of where her feet landed on the filthy ground.

"Not necessarily. Settlers built this level during the early colonization of New England, although there are no records. The type of stonework and skill tell the story. Not until the Civil War was its use documented, which was for the detainment of Confederate prisoners. Since that era and before the war, we presume, these cells have held many men and creatures."

"Cells as in plural? How many are there? Is anyone else locked up now?" Cristiane took a couple of quick steps to the next vault-like door, placing her hand on the rough surface. As she closed her eyes, she felt her mind pick up breathing and a heartbeat. She noticed two hallways about thirty feet away on either side, jutting out in opposite directions. A shiver ran through her as she sensed several others in the caverns. "No windows? Tell me there is air circulation, at least. How do you expect people to survive?"

Xirnan twitched as he stepped past her. "No windows. It's not my concern if those held captive inside live or die." His monotone illustrated his lack of interest in the conversation. "Follow me. You may ask Nissa your questions. I doubt she will entertain them, but that is up to her."

Cristiane followed along with Xirnan through the underground walkway. The broad hall soon opened to a sizable chamber with a dry-stacked stone staircase, two-stories high, lining the far wall built from boulders. Two black industrial chandeliers hung from the ceiling, bathing the room in bright light. The double doors at the top of the staircase were at least ten-feet tall with ornate carvings etched from ceiling to floor. As Cristiane approached the stairs, she noticed mortar filled sporadic spots around the boulders.

"Why the mortar? I thought boulders made a strong wall."

Xirnan rolled his bulbous eyes. "Erosion from the Long Island Sound over the years." He waved an upward palm, gesturing for Cristiane to ascend the stairs. "Now, if you'd please."

So they were not in Andover. Cristiane ambled up, turning her head every three or four steps to note how close Xirnan was to her as they journeyed toward the double doors. Xirnan kept several paces behind, which was fine by her. Once at the landing, Cristiane waited for Xirnan to open the doors.

"Simply grasp the handle and push. The doors are not locked."

"Oh." Cristiane turned the handle and pushed but the door barely moved.

"Weak." Xirnan watched as Cristiane put her shoulder against the door. He craned his neck with eyebrows raised, amused at Cristiane's use of brute strength, trying to open the doors. "You are a witch, are you not?"

"Oh, stop it. If you can do better, just open the damn thing." The color rose on Cristiane's cheeks as she stepped aside and crossed her arms over her chest. She hadn't thought to use her magic. How was she going to escape this place if she didn't always think like a witch?

"I wouldn't dare come to your aid. After witnessing you dispense Malin, I am confident this wooden slab cannot defeat you."

Infuriated by entertaining Xirnan with her lack of physical strength, she flung a wrist at the door. It burst open, swinging furiously on its hinges, banging against the wall in response. "Fine."

Xirnan clapped his hands, chuckling. "Oh, splendid."

"Shut up." Cristiane stomped through the entryway. "By the way, why didn't you tell Nissa about my capabilities? I bet she wasn't pleased with you."

Her attendant shook his head and sneered as his fists clasped behind his back. He glided through the open door past Cristiane. "This way."

They came upon a modern kitchen, lined with picture windows showcasing a gorgeous water view, which led into the middle of a lengthy hallway. As they approached another staircase, this one lined with photos and handrails on each side, Cristiane glanced back to the opposite end of the corridor, toward another set of double doors. A knot formed in her stomach. Something about the corridor was familiar, but she didn't understand. She'd never been to Long Island.

Xirnan waited on the landing for Cristiane to reach him. As she approached, he started up another flight of stairs. They came to an expansive bedroom, furnished with a four-poster king-size bed and ornate furniture. A wardrobe and vanity filled the primary space. At the far end was a sitting area furnished with two Victorian chairs and a small sofa. On the cocktail table, a tray of fruit, cheese, and other bite-sized items accompanied a cut-glass pitcher and drinking glass.

Xirnan floated into the room, peering at Cristiane as she followed him. "There is a full bathroom beyond the sitting room, so you may freshen up. Have something to eat, make yourself comfortable. The wardrobe has an assortment of clothes. I'm sure you will find something to fit." Xirnan stepped near the night table and pointed to an old rotary phone. "It is an internal system. Simply pick up and it will ring Ms. Marissa, the housekeeper, if you need anything. Questions?"

"What's stopping me from walking out of here?"

"The exits are the door or the windows. I lock the door and it is as impenetrable as the locks on the chamber doors below. The windows—well, be my guest." Cristiane gazed out the nearest window. "You're about thirty feet above the concrete. Unless you've mastered piercing bulletproof glass and levitation, I don't think Nissa will be concerned about an escape. She will expect you for dinner, and not a moment earlier."

As Cristiane took in her surroundings, she sat on the edge of the bed. Tired, hungry, and dirtier than at any other point in her life, she resigned herself to the situation. Xirnan nodded and left her in the bedroom's solitude, closing the heavy doors behind him. Cristiane heard the click and clack of locks once the door shut, then a wisp of magic. A small flame danced along the door, then disappeared. Xirnan had enchanted the entry.

She made a dash to the water pitcher and drank two glasses before taking a bite of food. Although every morsel looked delicious, Cristiane's priority was a shower, clean clothes, and shoes for her feet so she could find a way out.

After notifying Sarah of Cristiane's disappearance, Jarvis and Beatrice contacted the police department. Jarvis was able to rush a missing person's alert for Cristiane because of her close ties to David Howson. Due to the ongoing investigation and brutality of David's murder, a Coordinated Law Enforcement Adult Rescue (CLEAR) alert was issued. The alert was constructed to help law enforcement find and rescue adults who were in direct danger, as well as to provide additional resources in the effort to find probable suspects. Once Jarvis filed the alert, he and Beatrice rushed to Sarah's, the coven's headquarters.

Jarvis rallied members in the large banquet room as Sarah asked to speak with Beatrice. Sarah and Isadora had spent hours going through the items in the trunk Jarvis had delivered a few days before. They had a clearer grasp of Nissa and her tactics, as well as Beatrice's involvement in the group in recent years. However, for the coven to trust Beatrice, Sarah wanted a private word and to hear Beatrice fill in the gaps since they were college roommates. Sarah couldn't let a stone go unturned if they were to find Cristiane alive.

As Beatrice spoke with Sarah, Cristiane was far away, getting Nissa's spin on her mother's former life.

Cristiane felt more like herself after spending the afternoon in the well-accommodated prison room. Although held captive, she cleaned up and used a bit of healing magic, thanks to the Horned God and Mother Goddess binding the coven's powers to her, to repair her gashed feet and bruises on various spots along her body. Refreshed, she sat opposite Nissa, at one end of a long 17th-century dining table in a pair of jeans, crop top, and button-down shirt that fit her well. The Doc Martens boots were a tad too small, but they beat the only other pair of shoes in the wardrobe that she could slide her foot into, chunky leather sandals with dry-rotted buckles.

Nissa was dressed in cerulean blue, wide-leg dress capris and a matching jacket with a cream lace blouse. She wore dignified flats in a stripe pattern, matching the colors of her outfit. After seating Cristiane at the table, Ms. Marissa brought the women soup and then filled their wine glasses. As their server stepped out of the room, Nissa raised her glass. "To never throwing out guests' clothes. I'm glad to see your mother's old pieces fit you so well. I wasn't sure they would be of use after so many years."

"These were my mother's?" Cristiane tugged at the shirt collar. She eyed the wine, but waited for Nissa to first eat or drink what Marissa had served to them.

"Yes, so many years ago. I'd say at least 25 years now." Nissa took a sip and waited for Cristiane to do the same. "Has Beatrice told you of her time here?"

"Some. She told me, I mean us, my dad and me, about Michael."

"Michael?" Nissa waved a hand. "Oh, I guess she gave it a name. A name to who she thought was her baby, anyway."

"What does that mean?"

"All those years ago, I gave your mother a home, love, and support as her belly swelled with her lover's child."

"You mean Luke. The baby's father was Luke."

"Ah yes, Luke." Nissa loudly slurped a spoonful of soup.

Cristiane wrinkled a nostril at the sound. "What did you mean about the baby?"

"It was so long ago, I suppose it doesn't hurt to tell the truth now, does it?" Nissa set the spoon down and took the napkin to wipe her mouth. She took her drink and leaned back in her seat. "Your mother stayed here for many months, waiting for her child to be born. She wasn't strong like you, always fretting over our gatherings. She loathed casting the few tokens of protection I asked her to deliver over the festivities in payment for giving her so much. But alas, she worked herself up into such a frenzy, losing her precious child, or so she thought, that I couldn't wait to send her packing.

"If she'd taken the blood oath, she would have learned that Michael was alive and well. I would have given her baby back." Nissa shrugged. "But she still wouldn't take the oath.

It was quite frustrating to see the depression swallow her up during the last few weeks she spent here."

"Again, what about the baby? You said, 'who she thought'-what did you mean by that?" Irritated, Cristiane tightened her fists under the table.

"Pardon me. The ruse was to push your mother over the edge to take the blood oath. The ruse being that her baby died shortly after birth, giving her nothing to cling to other than my friendship and support. But I didn't harm the child. I raised and protected him—for a while anyway." Nissa again waved a dismissive hand as she picked up a large coin from the table with her other and toyed with it, flipping it over and over with her fingers. "Anyway, I gave her a changeling. You know they take on any form, but they adore portraying children. It worked well, I have to say. The slight, feral creature stayed in her arms for hours, enjoying the warmth of her bosom, playing dead. I had to reward the devil; his performance was extraordinary."

Cristiane seethed. "What happened to Michael?"

"He lived here for several years with another child, raised to be a member of our sect, my protégé. If I couldn't have his mother, I planned to raise the witch child and groom him for the seven. Did you know seven, as a lucky number, dates to the Mesopotamian era? Lamashtu kept an intimate circle of seven devout mystics. If one died, she withheld favor from the remaining until another powerful witch or demon filled the void. It's my goal to reconstruct the seven and serve as her most trusted ambassador. It all was going wonderfully until Luke appeared." Nissa rolled her eyes.

As the fire flitted in her opponent's eyes, Cristiane noticed the coin was the same totem Nissa had at Javier's. Nissa must need the charm to funnel Lamashtu's gifts. "But you have little power. How would you serve as her representative?"

Cristiane smirked as doubt flashed across Nissa's eyes.

Doubt turned to fire as heat flushed Nissa's face. "You know nothing of my power."

"We'll see. Anyway, you said Luke was here?" Cristiane sat straighter. She understood Beatrice's comments about Nissa's power being weak. Nissa had none of her own.

"Yes. That sneaky little bastard showed up years later. I believe when Quinn—that's the name I gave him, was around ten. Luke kidnapped my boy, along with the other child. He must have planned it for ages. We found a small boat with supplies in the boat shed as we looked for the children, but he had a car nearby or stole one. Our search was around the Sound for far too long. Had we realized he'd left in a car sooner, we might have found the boys.

"I'd dispatched everyone for the search, but it was fruitless, until I sent two of my dear changelings, Pux and Lam, toward the park preserve. Only one returned. The other poor creature, Pux, must have come across Luke leaving and attempted to stop him. We found the car the next day smashed against a tree. My poor Pux lost his head."

Cristiane squinted and pursed her lips.

"Literally, he lost his head. Cut clean off." Nissa ran a finger across her throat. "We searched the woods for weeks for the two boys until we found remains deep in the forests. Young male bears can be quite ferocious beasts in the wild. Of course, it could have also been wolves or even a werewolf. Who knows?

"But I was a good citizen and called the police about the discovery. They sent wildlife experts and forensics to collect evidence. The state park preserve was deserted for weeks as the posters, highlighting a recent mauling of children, scared everyone away. But there was no record of Quinn or the other boy, Tony, in any database or missing child alerts. The police wrote the remains off as unknown, undocumented or what have you, and that was the end."

Nissa spoke without a hint of care or remorse, a true sociopath and narcissist. Cristiane knew there would be no reasoning with her captor. "What purpose did the children serve?"

"I seized them for sacrifice, of course. I kept Quinn for myself, hoping his powers would evolve and serve as one of the seven. Tony had no powers or abilities worthy of our needs but he was a friend to Quinn. Like many other adults and children before and after, we sacrifice for Lamashtu, so she will bestow her blessings and riches to her loyal followers in brief bursts after such events. Mysterious moments which I live for until the joining. Once I gather powerful mystics who choose the blood oath, she will finally offer us, the seven, her complete chaotic grace. She will do the same for you. Take the blood oath that your mother would not and see what grand riches await you." Nissa stood and walked around the long table, placing a hand on Cristiane's shoulder.

"You're insane. What twisted fuck kills children and conducts human sacrifice? You are a top-tier psycho bitch. I told you at the club, it's never going to happen." Still seated, Cristiane's eyes moved from Nissa's hand to her face. As she glared at Nissa, she caught Xirnan's approach from the far corner. "You can tell your goon, Xirnan, to back off. I'm not afraid of you."

A burst of belly laughter from Nissa roared through the room. "You have more spunk than Beatrice. I'll give you that." She stepped away and strolled back toward her chair. "We could use that fire at our gatherings. The crowd is dull at the club these days. Most are bored couples, or mid-life crisis wanderers looking to spice things up after blowing up their marriages. Oh, it's fun, but that's not where the real magic happens. Simple theatrics for the people so they'll finance my indulgences. Such an exclusive reputation brings clients with open wallets. The genuine thrill is after, with individuals seeking unimaginable transcendent power."

Cristiane examined Nissa, lost in her own reminiscing. Xirnan stepped back into the shadows, but Cristiane felt his presence as Ms. Marissa came into the room with dinner.

Cristiane wondered if the maid had heard the conversation. Was she hired help for the house, or was she more to Nissa? Cristiane sensed no mystical energy from the woman as Marissa cleared the soup bowls and filled glasses. "My mother mentioned your gatherings. Do you not have the meetings in this house anymore?"

"Beatrice told you of the meetings. How interesting." Nissa tapped her nails on the table.

"Not until recently, but we found most of the details on the tapes." Cristiane stared at Nissa, watching as her cheeks turned red and her jaw clenched. "You know, the details of how you drain the person's blood and then carve symbols into the chest, praying to your crazy-ass demon."

Nissa's hand slammed on the table as she stood. "What tapes? Where are they?" Her thunderous voice echoed throughout the room.

The skeletal demon marched into the room between the two women. Ms. Marissa hurried in and, startled at seeing Xirnan, froze. He quickly flung the cloak's hood over his head, covering his face, then waved her off. "Leave us." The hood turned an inch as he waited for the frightened woman to go away.

"I have no idea where they are now. I gave them, along with a bunch of other stuff, to a police officer." Cristiane remembered touching the artifact that spoke to her. Her hands went to the seat edge as she twisted slightly and crossed her legs, then leaned back in the chair. "Oh, and by the way, what demon did you piss off? I'm guessing it's still looking for Michael, or Quinn, whatever you call him. It was quite disappointed to make my acquaintance. It wanted the 'child' promised—the first-born son, I believe. You shouldn't play with dark magic. It has a way of biting back."

Nissa stumbled away from the table. Her face flushed, jaw convulsing, as she glared at Cristiane. "You're making that up. What lies has Beatrice fed you?"

Cristiane stood, knocking the chair over in the process, and took a defensive posture, ready to throw fireballs. "I didn't make up an ugly ass animal hybrid with bird feet roaring at me from the pits of hell. My guess…" Cristiane waved her hands in the air. "And I'm giving this my novice shot—being a baby witch and all. But you tried to pull a fast one with Lamashtu or whatever, by keeping Michael to yourself. You made promises you didn't keep and it's pissed off. My mother's been holding that artifact and the other cursed shit for years."

Xirnan slithered near Nissa. "Did you pledge Quinn to your goddess?"

Nissa backed away. "You don't question me, Xirnan. You serve me. Don't forget it."

"Check your tone, human," Xirnan growled as the flames danced wildly in his eyes.

Nissa smacked the demon. "You serve me!"

Xirnan swept Nissa into a vortex of smoky haze. The whirlwind snapped and hissed as if alive, as the two evils thwarted each other. Xirnan pulled himself out of the rushing winds and held Nissa suspended in the mix. "I serve you, but my decree is to Draigh." Xirnan closed the distance between the two in a flash. "Your infatuation with chaos cannot interfere. My punishment was to serve you, but I will deal with your incredulous actions if necessary."

Cristiane couldn't hear as the two glared at each other. While the disagreement kept them distracted, she searched for an exit. Her attention went to the swinging door to her left, which Marissa rushed through during her exit. If Cristiane could reach the doorway while Xirnan focused on Nissa, she might be able to flee. Her feet stretched over the carpet, slowly, so as to not make a sound. Looking over her left shoulder at the door, she needed just a couple more seconds to close the gap.

As Cristiane turned to dash for the exit, her body ceased and fell, banging her face into the floor with a thud. Blood erupted from her nose. She wrestled against the feeling of being bound as a pool of crimson spread under her head.

Xirnan stood next to her and flipped her over with a finger flick. "Where do you think you're going?"

Nissa came up behind him.

Cristiane hissed back. "You broke my nose!"

As Nissa peered over Xirnan's shoulder at Cristiane, Nissa's hands flew to her mouth as her nose twitched up and down. "Ouch. I think he did."

"I will take her to the room." Xirnan brandished a hand about the air, which righted Cristiane, having her stand upright as blood dripped down her face. He waved a finger in circles twice, unraveling the glistening twine from her legs so she could walk.

Once Xirnan escorted Cristiane back into the bedroom, he removed the mystical rope from the rest of her body. "You will remain here." He left without another word, enchanting the door as locks clicked into place.

Cristiane had to escape. Xirnan and Nissa were at odds, but both saw her as the enemy. She ran various spells through her head, trying to find an idea that would help her flee. She noticed her wrists gleaming gold and silver. The blessings from the gods were trying to tell her something. Cristiane closed her eyes, concentrating on receiving the message. What did they want her to know? Jarvis, her parents, and Isadora came to mind. She felt at peace and a sudden urge to travel, to move. Encouraged, she looked at her wrists and the threads of gold and silver glistened, moving as waves below her hands. The faces of those she loved became clearer as a pull to move worked through her core.

She could teleport. She hadn't attempted the magic spell given by the Mother Goddess. As suddenly as the thought came to her, Cristiane filled with panic. Yet home and her loved ones were so far away. Could she make the trip—or survive it? The alternative was to remain Nissa's prisoner and witness a sacrifice—or become the sacrifice. Cristiane had little choice; she must leave.

The Mother Goddess entered Cristiane's mind as her skin tingled and glistened with the Horned God's strength. Mother Goddess said, "You are a powerful witch. Do not allow fear control over you. You have my blessing, and we offered you the energy of the five elements. Believe in the divine strength and your own witchiness. You can do anything you set your mind to do. Believe as I believe in you."

Calmness washed over Cristiane as confidence in herself gripped her soul unlike any trust she'd ever had. The ever-present anxiety was gone. Again, she thought of her family and friends. An internal pull gripped her, tugging at her senses, willing her to move. And as quickly as she thought to travel to those who cared for her, she vanished.

A bump into a wall caused Cristiane to stumble backward until she regained her footing. She looked around, not recognizing the foyer. But voices trailed from two directions. Her mother spoke behind the door to her right as she made out Jarvis's voice coming from a far-left corner. As she turned to find Jarvis, he rushed to her side.

"Cristiane! Are you okay? You're bleeding." Jarvis cupped her face in his hands, turning her side to side.

"I'm okay. He broke my nose. That's all. I'm fine." Cristiane covered his hands with her own. "Where am I?"

"We're at the coven headquarters. Sarah's place."

"Where's Sarah? Is my mom here, too? I need to talk to them."

Jarvis pointed, while Cristiane followed his hand and pushed through the door.

TWENTY-FOUR

"I need to talk with you." Cristiane hollered as the door banged against the wall.

Jarvis stopped it from slamming into his face and gently closed the door behind him as he followed Cristiane into the study. Sarah faced the door and rose as the two young witches entered.

Beatrice jumped up. "Oh! Thank god you're here." She hugged her daughter tight, not wanting to let go. As she pulled back and held Cristiane's shoulders, she scrutinized the damage to Cristiane's face. "Broken?

"Yes, but I'm okay." Cristiane squeezed Beatrice's arms and looked down at her own body, tapping her hands along her sides and legs. "It's good to see you. Thankfully, I'm in one piece. Teleportation feels like it's pulling you apart until the second you stop."

"So, Mother Goddess's blessings came in handy." Sarah gave the young witch a quick hug. She waved a hand in a circle three times as a warm, damp cloth materialized. It hovered in front of Cristiane, waiting for her to take it.

"Yes. I don't know what I would have done without them." Cristiane plucked the damp washcloth from the air and wiped blood from her face, keeping a delicate touch around her swollen nose. She looked around to put the blood-filled cloth somewhere as Sarah took it from her hands and twirled it in the air, gone from sight.

"It will hurt, but I can fix the break for you. You'll be good as new in a couple of hours," Beatrice offered, waiting for Cristiane to answer.

"Sure, that'd be great."

With a short mantra and a flick of Beatrice's index fingers, she cast the bone healing spell.

Sarah and Jarvis cringed as they listened to Cristiane's nose crack into place. While a gasp left her lips. "Ouch!" Cristiane wrinkled her nose and twisted her lips back and forth a few times. Other than the swelling, her nose felt normal.

Sarah sat in one of the two accent chairs as Beatrice stepped toward the other. Sarah gestured Jarvis and Cristiane toward the rigid camel back loveseat. "So, you said you had to speak with us?"

"Yes, but first I have to tell Mom something." Cristiane grabbed her mother's hand. "Mom, Michael wasn't stillborn."

"What are you talking about? I held him in my arms. He was not alive."

"No. Nissa switched him with a changeling. Michael lived for another decade but died during the escape with Luke. That's what my dream has been about and why Luke's spirit has been around us. Michael and another boy, Tony, died in the woods after the car accident. The orb isn't Michael. It was another of Nissa's changelings."

"Michael was alive and Nissa was raising him? That woman is evil!" Beatrice jumped up and paced the floor.

Cristiane took in the room's décor as she settled next to Jarvis while monitoring her mother process the news.

The walls were a calming shade of green. Two large bookcases stacked with books from floor to ceiling lined the far wall between two picture windows facing the front yard. A small wine refrigerator rested against the adjacent wall with an ornate bar cart and a small desk nearby. "Can I get a drink or something? It's been a crazy minute."

Sarah looked at the tumblers on the cart in the far corner of the room, said a brief verse that sounded like a haiku, and then winked. The other three looked on as drink glasses filled with pinkish-orange liquid. An orange slice slipped onto the rim of each glass. One beverage floated to Beatrice, who grabbed it with a terse nod of thanks. She stopped her pacing but remained standing while the drinks moved to the others in the room.

"Thanks." Cristiane drew a sip and smiled. Her favorite, Tequila Sunrise.

Once she'd had a moment to relax, Cristiane began describing her kidnapping experience. She shared details of the holding cells and then the transfer to the bedroom where her mother used to stay. Cristiane described the discussion she had with Nissa, and then the ensuing rift between Nissa and Xirnan. She provided specifics regarding Nissa's reaction to the videotapes and Nissa's extreme agitation over the news that a spirit had spoken to Cristiane. Finally, Cristiane described Xirnan's challenge to Nissa before he caught Cristiane trying to escape.

Cristiane hit the important points, but Sarah and Beatrice appeared to follow without concern.

"So, Beatrice, Cristiane's account confirms Draigh Vossen." Sarah nodded to Beatrice as she made a heavy draw of her drink. "Cris, you said Xirnan left you quickly to return to Nissa."

"Yes." Cristiane wondered where Sarah was going with her question. "I'm certain they continued the disagreement after he locked me back in the bedroom. Xirnan seemed excited, as if Nissa revealed an opportunity he needed to evaluate."

"Did you get the impression Nissa was afraid of Xirnan and the artifact?"

"Definitely."

"Beatrice, do you have insight into Xirnan's history before he joined with Nissa?"

"Not much. As far as I can remember, he has served her with a sense of disdain, like he was superior and loathed having to help her. The body that he inhabits is quite beyond its usefulness, but without Draigh's approval, Xirnan has been forced to remain in it. He's tried to transfer to another host without success. I believe the only other option for him to move to a stronger host is if he proves himself to be more valuable to Draigh."

"What do you think Xirnan could do to prove more valuable?" Sarah asked as she pulled a small notebook and pen from the end table drawer. She lifted the pen to her temple and tapped it twice against her head, then placed it straight up over the notebook before tapping the tip twice on the paper. The pen remained in position as Sarah pulled her hand away. As Beatrice spoke, the pen moved over the paper.

"Nothing. I only saw Draigh once from afar. I've never met him or talked with him. The impression I had was that Xirnan committed a grave mistake and Draigh no longer trusted him. He placed Xirnan with Nissa to have someone close to her to report back how she conducted meetings or gathered followers. If Xirnan proved he could serve Nissa without incident, perhaps he would win favor with Draigh. But as I told Jarvis and my family earlier, I believe Draigh is through with Xirnan. That's what I feel is behind the relationship. It's a compulsory pairing between Xirnan and Nissa. Neither are happy about it.

"Nissa needs Xirnan's powers and mine or others like me to protect her, so she can play her games and continue her quest for the seven. It's nonsense, but to her, it is real. Without a powerful mage holding her up, Nissa is nothing more than a narcissistic performer to rich clientele for her own gain. To use magic, Nissa must wear or hold a totem. She plays with worshipping Lamashtu rather than being a serious leader. Her lack of true faith, and any failure to deliver, will be her downfall. Lamashtu, or Draigh, will seek revenge if Nissa has deceived either of them."

"So, as Cristiane witnessed, if there is now a rift between the two and Xirnan reports Nissa's misdeeds, Draigh could release Xirnan from his burden?"

"That's possible, yes. The error on Nissa's part would have to be extreme, but it's possible." Beatrice nodded and looked toward her daughter for confirmation.

Cristiane agreed. "I couldn't hear everything they said to each other, but Nissa was frightened of Xirnan. If he reports to Draigh, it may be too late to stop Xirnan or Nissa from harming others."

"What is the strength of Nissa's group? What are we up against?" Sarah gazed at Beatrice, then at Cristiane. "Cris, do you know how many people were in the house?"

Cristiane and Beatrice looked at each other and shrugged in confusion. Cristiane gestured for Beatrice to answer first.

Beatrice blew out her lips. "It's hard to say. The significant concerns are Xirnan and the half-dozen changelings she has at her New York estate. She's had a changeling or two at her home here in the past, but I haven't been there in years. It's important to remember, Nissa has little power herself unless it is directly after a ceremonial sacrifice. I don't know when she last held that type of meeting. When she was trying to recruit me years ago, some meetings were with animal sacrifice, but as you know from the tapes, the most extreme were humans, always men. What she does at Javier's is theatrics for elitists with a lot of money looking for a thrill. They're not around the club or her estate otherwise."

Cristiane nodded. "She has guards, two that I know of, maybe more."

"Yes. That's right. Fortney and Chuck are her paid personal guards, military trained. They go everywhere with her and live at her properties. Knox could be a problem. He's a bouncer, a Marine veteran, but I don't know whether he is just a bouncer, or he's involved in what goes on outside of the club. I've not seen him at a ceremony, but he's formidable." Beatrice glanced at her daughter. "I think that's it."

"She has a household staff at the New York location." Cristiane stood and walked about the room as she spoke. "There was a maid, Marissa, who seemed new. I got the impression that she either didn't know Xirnan or had limited contact with him. She was terrified when she had a good look at his face. A house of that size, there must be more staff."

"She used to have a groundskeeper and a couple of live-in maids. It wouldn't surprise me if that were still the case."

Cristiane stopped pacing and looked at her mother. "Who feeds the prisoners?"

"What prisoners?" Beatrice clutched her chest.

"In the basement where she held me captive. There are others. I felt their presence, possibly four or five. Xirnan dismissed my questions, but he said they kept people and creatures in the cell blocks. The holding cells are ancient, with thick walls and double locks on doors that are around a foot thick. We'll need a thumb print from Xirnan or Nissa for the modern locks, unless someone has magic that works on that sort of thing. The other is a huge deadbolt with a bank vault spindle to unlatch." Cristiane sat down next to Jarvis and reached for his hand. His fingers interlaced with her own as she squeezed close to him.

Beatrice shook her head. "Wow! I don't know. The large chamber at the base of the stairs was as far as I ventured below the house. I didn't know the basement was so vast beyond the meeting chamber. There were no chandeliers or electrical lighting that I remember. The illumination was by candlelight and the staircase covered from the main room. That's how I sneaked down the first time I witnessed a sacrifice. I doubt the maids or gardener know anything about the activities in the basement."

Sarah stood and straightened her back. "We must hasten. If there are others held captive, we must help before Nissa causes more harm or Xirnan regains his strength. I must consult with Isadora." Sarah started toward the door, then stopped and turned back to Cristiane and Jarvis. "Jarvis, take Cristiane upstairs and get a few hours' rest. We cannot wait until morning. They will realize she has escaped by breakfast. I will have a plan ready shortly. Beatrice, please join me."

Beatrice nodded and rose, following Sarah out the door.

Jeffrey rinsed the kitchen sink with the faucet sprayer as he heard a knock on the front door. He shut off the water and looked at the clock as he picked up the dish towel to dry his hands. *Who is stopping by at this hour?* Several knives, a sword, and the blow gun his buddy gave him when he left the service littered the kitchen countertop. He had spent the night sharpening and cleaning each weapon and every dart to take with him to Jarvis's apartment. Jeffrey covered the display with two dishtowels, but the darts remained visible. Instead of tinkering with the items he'd laid out as if he were readying for a military inspection, he grabbed the darts and shoved them in the cargo pocket of his pants before walking to the door.

Another rap on the door as Jeffrey turned the knob.

Nissa Marth stood outside the door, casually dressed in black slacks and a chicory red quarter-zip pullover sweater. Tennis shoes, covered in dirt and grime, completed the mismatched ensemble. She smiled a broad, closed-mouth grin as she walked past Jeffrey into his house.

Stunned, Jeffrey clenched his jaw as he followed the woman inside and then closed the door behind him. He took a slow breath in and out as he watched her waltz into the living room, leaving muddy footprints in her wake, and sit in the recliner.

"Hello, Mr. Bradford, Jeffrey. May I call you Jeffrey?" Nissa raised her brows over bulging eyes as her smile remained plastered across her face.

Jeffrey had seen her twice before and neither occasion offered the opportunity for him to identify her characteristics. Yet now she seemed strange. Her features exaggerated, or perhaps she'd recently had a facelift or other plastic surgery. "Mr. Bradford is fine. Ms. Marth, isn't it?" Jeffrey moved a few paces to stand behind the sofa facing his unwelcome guest.

"Please, call me Nissa."

"What can I do for you at this late hour, Ms. Marth?"

"Oh, I see. Well, I learned about your daughter missing and thought I'd come by and offer a hand in her search. Is Beatrice home?" Nissa settled elbows on her knees and cupped a fist with her other hand under her chin.

"No, Beatrice isn't here. Thank you for the offer; we have the police and dozens of volunteers helping us. If you check at the police station tomorrow, someone can add you to a volunteer group." Jeffrey moved back to the front door. "Now if you don't mind. I'd like to finish cleaning up before Beatrice comes home."

"Oh, could I wait with you? I'm sure she'd like to hear the messages I have from the other members of our book club." Nissa blinked, fluttering her eyelashes.

What a strange woman. Jeffrey sighed. He knew the book club wasn't real, so what was Nissa doing at the house? Did she know where Cristiane was located? Did she take Cristiane? His fingers balled up in tight fists at his sides. He had to find out. "Fine. Would you like a glass of water or something? I think we have wine."

Nissa rubbed her hands together. "Wine would be lovely. Thank you."

Jeffrey gave her a meek smile as he headed toward the kitchen and flipped light switches for both rooms. Remembering the weapons laid out on the counter, he hesitated in the doorway and turned toward Nissa. Her face and hands were pale white. Her fingers were extraordinarily long as she tucked a loose strand of hair behind a pallid, pointed ear. As he studied her form in more detail, her arms seemed too long, disproportionate to her body. He swallowed hard.

What was she?

He took another step into the kitchen and pulled the blowgun from under the towels. "White or red?" Jeffrey made noise with opening and closing a cupboard and drawers as he slid the combat and survival tactical knives into the back waistband of his pants.

"Red, please."

His phone vibrated. He snatched it off the counter. He couldn't believe what he read from Beatrice. Cristiane was safe. Relieved, he typed back that Nissa was in their living room, wanting to see her.

His jaw fell open when he read her reply.

"That's not Nissa. She's in New York. I'll be there as soon as I can."

"Don't worry. I got it." Jeffrey slid the phone into his side pocket and then pulled out the handful of darts. He shifted to the doorway and peered around to the living room. In the moonlight through the picture window, the creature's hair color morphed in waves of varying hues. Jeffrey shuddered at the sight. Nissa, or what they called a changeling, stood near the framed prints on the mantle, peering at a family photo she held in her left hand. He took a quiet, long breath in and released it, then positioned the blowgun. Jeffrey had one chance before the creature would retaliate. He had to make it count.

He turned and planted his feet shoulder-width apart and took aim while drawing his lungs full. It'd been years since he'd practiced with the weapon, but he had no time for worry. He blew the dart and ducked back behind the doorway to reload. The piercing screech like a wild dog told him he'd made his goal. With another dart loaded, he rushed through the door, found his target pulling at the photo frame adhered to its hand while screaming in agony, and fired off another round at the creature's body. He continued rushing at the creature as the dart struck its eye.

Blood gushed as the fiend wrenched the photo frame from its hand and then yanked the dart from its eye. Jeffrey barreled into it, knocking it into the wall. They wrestled onto the table and fell over each other, scrambling onto the floor. Jeffrey reached for his waistband, but the contorted beast was strong, stronger than he had expected. Pinned down at his shoulders, he twisted and turned, holding the creature back the best he could as the snarling face revealed rows of sharp, dagger-like teeth. "Shit, what are you?"

His grip faltering against the creature. Jeffrey had to move. As he looked for something to use as leverage, the beast pressed its hand into his shoulder. Its lengthy claws dragged across him, tearing through Jeffrey's shirt as it found shoulder flesh, digging deeper across his upper body. The pain seared across Jeffrey's chest as blood oozed out everywhere.

Instinct kicked in and Jeffrey arched his back, throwing the creature off-balance for a split second. Jeffrey used the instant to pull his legs up under the beast and propel it across the room. It landed hard against the window. With no time to recover, Jeffrey jumped up and threw himself over the couch as he heard the shattering of glass and splintering of wood. The fiend bellowed an unholy screech as it lifted itself out of the window mount and dropped with a resounding thud on the floor.

Jeffrey pulled the knives from his waistband and took a couple of deep breaths. As he assessed his injury, he caught sucking sounds and glass pieces tinkle on the hardwood floor. The creature whistled as it inhaled.

"Nissa thought you were a wallflower, but you surprised me tonight." The creature dropped another piece of glass on the floor as Jeffrey stood up from behind the couch. It wheezed through another labored breath. Its skin was shiny, glistening across a contorted, evil sneer. "I heal much quicker than a human. We will finish this tonight and then I will find your daughter and finish her as well—just for fun."

"You will not leave here tonight breathing. If I die trying, I promise you, you will see no one again." Jeffrey tightened his grip on the knives hidden behind his thighs as he glared at the hideous creature. All hint of Nissa was gone. Clothes hung loosely over the thin, whitish frame. The shoes were gone, exposing elongated, skeletal feet with bird-like toes and daggers for nails.

The creature laughed a wet, gurgling chuckle. Then it leaped into the air and cast a wide swipe at Jeffrey as it whooshed past him to come down at his side. It landed on the area rug and continued to slide, losing its balance, and careened, bewildered, into the staircase.

Jeffrey rushed up onto the creature as it crawled, floundering on the stairs, trying to pull itself upright. He straightened his spine and opened his arms wide, standing a few feet away. He held the blades firmly at the hilts and swiped the blades as the creature turned to face him. The fresh, razor-sharp edges swished in the air, slicing through the flesh with ease.

A cry cut short as the changeling's mouth stood agape and its eyes clung to Jeffrey's for an instant. Blood dripped from the gashes on its neck before the head fell back and slumped to the stairs. The crimson fluid gushed over the headless corpse as Jeffrey stepped away from the expanding scene. Droplets fell from the knife tips at his sides, mingling with his own blood falling from his arms. He didn't know what to expect as his eyes followed the body's blood trails to the growing pool on the floor.

Jeffry shook as if chilled. His body throbbed, reminding him of his wounds. He looked at the claw marks along his chest and torso through his shirt. The blood had dried in places, but his arms were another story. The wounds were deep where the creature began dragging its nails across his shoulder and rib cage. Jeffrey realized it had slashed his arm as it jumped through the air past him. He needed stitches. As fatigue crept across his body, the door swung open.

Beatrice barged in with Sarah at her heels. As her eyes landed on the headless corpse, she froze. Her abrupt stop sent Sarah slamming into her backside as she caught sight of Jeffrey.

"Hi, ladies."

"Jeffrey!" Beatrice squatted down to him and looked over his injuries. "Thank the goddess you are all right."

Sarah walked past the couple to inspect the corpse littering the staircase. "You took its head clean off. That's impressive for a human against a changeling." She turned back toward Jeffrey, noticing the extent of his injuries for the first time. "What did you use?"

He raised his arms with both blades clutched at the handles.

"Impressive."

Beatrice moved to his side, being careful to slide her hand under his arm without touching the gash. "Help me move him to the chair. I can mend these injuries quickly."

Once the two women moved Jeffrey to the recliner, Beatrice darted about, gathering herbs and oils to make a salve. She gave Jeffrey some water and covered him with a blanket as she worked. She didn't want him to go into shock as she worked his wounds. "This will hurt in places, but we need to work fast. I need you." Beatrice glanced at Sarah. "We all need you to help tonight. Sarah will fill you in on your assignment as I clean you up."

Jeffrey had battled a shape-shifting creature and lived to tell the tale. He understood now more than ever what Beatrice had been keeping at bay all these years. "Don't worry about my pain. Do whatever you need to do so I can help."

Sarah nodded as Beatrice went to work making the salve. She shared the details of Cristiane's confinement and why she felt they needed to stop Xirnan and Nissa that night. Xirnan was the larger threat of the two. If he contacted Draigh and won favor, the power at his disposal would be infinitely more difficult to fight than what they faced at this moment.

TWENTY-FIVE

Jeffrey fell against the wall as the trio teleported into the grand foyer of Sarah's home.

"Holy crap!" Jeffrey scrambled to get on his feet. He looked over his body and then at his surroundings in disbelief. "Don't tell me you do it all the time."

Amused, Sarah gave him a pat on the shoulder before she started for the stairs. "Rarely. When circumstances necessitate its use. We can't pop in and out in front of the public now, can we? That would draw too much attention." She paused on the first step. "Please go through the main floor and gather everyone to the back patio. I will collect those upstairs. We must hurry."

As the crowd grew in the expansive courtyard, whispers and questions flourished in anticipation of the battle ahead. Members, young and old, joined the fray as the minutes ticked by. Claire and Robyn stood with a few people Cristiane did not know. Not all the coven members could meet the tight timelines. Others would arrive at headquarters to care for injured as needed throughout the night. The two young witches who were initiated when Cristiane was dismissed stood off from most of the other coven members. They looked at Cristiane through the crowd and bowed their heads in acknowledgement. She smiled with a brief nod in reply. Cristiane had joined her father as soon as she heard he was at the coven headquarters. She hugged him tight before looking over the fresh scars on his arm.

"Your mother worked her magic. I'm as good as new. Those marks will fade away soon." Jeffrey reached for his daughter's hand and gave it a squeeze. "Your dad's going to give 'em hell tonight."

"Dad, you're too funny." Cristiane leaned against her dad for a side hug. "So that creature thought you were a wuss, huh? I don't believe anyone will make that mistake again."

"Not tonight. I guarantee it." Jeffrey saw Jarvis and Robby walk through the back door, followed by Sarah, Isadora, and Beatrice. He gestured with his chin toward the doorway. "I think we're getting underway."

The trio of women stopped at the top of the steps. Sarah then stepped forward and put her hands out, waiting for the crowd's chatter to die down.

"Thank you for gathering so quickly to meet this urgent threat. You have each received your assignments and paired with your battle buddies. We have two missions tonight. The group with our non-magical brethren will gain control of Javier's basement chamber after the police clear out the nightclub. Jarvis is your lead. Robby, you are his second-in-command. The ceremony chamber must be cleared and all magical items packaged and delivered to Isadora's home for assessment and disposal. Do not bring items back here to our headquarters.

"The other group will teleport to New York, led by me, along with Beatrice and Cristiane Bradford. The New York estate is large, with underground holding cells, several of which hold people, and possibly creatures, captive. To open the cell doors, we need a fingerprint from Nissa or Xirnan. There are innocents among the magical in the home. Help the innocent to safety without endangering the mission. Xirnan, Nissa Marth, and her changelings are the enemy. Keep your guard up, there could be others."

Sarah gestured to Liam, holding a basket. "Liam will pass through the group. If you do not already have a sigil,

Liam can tattoo one in seconds. Those going with me will receive hex pouches. Always wear it. Xirnan is a powerful demon, and he is hungry for a new body to possess. If he's received Draigh's blessing, he may already be in a different host. We're in for a fight. Let's not give him an opportunity to inhabit one of us."

Jeffrey observed as a young witch received the tattoo. "What is the sigil tattoo?"

Isadora took a step forward. "The tattoo sigil is a modified mystical symbol encircled with runes and imbued with a demon protection spell. I also crafted this sigil to prevent changelings from duplicating your form. That is to prevent any doppelgänger confusion during conflict."

Cristiane accepted the sigil Liam offered and slipped a hex pouch around her neck.

"One last thing. Those injured beyond their capacity to fight are to return to our headquarters for help." Sarah watched as Liam weaved through the crowd. A hex pouch rose out of the basket and hovered in front of a witch, waiting for the recipient to snatch it and place the cord around her neck. Next, Liam stopped in front of Jeffrey as the tattoo quill hovered in the air. Sarah noted his hesitation. "You may refuse the tattoo, but you will not join us if you reject it. As Isadora mentioned, the sigil prevents Xirnan from inhabiting your body and it will prevent a changeling from causing added confusion in battle. You may take both if it makes you feel better. Questions?"

Jeffrey pulled the collar down, revealing his chest, and took the pouch with his free hand. As Liam inked him, he asked, "How many opponents do you expect at each location?"

"An excellent question, Mr. Bradford. At Javier's, we know there are two or three well-trained humans and possibly two changelings. Be careful, there could be more. Those of us traveling to New York, the threat is much larger, so we travel with coven members and experienced witches.

Only the mystical will travel to New York. We expect a dozen or more opponents. The prisoner count is an unknown as well as their threat level."

The crowd chatter rose as people talked to their neighbors. Once Liam returned from distributing the hex pouches, Sarah took one for herself and gave one to each of the women by her side.

Isadora held Sarah's hand. "Be careful, High Priestess. I cannot stand to hear tonight that Xirnan has taken another pupil I trained to lead us."

Beatrice scrunched her face. "What do you mean, another leader?"

Isadora faced Beatrice and took her hand. "The high priestess who led this coven after me served only a brief time before her death. Sarah has remained at the helm ever since. We weren't sure who killed Sarah's predecessor until we saw the ceremonial carvings in your hidden video. From what you've shared with us, the reasonable conclusion is that Xirnan killed Roberta. She bore similar symbols etched on her arms and torso when found in the front of this property. Battle-worn, she couldn't speak and died a few hours later. Although we thought Nissa and the cult might be involved in her murder, we had nothing substantial to support our hunch until now."

Guilt washed over Beatrice as she hung her head. "I wish I'd acted sooner. So much tragedy."

"You're here now. That's what matters." Sarah clasped her free hand over Beatrice's and closed the circle among the three women. "We have the power within us to defeat this evil. We will prevail."

Sarah led a chant. The crowd quieted to a comforting silence as Sarah's voice rose into the night air. The group soon joined in until the positive vibrations wove through everyone. Mother Goddess's mystical adrenaline graced each of them. After chanting several rounds, the three women raised their hands and in unison ended their prayer. "Blessed be."

Confident energy filled the midnight air as the larger group splintered into smaller groups or stood beside their battle buddies. Jarvis, Liam, and Robby stood with Jeffrey and a few others, ready to leave for the nightclub. Cristiane embraced Jarvis, then her father, and wished the group good luck. Zack hugged and kissed Liam before he made his way up the steps with Cristiane, his battle buddy, to join her mother and the high priestess.

Cristiane hugged Isadora and then turned to Sarah.

All awaited the high priestess's word.

Sarah returned to the gathering after saying farewell to Isadora. "It is time."

Jarvis and Liam rode together in a dark gray panel van to the nightclub. Shelves lined either side of the cargo area, loaded with containers and bags of all sizes to gather items found in the club's basement. Robby followed in his car with Jeffrey and two other witches, Darrell and Joe. As Jarvis and Robby parked their vehicles in the alley and the men opened the doors to step out, Jeffrey stopped and slid back into the car as a uniformed police officer turned the corner and walked toward them. Jarvis turned to his companions and motioned for everyone to stay where they were.

The officer recognized Jarvis. "Hey, Detective Morris. Good to see you." The man waved a thumb back over his shoulder. "We cleared the club without trouble. The fire department couldn't find a gas leak after all, but dispatch said you were coming over anyway. What's the problem?"

"Officer Jackson, right?" Jarvis kept walking toward the officer, closing the gap and keeping distance between the vehicles and the young, uniformed cop. "Looks like the owner is under investigation. We're waiting on the judge to authorize a search warrant, but with everyone cleared from the building, the boss let me come out and get a head start on the search. Is the owner still here?"

"Couldn't reach her. The manager is Knox. He's inside by the bar, still trying to reach Ms. Marth."

"Any other lingering employees?"

"I don't think so. It's quiet." Officer Jackson looked at his watch. "You need me to stick around and help?"

"No. You go on home. I have a few detectives with me. No need to keep you wrapped up in this if the judge denies the warrant." They shook hands and Jarvis thanked Jackson for waiting on him. Jarvis watched the young man walk back to the squad car and then drive off.

After the squad car was out of view, Jarvis waved to the others. "There's one guy, Knox, inside at the bar. Jackson didn't see anyone else, but there could be others."

Jeffrey stepped close to Jarvis. "Let me talk with Knox, one veteran to another. According to Cris, he's the Marine. It'll be obvious if he's going to be a problem. You do your thing to find anyone hiding before we pull out the equipment."

"That's a good plan. Robby, you lead the others through that side door. I'll go in the front with Mr. Bradford. If you don't have your weapons, grab them now."

Jarvis put a hand on his holster and lifted the snap that held his 9mm side-arm secure. He bent down and double-checked his backup piece, a .38 Special strapped above his ankle as he waited for the others to gather their weapons.

Robby opened the truck and the five men plunged in. The sound of metal clinking against metal bounced off the narrow alley walls, adding to the eeriness of the night.

After several seconds, Jeffrey came around the vehicle, shoving a .45 into the front of his pants. "Let's go."

Jarvis gazed at Cristiane's dad as he came closer. He had thought the man was quiet and unskilled, but tonight proved his usual demeanor was deceiving. The man walking toward him was anything but meek. He approached with purpose and a confidence military bearing. He knew how to fight. Jarvis nodded and let him pass by. As Jeffrey moved in front, Jarvis noted Cristiane's father had two blood-stained knives looped into his waistband. He smiled as they opened the front door.

"Hey, who the hell are you?" Knox rounded the end of the bar with a 12-gauge shotgun in his hands.

"Easy now. Knox, right? I'm Jeffrey Bradford. This is Detective Jarvis Morris. We'd like to talk with you about the gas leak and the owner." Jeffrey raised his hands as he closed the distance, showing his weapon as he approached. Jarvis followed with his weapon and shield visible. Jeffrey stood with his legs shoulder-width apart, positioning himself out from the bar counter, between Jarvis and Knox, but close enough to react if Knox moved a muscle. "That's a nice Mossberg 590. It'd be better for everyone if you lowered it."

"Sorry, man. It's been a crazy night." Knox put the shotgun behind the bar and offered his hand to Jarvis. Jarvis shook it, then motioned to take a seat at the bar. "I thought the cops left."

"The uniforms, yes, but I'm a detective. We have questions." Jarvis looked into the room's recesses. Not seeing another person, he turned his attention to Knox. "Anyone left in the building?"

"One guard is upstairs in the security room. Could be folks in the basement and the boss's office." Knox motioned toward each room above. "There wasn't a gas leak, was there? The cops didn't bother sweeping through every room to evacuate, just the patrons and the regular staff. What's going on?"

Knox sat on the bar stool casually, but Jeffrey noted both feet were on the floor and Knox was leaning forward, ready to move if the situation warranted action. Jeffrey took a step closer. "Do you have access to the basement?"

"No, that's Ms. Marth's building security and close associates only. I'm a bouncer, but since Malin has been missing, I've been the club manager, too." Knox stood up and Jeffrey put his hand on the pistol grip. Knox turned and faced him. "I've been cool, but you're making me anxious, Bradford. Someone mind telling me what the fuck this is about? Now."

Jarvis slapped a hand on the bar. "I'm going to ask Mr. Bradford to check the control room so we can access the basement. I have associates coming in from the alley. We suspect your boss of orchestrating the deaths of two individuals, your missing manager, Malin, and a young man, David Howson. Knox, we need to know if you're a threat and what other risks we face in this facility."

Knox lowered himself onto the stool and nodded that he understood. "I knew she was shady, but I needed the job. I take care of club clientele who get out of hand, but the other mess, I don't get involved. She keeps company with some bizarre people, to include her guards. Fortney is in the security room now." Knox tossed his chin in the direction of the control room above the dance floor.

Jarvis called to Robby to head toward the security office, then nodded to Jeffrey to go ahead. "I'll tell Knox what's going on. Let me know if you guys need backup."

"Ms. Marth's office should be empty, but I rarely go there unless she calls me. Hide that pistol. Security has cameras covering the club."

"Little late for that." Jeffrey turned toward the staircase. Knox's eyes were drawn to the two blood-stained combat knives strapped to Bradford's back as he walked away.

Jarvis stayed and told Knox about the cult and Nissa's ceremonies, the sacrifices, and the video and photos he and others had of the basement rooms. Jarvis spoke cautiously of Xirnan and asked if Knox had witnessed activities that were hard to explain. "Keep an open mind. If you remember seeing something out of the ordinary, tell me."

"Hey, Xirnan is a creepy bastard, but I haven't seen him do anything weird. The dude's been dead for years, except no one's told him." Knox rubbed the scruff on his chin. "I've seen some crazy shit while in the Corps. Get to whatever you're dancing around. I'll help however I can."

Jarvis studied Knox for a moment. "I have no police authority to be here, but it's imperative that we strike tonight. She has supernatural beings, changelings, around her always. We need to eliminate them. Ms. Marth held a friend of David Howson's prisoner in New York last night until she could escape and make it back to Andover. Nissa Marth has security and these creatures at both locations. We have a brief window to act and break up this cult, capture Ms. Marth, and possibly destroy Xirnan."

"Destroy Xirnan? That geriatric bag of bones is going to die any day."

"That bag of bones is not human. He is a demon." Jarvis stopped to see how Knox received the information, but Knox appeared unfazed. "If he changes hosts, as we suspect he will any day, he'll be much harder to defeat. I don't have time to give you a lesson on mystical creatures. We're up against evil. As a Marine, I know you've encountered evil, but this is a darkness few humans face without dire consequences. If you can keep the front clear, we'll handle anything or anyone in the remainder of the building."

Knox stood and turned the corner of the bar, grabbing the 12-gauge.

Jarvis stood, placing a hand on his 9mm side arm, ready to draw.

Knox pointed the shotgun barrel toward the ceiling as he met Jarvis's eyes. "Of course I can help, but I can't sit and watch a door. I am responsible for this business while my boss is away. I go where you go." Knox pumped the tactical 9-shot with one swift motion, defying the hefty weight of the weapon.

"Fine but stay behind me. I can't have civilians getting hurt." Jarvis tugged on his side arm and chambered a round as both heard a crash, then gunfire.

"They're in the security room."

Nissa's guard, Fortney, turned from the club's security office monitors as Jeffrey strode across the nightclub floor toward the stairs. Confused by Knox chatting with the armed man, she waited for the visitor to come through her door.

It was taking too long.

Fortney turned back to the monitors. Knox had the shotgun in his hand but wasn't shooting. Whatever was happening, a bad feeling grew in the pit of her stomach.

Jeffrey knocked on the security room door then stepped away, along the wall. "Jeffrey Bradford, Beatrice's husband. I'd like to talk with you."

"You came to talk carrying a pistol and knives? I don't think so. Get out of here." Fortney pulled a pistol from the drop-leg holster attached to her right hip and aimed it at the door.

"I'd hoped you'd be reasonable. We simply need the keys to investigate the basement."

"Drop dead, asshole." Fortney fired a warning shot through the door.

Jeffrey remained a few feet away while Robby and the other witches moved up the stairs without a sound. They joined him as the bullet flew by. Jeffrey said, "Fortney, the guard inside, will not cooperate. Keys to the basement are in here. Knox doesn't know if anyone is in Nissa's office. It should be empty but stay sharp."

"You still there, Mr. Bradford?"

The snarl in her voice grated Robby. He tilted his head and raised a brow as he leaned in close to Jeffrey. "I don't think she's happy with you."

Jeffrey shook his head. "She didn't give me a chance to flash my charm."

Robby nodded as he motioned Liam and Darrel toward Nissa's office. The two witches rose into the air and glided past the security door, and then dropped to stroll the rest of the catwalk toward Nissa's office, leaving Jeffrey, Robby, and Joe to handle the security room. "Once I get the door open, you two be ready." Robby stepped away from the wall with his fingers curled as a ball of light formed and grew between his hands. Within seconds, the mass of churning electrons pulsed.

Robby thrust the ball of energy toward the wooden door, shattering it to pieces. As he dodged to the side, a round flew over his head. Joe flung a mystical shield as he tumbled sideways into the room, blocking the continuing fire from the guard. Joe's barricade allowed Jeffrey and Robby to follow him into the expansive space. Two rows of monitors lined the opposite wall with a console that stretched the length of the room and two tall-back executive chairs in front of the console so security could watch over the club's activities.

Jeffrey discovered Fortney ducking behind a chair while aiming for Joe, just below his shield. Jeffrey squeezed a round into her lower leg. The bullet passed through her flesh and landed in the wall under the desk. She screamed in agony as the shot meant for Joe embedded in the ceiling. She dropped the pistol and reached toward her foot. Jeffrey looked for the wound and found the stippling mark just above the ankle, blood now oozing from the injury. Robby raised the woman into the air as she pulled a small revolver from the holster under her opposite arm and fired two shots toward Jeffrey.

As the bullet whizzed by, Jeffrey canted in the opposite direction. He felt heat near his eye and raised fingers to his temple. Blood. Jeffrey responded with a round to her shoulder and one to her forehead. Fortney's head dropped to her chest. Robby let his hand fall to his side, allowing their target to drop to the floor in a heap.

Liam and Darrel appeared in the doorway as Joe tossed a keyring to Robby. Liam peered around the room, noting each of his teammates was safe. He went to Jeffrey and assessed the wound. "It grazed the surface. The bleeding is already stopping."

"Thanks. It can wait, then."

Robby flipped through the keys, looking at the labels. "Anyone in Nissa's office?"

"No one's there, but there are some odd artifacts. We need to take some items to Isadora for analysis," Darrel said as he walked to the monitoring station and sat down in the chair not occupied by Fortney's dead body. He twirled in the seat toward his companions. "Jarvis may want to search through the tapes here, too."

"Agreed, but let's get the basement chamber secured first." Robby held up a key and shook it. "I think this is it."

The witches and Jeffrey met Knox and Jarvis at the stairs.

Robby handed Jarvis the key. "I think this is what we need. Fortney is dead."

Jarvis turned to Knox. "Last chance. You don't need to get into this."

"I told you, I go where you go."

The witches teleported to the second floor of Nissa's New York estate. Because both Beatrice and Cristiane knew the location, the group could travel together without incident. After Beatrice pointed out rooms on the second floor and told Zack and Cristiane to wait for their return, she and Sarah vanished from sight. After ten minutes, they reappeared without explanation.

Beatrice smiled at her daughter's quizzical stare as Sarah gathered the group for a final word.

The teams dispersed after Sarah gave their assignments—one team to find the staff and take them to a safe location, and the other to the basement chambers. If they could not breach the holding cells, then they were to wait for the fingerprint delivery.

Beatrice and Sarah started in front of the door where Cristiane was captive a few hours earlier, the same room Beatrice had previously occupied decades ago. The door stood ajar, indicating Xirnan knew Cristiane had escaped, but did he know when? Sarah and Beatrice, along with Cristiane and Zack, were to start on the second floor and work their way to the basement level and help escort prisoners from the holding cells once they had the thumb print to open locks.

Sarah turned to Beatrice and the two young witches. "Zack and Cristiane, you two are battle buddies, but the four of us are going to stay together as much as possible. Cristiane and I can communicate telepathically if we separate."

"We can? I don't know. Xirnan could reach me, but I haven't tried it myself." Cristiane bit at her nails while she tapped a foot on the floor.

"Don't worry." Sarah put a hand on Cristiane's shoulder. "We don't have time to practice. I'm sure it will work. Let's search this floor starting over here. Try to draw on that power as we proceed. I'll let you know when I hear you." Sarah moved right and continued down the hall.

"Okay. I guess." Cristiane bent her head, uncertain if she could muster the power on a whim. She followed next to Zack as the two older witches led the way.

Cristiane found Nissa's guard, Chuck, in the first room and cast a sound sleep spell to keep him from waking. Zack and Beatrice bound and gagged him as Sarah waited to transport him to the coven headquarters so they could continue their quest.

Once Sarah returned, the foursome went on with their mission.

After searching most of the second floor, the witches found nothing of concern. To the left of Nissa's bedchamber, the witches hesitated in the doorway of a room stocked with charmed figures. A bookshelf dedicated to the dark arts and an uncanny obsession with demon figurines lined a wall. It felt as if each figurine followed them about the room with sparkling eyes made of gems, each demon with a different eye color. Centered between two windows was the largest figure of all, a representation of Lamashtu with the features engorged and exaggerated. Cristiane shuddered as she glared into its eyes, remembering the artifact she'd touched from her mother's trunk. The spirit that had materialized from within her mind looked eerily similar. The figurine in front of her was more elaborate, but the eyes haunted Cristiane. As she turned to move to the next figure, she glanced back, thinking she'd noticed the eyes brighten. Beatrice caught her attention and Cristiane moved over to see what her mother had found.

Inscribed on the second largest figure was the word Rolvachi. The sculpture sat off from the others. "This figurine doesn't belong in a room of unnamed demons surrounding the demon goddess. Lamashtu is obviously the centerpiece." Beatrice considered the statue, being careful not to touch it. She peered along the back and found an inscription on the base.

"When your obsession fades, I will welcome you home. ~ Draigh."

"That's a fascinating piece, Beatrice." Sarah came up along the opposite side and studied the sculpture. "It appears new, unlike the others. I don't sense an enchantment, do you?"

"It's an odd addition to the collection. Rolvachi is a whole different league. It doesn't fit. To add to the peculiarity, I agree, it is not an artifact, but crafted within the past few years." Beatrice stepped back so she could look over the entire collection.

"What is a Rolvachi?" Zack asked Beatrice as he and Cristiane came to her side.

"Rolvachi is one of the greatest mysterious creatures in recorded history. Folklore varies throughout the world, but most agree on his origins. He leads legions of demons and has superior power to command the dead. Modern culture would have you believe vampires are a recent phenomenon—myth, but Rolvachi dates to the Indus Valley, one of the first civilizations on earth. Of course, Lamashtu dates back to the same era, but to the Mesopotamian civilization. Perhaps that period is the connection, but recent discoveries suggest the Indus Valley predates Mesopotamia by as much as 200 years."

"This is important, but we must remain mission focused. Thank you, Beatrice." Sarah glanced over the figures one last time, then exited toward the last room to explore. While Cristiane filed out of the room behind the others, she caught a movement in the corner of her eye. As she glanced back at Lamashtu, she thought the figure had moved, but as she looked on, she shook her head and left.

Sarah reached Nissa's double doors as the others joined her. She eased the entry open without a sound. The group moved into the room in silence, gathering around the occupant. Nissa dozed in a palatial canopy bed that sat high above the floor. Cristiane and Zack looked at each other as Beatrice leaned over her tormentor. With a set jaw, a darkness flitted across her eyes. Sarah's fingers brushed Beatrice's arm to move her back.

Nissa sprang, clutched Beatrice by the neck with one hand and clawed at her face with the other. Sarah brandished a shield as she threw fire at their target from her other hand to no avail.

Deflected by an invisible barrier, the fireballs flew instead toward Cristiane and Zack as they ducked and sought cover. The curtains, rugs, and other fabrics caught fire and smoke began to fill the room. Cristiane and Zack flung water orbs at the growing flames, creating more blinding smoke as they worked at a feverish pace.

Beatrice conjured sharp spikes and jabbed Nissa across her face and body. Nissa let go and reeled from the pain, flinging herself toward Cristiane and Zack. Cristiane raised a shield as she stepped back toward the doorway.

Sarah thwarted the flames on her side of the room and saw Nissa fall. "Bind her now!"

Cristiane felt a mysterious tremor in her head before she registered the command. "Huh?"

Zack acted and whipped a magical thread toward Nissa. As the thread curled around a leg, the room spun with a violent wind. A thunderous boom blasted the witches to every corner. Cristiane's body flew out the door, turning over itself before banging into a wall at the hall's far end. Sarah and Beatrice slammed into furniture as Zack fell, hitting his head against a table corner.

Sarah shook the fog from her head and peered through the smoke-filled room for her witches. She shook Beatrice awake and found Zack lying at the room's entrance. As she pulled him close, her eyes searched for the missing witch. "Where is Cristiane?"

Beatrice waved a hand and cleared the air. A few lingering flames dwindled away, revealing a massive energy dome mere feet from the witches. Inside, Nissa hovered at the hand of a massive churning shadow taking shape. As Cristiane crawled in from the hallway, the murky figure took shape as Beatrice pulled her daughter close. Lamashtu.

"Niiiissaaaa." Lamashtu pulled her close. "Yooou hid him from meeee. Wheeere is the boy chiiiild?"

"H-h-he's gone. D-dead," Nissa choked while clawing at her throat. Her hands flew to her sides, rigid, as her body inched higher in the air.

"Yooou faaaailed."

"No! No! No! I c-can get you another—his sister is there. There, behind you."

Silence filled the room for several seconds. Then Nissa bellowed a blood-curdling scream as blood dripped from her hairline. She thrashed while the shadow pulled flesh away from bone and muscle. As the screams continued, Sarah motioned for her group to clear the room. Cristiane crawled out first, followed by Zack and the two senior witches. They rose and stared as the skin pulled down Nissa's face and neck. The whites of her eyes and teeth were awash in a sea of crimson through the agonizing screams. Lamashtu lapped at the blood with its tongue as gurgling laughter continued while it ignored the surrounding witches. Nissa's hide hung as if the demon were preparing an animal leather for the market. While the skinning persisted, Sarah ushered the others toward the exit. As the Beatrice followed the others out the door, the demon spirit ripped at Nissa's body. The backdrop of crunching and popping bones and cartilage caused them all to jump and shudder as they turned back to see the carnage. Lamashtu's figure formed massive teeth and jaws and drilled its teeth into Nissa's skinless shoulder.

Nissa's shrieks fell silent.

Beatrice hurried to close the doors and ward them with locking spells.

Zack blew out a shaky breath. "Should we continue searching for Xirnan?"

"We must." Sarah turned toward the doors again. "I'll remain here. If this entity moves beyond Nissa, we must leave."

"You can't stay here!" Beatrice insisted in a faint voice as she glared at Sarah. "Lamashtu will destroy anyone in her path."

"Normally I would agree, but if that were her intent, she would have killed us. Nissa was her target—for betrayal. Lamashtu was after payback. Your blood drew her in, like Cristiane's blood did in your altar room." Sarah kept her eye on the door as she shoved Beatrice forward. "But now we must find Xirnan. Go!"

TWENTY-SIX

Back at Javier's, the men amassed in the basement. Witches guided the way, establishing a semi-circle formation around Jeffrey and Knox as they crept forward. Jarvis flicked on the lights and led from the front. Jeffrey and Knox followed in the middle as they approached the ceremony chamber doors. As they passed a door on their right, a creature burst through and clawed at Darrel, sending him to the floor. Liam reacted by casting the demonic elf to the wall, impeding the demon's chance at escape, its elongated appendages flailing. It screeched, wriggling under confinement. Its gray skin appeared to molt and move as its hair morphed into shades of green, blue, and pink over and over. The face mutated between an angelic childlike cupid to a harsh, white hellish face with black and red eyes.

With mouth agape, Knox moved close, holding the shotgun, ready to fire. Within inches, he eyed the creature squirm and mutate through its changes. "What the hell? Shiiiiit!"

"Met my first one tonight, too, brother. Best advice— shoot that abomination's head clean off before it gets free." Jeffrey pulled his knives out, ready to finish the changeling off if Knox didn't.

Knox stared as the creature transformed into his own face. "Oh, hell no." He took a step back and squeezed the trigger. Bits of flesh scattered through the grand hall, landing on the floor as gelatinous goo. The body, fixed in a thin, whitish form, slid to the ground and dissolved into the same mess as the head. Knox swallowed the bile that rose in his throat.

"Nasty bastards." Jeffrey assessed Darrel's wound. "Go back to headquarters if you're mauled again. Those are some deep cuts."

"I'm good. Thanks." Darrel cast a healing spell over the wounds, then took his place in the formation. "Let's get this over with."

Jarvis nodded and stepped toward the chamber wall. He'd studied David's photos multiple times to ensure he knew the layout. Everyone knew it forward and backward but Knox. If he was telling the truth, he was going in blind. "Knox, you stay close. Touch nothing." Once Knox acknowledged, Jarvis slid the door and stepped inside, providing cover as the men followed him into the darkness.

As the men waited for their eyes to adjust to the dark, Jarvis shifted to his left and found a light switch. The room lit up like a high school gymnasium. A chorus of groans erupted.

"Jeez, man. A little warning next time." Joe covered his eyes, mumbling under his breath.

The men dispersed after the commotion ended. Jarvis noticed the room appeared the same as the photos David provided to Cristiane. The big identifiers remained a large tapestry with the goat's face hung on the wall, shelves held the same artifacts, and the blood-stained altar appeared as they were in the pictures. As Jarvis stood in the middle of the room and snapped photos in full light, many of the items appeared staged. These ceremonies weren't for real. They were gimmicks to lure rich clientele, wanting a titillating experience, something way off the beaten track. Still, Jarvis remembered, Beatrice said the true rituals were infrequent. There could be evidence to preserve, and cursed objects mixed in with the superficial.

Jarvis watched as the men investigated every oddity. David's photos didn't cover the far-left room, so Jarvis headed in that direction. He heard muted voices and rattling metal as he approached the door. Jarvis motioned for the other men to be quiet as he pulled the pistol from its holster. Once the others were near, the knob turned under his command. The door swung open.

A creature jumped into Jarvis's face. He forced it against the wall and blasted a shot under its gnashing jaws as a flurry of commotion rushed behind him. Another round and razor-sharp teeth flew out with bits of its head as Jarvis let it drop to the deck. Sticky goo spread out as Jarvis stepped over the mess.

Jeffrey struggled with a changeling chewing on his shoulder. He slit its throat but fell, clutching his bloody shoulder as the monster reached for him. Jarvis rushed in and pulled the ugly elf through the air by its head, smashing it into cages lining the wall. Two rounds finished the job. Jarvis shoved his palm onto Jeffrey's shoulder to fend off the blood flow.

A tiny, lithe creature jumped onto Knox's shoulder. He snatched it by the head and flung it across the room. Nails caught his face. Knox couldn't believe how fast the bugger was as he watched it hop over and among the shelves all while Knox blasted holes into the ceiling and walls. He managed a shot to the creature's arm, leaving its hand dangling with slop as it scurried to the tall corner of a shelf. Knox stacked cages and climbed atop them as the chaos and carnage mounted behind him.

A tall one hopped at Robby, taking a tip of his ear as it hurtled past.

Robby summoned the wind in reply.

The monster's lengthy hands clutched a shelf as the vortex gathered strength. It gnashed and growled as tornado-like tendrils pulled tufts of colored hair from its head. As the hair fell to the floor, each batch turned a matte gray before mutating to slime.

Liam struggled to contain another with Joe as Darrel fought two creatures on his own. Within seconds, they littered Darrel with bite marks. One beast climbed Darrel like a tree, using its jagged teeth to rip through the witch's neck and rip out vertebrae. Darrel slumped to the ground in a heap. The two creatures crawled onto Darrel as he screamed, blood gushing from the hole at the base of his skull. The creatures clenched onto joints and snarled as they pulled at their prize, sucking on synovial fluid with greed.

"Darrel!" Liam blasted the creature he was holding off with a fireball and ran to Darrel's side as Joe flung daggers at their target.

Liam hurled more fireballs at the two creatures as they chomped at Darrel's joints like ravenous dogs. Without regard to the fire scorching their flesh, the child-size beasts ate their feast as Darrel ceased to breathe.

Jarvis grabbed Jeffrey's hand and jammed it over the wounded shoulder. "Don't move this." He stood and took his pistols, blasting round after round at one of the two creatures overtop Darrel.

Liam glared, his hands outstretched with fingers taut and curled at the tips, generating a crushing force-field around one feasting creature. As it stopped gnawing on Darrel's wrist and cowered, Liam tightened his hold. Cartilage cracked and its body oozed as Liam constricted the evil elf until the pressure squashed it.

Shocked, Jarvis and Joe stood motionless as the crumpled creature oozed onto the floor.

The maelstrom Robby gathered around his target broke off thick arm-like extensions and pulled the panicked creature from the shelf edge. It barred its teeth while reaching for Robby. With one quick motion, the whirlwind whipped the monster's head until it flung away and bounced off the ceiling. Robby dropped his hands, exhausted. He noticed Darrel as he looked about the bloodshed.

A shotgun blast rang through the silence. Then another demon child flopped to the ground, half its head gone, as Knox jumped from the stacked cages.

Liam knelt beside Darrel. Gently, he lifted Darrel's head and placed it on his knees. He rocked back and forth while murmuring a prayer over his departed friend.

Jarvis and Knox helped Jeffrey to his feet. Robby and Joe put their hands on Liam's shoulders.

"Robby, I need you to take Darrel and Mr. Bradford back to the coven. Knox, you, too." Jarvis waved off Knox's attempt to debate. "Don't argue. We have a lot to clean up and remove. I can't be worrying about you touching the wrong thing."

Jeffrey released a ragged breath, turning to Knox. "He's right. They can work faster without us."

The three witches ran to the staircase and hurried down the steps. As they turned on the landing, Xirnan appeared. Beatrice and Zack rushed him, brandishing a shield as Cristiane teleported to the first floor behind Xirnan and blasted him forward into the shield.

Zack screamed, holding his head and buckling to his knees. Xirnan grinned as he levitated above the confusion and settled at the top of the stairs. Beatrice grabbed Zack and disappeared from sight.

Cristiane tried to reach Sarah. "Xirnan's on the second floor." But she didn't feel the connection. She saw his footstep down another tread. A split-second and Xirnan would see her. She vanished.

Cristiane banged her head on the cupboard edge as she materialized. "Shit!" Her fingers rubbed the growing knot on her forehead.

"Cris?" Beatrice slid the pantry door open a crack and peered out.

"Mom? What are you doing in there?" Cristiane threw a nervous glance down the hall as she approached the door.

"Zack, his mind is hostage. I'm not sure." Beatrice glanced over her shoulder at Zack, cowering in the corner, holding his head, whimpering in pain. "I can't figure out what's happening in there."

"What do I do?" Cristiane peered over her shoulder.

"I'll provide a distraction. We'll lure Xirnan to the far room, the study at the opposite end of the staircase, and we can corner him there."

"Yes, but he knows this house."

"The far room has a devil's trap drawn on the floor. He won't see it until we sweep the rug away. If we can get him standing in it, then he's caught. When Sarah and I vanished upstairs, we marked two snares in the house. The other trap is in the basement. Go now. There's a gun in the study's corner. Salt pellets." Beatrice rushed past Cristiane to the foot of the stairs.

Cristiane tried to connect her mind to Sarah and felt a slight awareness, but nothing more. As she peeked down the hallway, she saw Beatrice walking backward as Xirnan came into view.

Beatrice turned and ran in Cristiane's direction, throwing fire bolts as she went, but Xirnan was gaining ground.

His hands were behind his back as he glided toward her.

As Beatrice reached the room's entry point, Cristiane vanished, and then materialized along the interior wall opposite the entrance.

Xirnan disappeared from the hall and reappeared in front of Beatrice, inside the study, exactly where they wanted him.

Sarah felt Cristiane's voice tug at her mind, but she was busy warding off Nissa's room from the rest of the house. She had to contain the demon until the others were safe. This unknown was too big to handle in the chaotic mix. She reached out to Cristiane with the sight Mother Goddess gave her to see what Cristiane saw. "What's happening?"

Relieved, Cristiane answered in haste. "Xirnan—captured in the study."

"On my way." Sarah put the final enchantments on the room and warded half the hallway for good measure.

Cristiane stood her ground, clutching the gun in her hands as Xirnan banged into the devil's trap's invisible containment wall. She whisked the rug away, revealing the deception.

Caught unaware, Xirnan looked down, realizing his mistake. "Witches—your tricks cannot hold me." Yet his bony hands pressed out as he went around the circumference, desperate for escape.

Beatrice caught her breath. Pleased with his capture, she felt the years of torment and anguish well up, filling her with rage. "You and Nissa robbed years of happiness from my life. The vile evil I've had to witness because of your shroud of darkness attached to me. But no more. That twisted demon upstairs destroyed Nissa without a thought."

Xirnan took a step back in the circle. "Lamashtu killed Nissa? Then the betrayal was true." He shook his head as a sneer spread across his pale lips. "I can return to Draigh."

"I don't think so. You're not leaving here in one piece." Cristiane came up alongside her mother.

Sarah appeared in a flash.

"This is interesting. Didn't you two hate each other?" Xirnan glanced from Beatrice to Sarah, then back.

Beatrice snatched the salt gun from Cristiane. "Because you and that bitch twisted us against each other. Now it's your turn to writhe in pain."

Xirnan screeched as the salt pellets braised his skin. Black smoke trailed the marks. Beatrice hit him repeatedly until Sarah pulled the weapon from her hands. Murky smoke filled the room, smelling of charred flesh and decaying meat.

"We mustn't hurt the man while banishing the demon. Beatrice, I understand your anguish, but this is not the means." Sarah moved the gun and glanced at Cristiane. "Look for something we can use for containment, like an urn or large vase. The closure must be secure. Even a kitchen container will suffice if it has a sealed lid."

Cristiane popped into the kitchen and looked in on Zack. Curled into a ball and moaning, his hands and arms wrapped about, cradling his head. "Hang in there, Zack. Once we contain Xirnan, I think you'll be free." She slid the door but stopped as she saw glass canisters on a tall shelf. Searching, she located one with a tight clasp she thought was large enough to hold a demon's spirit, then she vanished back to the study.

As Cristiane emerged, she noticed Sarah battling an enormous dog. Her mother was teetering, holding onto the beast's hindquarters as her toes were close to smudging Xirnan's trap.

Sarah bellowed over the creature's growls. "I'm taking the werewolf. You handle Xirnan."

Beatrice jumped into the circle and then turned toward Sarah as a blood-curdling scream cut off.

Sarah and the lycanthrope vanished.

Xirnan grabbed Beatrice, suspending her by her neck. Cristiane jumped into the circle behind the demon. She dropped the canister, reaching for her iron knife, and stabbed Xirnan's side over and over, triggering the end of his magical grasp of Beatrice.

Her mother fell gasping.

"Mom. I got him." Cristiane held the blade deep into his side as Xirnan hissed. "Open the container. I can get him out."

Beatrice grabbed the container but opened the hex pouch around her neck at the same time. She grabbed a handful of its contents and threw it at him.

Iron pellets and salt elicited another cry from the demon as he coughed blood. His breath labored, he fought to spit out the words. "You bitch. You'll pay."

"Mom!" Cristiane pulled the silver rope from her bracelets into the air and bound Xirnan's body in place as she recited an incantation. "Stop burning him! We need that fingerprint, remember?"

"Ugh. Sorry. You're right." Beatrice sucked in and then blew out a deep breath.

Xirnan twisted against the Mother Goddess's silver threads.

Beatrice held Xirnan's head still with his mouth agape as Cristiane cast a spell to expand the salt in her pouch. Iron pellets and the other items dropped out as the bag filled with salt granules. Once it hung heavy from her neck, she opened the container and flipped it over. "Mom, I'm going to float above him and pour the salt. Keep his head still so Xirnan's spirit flows into the canister. Got it?"

"You can float?" Beatrice seemed surprised and almost let her hold on Xirnan slip.

"I have the coven's powers on loan, and a few gifts from the Horned One and Mother Goddess." Cristiane rolled her eyes. "Can we get this over with, please?"

"Yes, of course."

Cristiane hovered a few feet off the ground as the open pouch lifted over the demon's gaping mouth. As salt poured in, Xirnan fought to move out of the flow, to no avail. Beatrice held him firmly in place, his mouth stretched wide.

Cristiane peered into his face with the canister ready. Fire burned in his eyes as he willed the body to fight against the restraints. As a blackness mingled with the salt in his mouth, Cristiane felt his spirit fumble.

Sullied by the witches' magic, the earthly body grew lax as Xirnan's efforts turned internal. The shadow, his essence, searched for escape, an avenue for his spirit to live on. As if on fire, the murkiness rumbled from within the frail flesh, churning as it crawled upward.

Cristiane ensured escape was impossible. As the last of the salt fell, she shoved the container over the old man's mouth and watched as a blackness swirled, filling the canister. The body faltered. Cristiane clasped the canister lid, double-checking the latch to ensure the seal was firm.

Beatrice guided the body down to the floor as Cristiane's feet landed. An old man with a weak pulse and shallow breath remained. He wouldn't last much longer.

Cristiane placed Xirnan's spirit on the table and helped her mother carry the old man to the sofa. They covered him with a blanket and sat vigil.

A muffled groan under the blanket roused the witches from their seats. Beatrice placed a hand on his arm. "Hello? Can you tell us your name?"

Cristiane placed a finger on his neck. "His pulse is barely noticeable."

The man moved his lips. Beatrice moved closer and waited. He moved again. She looked at her daughter. "I can't make out what he's trying to say."

Cristiane leaned forward and concentrated on the old man. She blocked out every other noise and focused her intent until she finished watching his mouth, then she straightened. "Peter Hains. Is that your name?"

A faint nod.

"We're with you, Peter. Rest easy." Beatrice held his hand.

Within minutes, Cristiane watched as Peter's spirit rose from his body and paused. "It's okay. Go toward the others. The demon is gone. You're free."

He bowed and turned, his apparition disappearing through the far wall.

"Is he gone?" Beatrice followed Cristiane's eyes to the wall as she pulled the blanket away from a lifeless hand.

"Yes. You can take the finger now."

TWENTY-SEVEN

Sarah's New York team lost one member, Claire, to the werewolf, the only creature in the basement prison. He had spent weeks locked in the putrid holding cell, undermining the integrity of the door by banging against it and clawing at the surrounding stones. The witches sensed the surrounding damage and focused efforts to release the prisoner. Unwittingly, the witches cast release spells against the compromised door of the lycanthrope. The enraged beast met the witches as it barreled through the opening, seeking escape. It came out fighting—and the witches lost Claire in the ensuing battle.

Later, Peter Hains' finger opened the remaining prison doors. Several were empty, but they found three scared and hungry humans in the search. Zack escorted them; a pregnant woman, a small child, and a man, to the local police department. The adult survivors would explain their capture and circumstances to authorities. All hoped someone would soon reunite the young boy with his family.

As Beatrice and Sarah waited for Zack's return, Beatrice healed Sarah's many injuries from the werewolf. Two were deep and would leave scars, but the other wounds vanished from sight over time.

Although the werewolf attack resulted from a simple misunderstanding while the witches were freeing him from captivity, the beast raged out of the basement and carved deep wounds into Sarah's flesh before she could protect herself. The werewolf assaulted her with full force, and it took all her strength to gain the advantage. She contained him with magical wards after much struggle and waited for his transformation. Once he changed back to his human form, Sarah and the man, Eric, could have a conversation. Remorseful after he realized his transgression in killing the innocent witch, Claire, Eric offered future assistance if the coven was ever in need. They reached an understanding before he took his leave. As werewolves and witches were once prosecuted side-by-side, Sarah extended an invitation to discuss an alliance. The current situation highlighted a common enemy, but the artifacts yet to be analyzed could reveal others.

Cristiane teleported the other witches to the coven headquarters, leaving her mother and Sarah at the estate to deal with Lamashtu's spirit. The pair would join the others at the coven headquarters in a few days.

Once the others were gone, Sarah and Beatrice set to their task. The wards Sarah placed earlier were outside of the room, yet they set about creating barriers within the bedroom to protect them once the doors were open. Shields braced to their front, Sarah twisted her fingers, unlocking the wards, hindering the creature's exit. Beatrice stood by her side with arcane laser spikes pointed toward the room, ready to cast them forward at a moment's notice.

As the doors swung open, a rotten, metallic stink assaulted their airways. Beatrice coughed and gagged until Sarah cast a clean air spell that vanquished the scent from their path. Their eyes locked on an odd, contorting corporeal beast that writhed on Nissa's blood-soaked bed. Pieces of bone and flesh lay strewn throughout the room and Sarah's eyes found Nissa's skull at the base of the wardrobe. She caught Beatrice's gaze and nodded toward the wardrobe.

Beatrice shuddered as her eyes locked on Nissa's vacant sockets surrounded by bits of soft tissue and a screech assaulted her ears. Still armed with the spikes, Beatrice turned toward the noise, ready to strike.

Sarah succeeded at crafting a devil's trap around the bed as Beatrice glowered at the mystical tangle, making the cacophony.

Beatrice constructed an extensive force-field around the area as an added layer of protection from the demon goddess.

The force-field held as Sarah drew closer to the beast, staring at its strangeness. It mutated from raw flesh to murky plumes and then back, as if it could not decide which structure to choose. Bone fragments shook and moved close to the mutation, like the creature was attempting to build itself into a human. After several seconds, the vibrating skeletal fragments would stop and another shriek rang out from the throbbing mass.

"You do not have enough strength to maintain a human form, Lamashtu." Beatrice caught sight of a coin on the night table and snatched it. "You should have taken over her body before you ripped it to pieces."

"Yoou faailed mee." A dark apparition formed with a jackal's pointed snout above the contorted mass of flesh.

"I didn't fail you. Nissa did. She made promises to you that she could not keep," Beatrice said while glancing at the glistening spikes above her hand, ensuring they were still accessible. She inched toward Sarah and displayed the totem coin marked with runes for the witch.

"Shee proomised yoou aand yoour son tooo meee." The apparition faded in and out as the flesh seemed to pull it back, trying to complete a physical presence.

"He was never hers. I never agreed to be part of the seven mages. Never!" Heat crawled up Beatrice's neck to her cheeks. She balled her fists and looked down as the mystical spikes disappeared.

The jackal lunged at Beatrice but jerked to a sudden stop. The bloody mass of flesh held it back.

Sarah took the coin and studied the markings on either side. Her face lit up. "Beatrice, while I grab the figurine."

Beatrice tipped her head toward Sarah. "I don't think Lamashtu's going anywhere. Go ahead."

While Sarah ran out of the room, Beatrice watched as the form charged toward her and then either hit the barrier or got pulled back by the fleshy mound. It charged again and was once more bounced around the contained area. She chuckled, which infuriated the beast even more.

"Yoou daaare toooo laaaugh at meee?"

"I think it's sad. Nissa did not possess powers and, in reality, she did not know how to bring magical witches or sorcerers together to serve you. It was non-winnable from the start," Beatrice answered.

"Buut Xirnan served—"

"No, Xirnan aided Nissa by order of *his* master. That master was not you."

"Liiiiiies!" Lamashtu thrashed and bellowed a long, raucous growl. The effort pulled the spirit away from its corporeal weight.

Beatrice stepped back.

Sarah rushed in with the Lamashtu figurine and set it down on the floor. She rushed back into the hall and returned with a glass container and opened it. "So I have a plan. But it's risky."

"What other kind of plan is there when dealing with a demon?" Beatrice twisted her mouth while raising a brow.

Lamashtu hovered in its mysterious enclosure, shifting its attention from one to the other while still tethered to the morphing mound of flesh.

"True." Sarah touched the hex pouch hanging from her neck. "Is part of Lamashtu's spirit in this figure?"

"I don't know. Maybe. Since it came in here after Nissa, all of it could writhe in front of us." Beatrice waved a hand toward the monstrous creature.

Sarah held up the coin. "Not all of it."

"Shit."

"You're not going to like my next suggestion, either." Sarah took a deep breath. She spoke to Beatrice telepathically, spelling out what she needed Beatrice to do.

"You know I can't respond through my head, right?" Beatrice shook her head, but then a moment later sighed. "Fine."

Sarah gave a nod and constructed a large sledgehammer from items in the room. She pounded the figurine until it crumbled to the floor. Dust hung in the air, but nothing mystical or demonic rushed the witches.

Beatrice blew out. "One down, one to go."

Sarah cast an energy field around the coin, then placed it in the glass jar. "You ready?"

Beatrice looked above her head at the glistening spikes set in a row. She pulled her sleeves up and her hands were aglow with armored gloves to her elbows. "Toss me that pouch and I will be."

Sarah tossed her hex pouch to Beatrice and watched as her old friend poured the contents into her own. As Beatrice tossed the empty pouch aside, Sarah took the glass jar and stood opposite Beatrice, Lamashtu in between them.

Lamashtu twisted from one to the other, pulling the flesh blob as it contorted, trying to reel the apparition into the physical realm. Once Beatrice stood with her hands braced, Sarah said, "On my count."

Beatrice bobbed her head.

As Sarah broke the devil's trap with the open end of the glass jar, Beatrice plunged her hands through the force-field, grabbing the mass of flesh with one hand and pouring the hex pouch contents over it with the other.

The flesh of Lamashtu thrashed and boiled as salt and iron made contact.

Straining to keep her head and shoulders outside of the containment plane, the bloody mass within constructed talons and raked them across Beatrice's forearms trying to release her grasp. The gloves protected her, but her grip was slipping.

The spirit Lamashtu rose to escape the salt and iron pellets raining over its fleshy tumor. Its snarling spirit crafted larger claws from the flesh and lashed at Beatrice.

Caught above the glove, Beatrice screamed as a gash opened and a glove peeled off.

Sarah threw fireballs at Lamashtu as she concentrated on the salt and iron pellets, multiplying their mass to push the spirit closer to her and the glass container.

Beatrice shuddered under the pain. The barbs above her head slammed toward the mass in her hand. With each strike, Lamashtu's growl reverberated through the house.

A thunderous strike threw Beatrice back as her last spike pierced her hand that held onto the mass. Beatrice cried out and shook with pain. She peered through cloudy eyes to see the tether reduced to a thin thread.

Salt and iron pellets filled half of the contained space, yet Lamashtu failed to rush toward the break she'd created in the devil's trap. Looking down, Sarah noticed the mouth of the container had not smudged the outer ring as she'd thought. She reached out and wiped away the intended spot.

A brutish demonic howl assaulted their ears.

Beatrice had crafted daggers from the iron pellets and jabbed at the binding thread until it gave way, releasing Lamashtu's full spirit into the contained area away from the warping pile of flesh. She fell back with the bloody mass attached to her hand by her own shiny, mystical spike.

The containment area continued to fill with salt and iron. The demon spirit darted about, then paused as a murky, tooth-filled snout turned toward Sarah. She'd smudged the trap directly under the glass container and Lamashtu sensed the weakened location. Her hands were in the trap wrapped around the jar's edge as she knelt over the container, bracing it in place with her body.

Beatrice crawled to Sarah and curled up behind her, reinforcing their hold for the anticipated impact. Crimson poured from her hand and arm as a blood trail snaked toward the devil's trap.

"Yoou will beee miine aafter aall," Lamashtu snarled at Beatrice.

Beatrice fought to remain conscious as she turned to Sarah. "What does it mean?"

As Sarah turned to respond, she halted, noticing the blood cross the devil's trap plane and swiped a finger of blood into the glass container. She collapsed the energy field over the totem coin, crushing it in the jar. The bit of Lamashtu's demonic energy with Beatrice's blood caught the larger entity's attention. She tilted the container opening to the floor as Lamashtu's spirit lunged for Beatrice's blood.

The devil's trap filled with salt, forcing Lamashtu's spirit farther into the container.

As Sarah pressed to close the lid, black tentacles lashed at her hands, peeling away skin from her knuckles and ripping muscle from her fingers. After an agonizing flash, the lid was in place. Beatrice reached over and pressed the lock down and slid the container from Sarah's grasp.

Stunned, Sarah stared at the exposed bone of her curled fingers as blood dripped from the tips.

Beatrice reached into a pocket and dabbed salve on Sarah's fingers and then along her own punctured hand and lacerated arm to stop the bleeding. Exhausted, she slipped back to the floor and closed her eyes.

Sarah lay near Beatrice and soon she, too, was fast asleep.

Sarah woke to Cristiane's voice in her head. She responded that she and her mother were fine and would return soon. As she nudged Beatrice awake, Sarah took in their surroundings. It looked like a war zone.

Beatrice pulled herself up and began healing their injuries. Once the two witches were mended enough for travel, they would clean up the house and return to Sarah's home.

Goodbyes to Claire and Darrel pained the coven, and many members took to their duties with solemn vigor in honor of their sacrifice. Cristiane learned it had been many years since a member's death, and all suffered in the recent loss.

Clean-up efforts took weeks to unravel and dispose of cursed and enchanted totems and other objects. Everyone stayed busy, with Isadora and Sarah directing the schedule and coordinating efforts for transportation, cleaning, or disposal from both locations. Nissa owned so many artifacts that Sarah and Isadora stored several items to study later.

Jarvis took the lead for the coven and the police at Javier's and Nissa's local residence. The announcement of Nissa's death made it straightforward to close the nightclub. Changeling remains were removed, and the backroom cleared of cursed or dangerous objects before the police came into the basement for investigation. Once Jarvis conducted his coven business, he provided David's photos into evidence at the station. Jarvis also served as liaison to the New York police on the investigation and to notify Peter Hains' family of his death. The police had everything needed to conduct a thorough search of the club and Nissa's ceremony chamber. Knox became a valuable ally to the coven and the police department during their investigations by offering access to Nissa's business files and answering their questions.

As the witches' task lists filled with completions, the Bradfords spent more time at home and less at the coven headquarters. Jeffrey and Beatrice took a couple's retreat and become reacquainted with who they were together and as individuals. One condition they each had for the other was to keep an open mind as they shared their interests. Beatrice promised to teach Jeffrey about witchcraft and share what she knew of her ancestry with her family. Jeffrey pledged to open up about his combat and military service.

To Cristiane's surprise, her parents returned from the trip with renewed passion and energy to explore. Her mother decided to expand her small business and travel in search of unique items for her new theme. To do so, she was closing for a month with plans to reopen as an apothecary—a spiritual and metaphysical shop—to coincide with the other products she already offered. Jeffrey came home discussing various herbs and balms with his wife. He wanted to learn more and open a unique self-defense academy that offered natural balms and remedies in a few years.

Jeffrey spent a fair bit of time with Cristiane, sharing stories of his military service and discussing the jobs he had before his most recent corporate career. He shared tales of his misadventures and tours in combat that he hadn't even shared with her mother until their retreat, moments he'd kept hidden due to a sense of pride or fear. But he realized keeping his experiences from his family created his own shell. A shell he needed to discard to illustrate to Cristiane that life's path is turbulent, and plans are bound to change.

While Cristiane and Jeffrey were putting away photos one evening, Beatrice came in to sit with them. As Cristiane closed the photo box, Luke and the orb drifted in from a corner. Cristiane hadn't given Luke much thought, but she realized he hadn't come around since Nissa was gone.

"Luke, where have you been?"

Beatrice and Jeffrey peered at each other.

"I mean, umm. Do you need me?"

Luke shook his head no.

"Mom, I don't understand. Luke doesn't need anything." Cristiane thought for a moment. "We know the boys, Michael and Tony, died in the woods?"

He nodded, but then scrunched up his face and shook it no.

"It was a changeling in the car with you. The orb—that's why I've not been able to see its authentic form. It's not a human soul."

He gave a thumbs up and the orb flickered out of sight. Luke's spirit looked down at his side, relieved.

"I don't understand. Why are you still here?"

Smiling, he waved and then clutched his heart.

"Oh, Mom. He's saying goodbye." Cristiane clasped her hands over her heart, too.

With a brief bow of acknowledgement and thanks, Luke turned and drifted from sight.

"Wow, I'm touched. He finally crossed over."

Beatrice came to her side, squeezing her shoulders. "Thank you for helping him and me to understand what happened."

"Of course, Mom. It's part of what I do now. Help souls. It's part of who I am.

"That leads back to our conversation, in a way. We're so proud of your work ethic and how studious you've been at college. But as the past few months have revealed to all of us, and what we just witnessed in this room, relationships and friendships are important. Be open to experiences and, primarily, be honest with yourself. The rest will follow."

"Thanks, Dad. I appreciate the sage advice. There are two classes before graduation, but I have ideas about what I'd like to do with my future. I didn't before all this chaos, but I believe in who I am more than ever and what I can accomplish. The future is exciting, which is a new feeling."

"We're glad to hear that, sweetie. I'm sorry I haven't been a great mom, but I hope to make it up to you as much as I can. With that in mind, I have a favor to ask." Beatrice sat beside Jeffrey and reached for Cristiane's hand.

"Sure, Mom. What is it?"

"Will you wait to take your classes in the fall?"

"Sure, I can stay. I missed the summer cut-off, anyway. Why?"

"Stay with us. I'm closing the store for a while and your dad's taking a sabbatical. We want to spend time together as a family."

"Count me in." Cristiane beamed and drew her parents together for a group hug.

TWENTY-EIGHT

"Isn't it beautiful?" Cristiane snuggled closer to Jarvis in the cool mountain air. "It's the perfect resting place for David." The minor chill gave her a soothing quiver as she pulled her sweater tight. A breeze ruffled the overhead leaves, providing glimpses of the mid-morning sun as it worked its way farther up the sky. The thick canopy of limbs kept the ground cool and out of reach from the sun's warming rays. Cristiane smiled as she let the sense of peace wash over her.

Carol Howson and Joyce stood side-by-side as the dedication ceremony ended in the forest covering of the Berkshire mountains. Joyce knelt near the wood disc, engraved with David's name, and ran a hand over the dedication plaque. She stayed at the base of David's memorial tree as Cristiane came to her side. Joyce offered a gentle smile. "It's a tiny piece of magic—choosing this tree and knowing he will be a part of nature, always here, nourishing the earth, and sort of, continuing to live with us. He's at peace. I don't know how I know it, but he is."

Cristiane stood with Joyce and gave her a hug. "I'm sure he is, too. This is perfect." As Cristiane opened her eyes, she saw her old friend's spirit standing off to the side of the attendees. Her eyes welled with tears as she struggled to hold them back. She pulled away and peered into Joyce's and Mrs. Howson's eyes. "He's here."

"He is!" Mrs. Howson clutched her heart as she looked about.

Cristiane nodded, more to David's apparition as he moved toward them than to the women. "Don't be frightened. He's coming closer. You may feel cold, or a sensation, or a warmth run through you." She stopped talking and let his presence fill their souls. Cristiane waited as David came up.

Between the two women in his life, he embraced them. His mother rubbed her shoulder where David had his hand. Joyce did the same but seemed to grab and hold his hand tight. He kissed them each on the cheek before giving a thoughtful bow to Cristiane. David turned and drifted into the thick forest.

"He's left."

Mrs. Howson allowed the tears to fall from closed lids. "That was beautiful and peaceful, and so full of love."

"I couldn't agree more." Joyce blinked as the tears flowed and she gave Carol a hug.

They pulled Cristiane back into a group hug and thanked her for informing them of David's presence. It made an otherwise distressing day full of wonder and love. Robby and Tina joined in the hug fest while tears of celebration and mutual love filled the air. The morning was a miraculous farewell to their friend, lover, and son.

After a few moments, Cristiane pulled away and looked for Jarvis. Joyce touched her arm and drew her back to the group.

"Before any of you leave, I have an announcement to make." Joyce wiped at her face and cleared her throat.

"*We* have an announcement to make." Mrs. Howson put an arm around Joyce and pulled her close.

"You're right. *We* are going on an adventure. David's mother is traveling with me as I conduct summer climbing courses to camping students. We'll be gone for several months, or longer if we continue into the southern states through the fall.”

“We’ll stay in touch, of course. But I am so happy Joyce shared her sense of adventure and love of nature with David, and now I can get back to old hobbies I enjoyed years ago. When Joyce asked if I would join her, I couldn’t refuse.” Carol Howson beamed with excitement.

Tina and Robby gave their congratulations, as did Cristiane. Jarvis strolled over during the big announcement and shared his enthusiasm for their upcoming adventures. The crowd grew as Cristiane’s parents, Isadora, and the other attendees gathered to find out what all the fuss was about. Congratulations and side conversations went on for a half hour.

As people said their goodbyes and splintered off, the Bradfords pulled Isadora aside.

Beatrice nervously looked at Jeffrey and then Isadora. “We’d like to have you over for dinner this evening, if you’re available. You’ve been a big part of Cristiane’s life the past few years. We’d like to get to know you and stay in touch.”

Moved, Isadora grasped each of them by the hands. “I’d be honored. What time?” She gave them a huge smile, scrunching up the wrinkles around her eyes.

“Seven?”

“Wonderful! I wouldn’t miss it for the world.”

Jarvis and Cristiane were seated side-by-side with Jeffrey and Beatrice placed opposite, while they perched Isadora on a cushion at the head of the table. Who would guess she was 96 years old with her energy? Dinner with Isadora was anything but uneventful.

She shared stories of chasing monsters and demons around the globe. Once, she met a lovely man while at a conference in New Orleans. They talked each evening in the hotel's restaurant, where she learned of the delightful Brandy Alexander. It'd become one of her favorite drinks. No, the drink was not named after the man she'd met. Unfortunately, the handsome fellow turned out to be a vampire, and she'd had to stake his heart at the end of her trip.

Jarvis was sipping on coffee as she coolly spoke of killing the creature. Shocked, he spat the drink across the table.

The fog of dread was gone from Cristiane's home. She smiled, taking in the ease of conversation with her family. This was the first of many more refreshing evenings together. Content, she squeezed Jarvis's hand under the table and gave him a kiss on the cheek as the others continued their banter.

A knock on the door quieted everyone at the dining table. Isadora gave a bewildered look with a motion, appearing impish rather than perplexed. Cristiane ran to open the door and came back with Sarah Killian by her side.

"Sarah, it's wonderful to see you. Care for coffee and a slice of pie?" Beatrice was up pouring the coffee before Sarah could answer.

"Thank you. I think I will." Sarah pulled up a chair and joined in Isadora's tales.

After a time, Isadora placed her hands on the table and stood. "Ahem."

She waited for everyone to quiet down.

"Sarah, do you think it's time?"

Sarah wiped her mouth and placed the napkin on the table. She slid out of the chair and pulled envelopes from her bag. "I do. Cristiane and Beatrice, would you also stand, please?"

Befuddled, the two women emerged from their seats.

"It's my great honor and privilege to deliver invitations to Cristiane and Beatrice Bradford to unite with our magical family, the Secret Pillars Coven." Sarah handed an envelope to each of the Bradford women. "I hope you both will consider the invite and officially join us."

Speechless, Beatrice looked at the envelope, then at Cristiane. "Are you sure? I-I understand Cristiane's invitation, but are you certain you want me?"

Sarah went to Beatrice and wrapped her arms around her old friend, giving her a tight, warm embrace. "Absolutely certain."

Beatrice swallowed the lump in her throat.

Cristiane watched with tears running down her cheeks.

"Well, I'm a solid yes. What do ya say, Mom? Shall we do this together?"

"Let's do it." Beatrice attempted to blink back tears but failed as she smiled at her family.

Isadora patted Beatrice's arm. "You're home, darlin'. You're back where you belong."

As congratulations went around the table, Cristiane felt a warmth of intensity surge through her. She peered at her arms and noticed her wrists glisten. Sparkling ringlets pulsed with colors. Her forearms radiated a shimmering glow.

Alarmed, Jeffrey tapped Sarah on the shoulder. "What's happening to my daughter?"

"Nothing to cause alarm. I believe the Horned One and Mother Goddess are letting their approval be known. You have an incredibly special daughter, and we welcome your wife with their blessing."

"Cris, you're literally glowing." Jarvis, awestruck, rose from his seat, staring at her.

Laughing, Cristiane went to a mirror to see for herself. The glow grew bright for a few seconds, then slowly faded. Bracelets around her wrists did the same as they soon disappeared. But the afterglow around the table, the unity and affection endured.

It was truly a magical night, felt and viewed by all. Crone, mother, maiden together and blessed by the gods. Sarah felt the burden and joy of soon having these powerful witches in her coven. The path ahead, an honest path full of love, truth, and pain—they would walk together.

Cristiane pulled Jarvis close to her side as she looked around the dining room at her family and friends. Not friends—they were all her family now. It'd been a long time since she'd felt so at peace and hopeful, especially in her parents' home. Her eyes caught Beatrice's across the room and the two women smiled at each other.

Blessed be.

ACKNOWLEDGEMENTS

As always, I wouldn't be able to do what I love without the encouragement and support of my husband and grown children. Stephen Anthony—thank you for being the steadfast person you are and making me laugh when I need it most. Elena—thanks for sharing your thoughts and pushing me to change things up in my scenes. Stephen J— thanks for hollering at me to get back to writing so I would keep on track. I want to also thank Wendy of Bruja Power Botanica for sharing her knowledge and insight as a 5th generation Bruja Curandera by lineage and initiated Shaman.

My beta readers: Stephanie, Elena, Chris, and Thom. Thank you for your thorough comments and invaluable input. Without your help, my editor would have had a much harder job to do. You each came at the story from a different angle, and all your feedback was extraordinarily beneficial. I can't imagine publishing without this step in the process.

Harley and Bruce—thanks for nudging me to get out of the chair and take play breaks throughout each day.

About Sirrah Medeiros

Thank you for reading. If you enjoyed this story, we hope you'll leave a review. We encourage you to sign up for Sirrah's newsletter as the Cristiane Bradford series unfolds, as well as discover her other upcoming releases and events at https://sirrahmedeiros.com.

SIRRAH MEDEIROS is an author of dark urban fantasy, horror, and thrillers. She's also an occasional poet and editor.

She is the author of several published horror short stories included in various anthologies (a list of which is on her website) and the author of the series prequel *The Emerald Curse*. Sirrah devoted much of her life moving and traveling around the world. She spent a sizable portion of her career as a technical communicator and program manager and now spends her time creating artwork, writing and editing fiction while enjoying a wonderful life pursuing her passions. Her other hobbies include hiking, drawing, travel, and once in a blue moon she'll crochet an ugly scarf.

Sirrah lives in Virginia with her family and two playful dogs.

Goodreads
https://www.goodreads.com/sirrahmed
Facebook
www.facebook.com/SirrahMedeirosWriter
Instagram
www.instagram.com/SirrahMedeiros
Twitter
@SirrahMedeiros

Other Tundra Swan Press books by this author include:

The Emerald Curse by Sirrah Medeiros

www.ingramcontent.com/pod-product-compliance
Lightning Source LLC
Chambersburg PA
CBHW070450300726
48975CB00007B/2105